A respectable looking French bank-clerk type was standing there. He wore an incongruously sporty cloth cap that had been set squarely on his head with a spirit level. "Good afternoon, monsieur," he said politely. "Is this your name?"

He held out some kind of an official-looking document so I could read the name on it. It was mine.

"It might be," I said. "Why?"

"I have a warrant for your arrest. Interpol."

He put the paper carefully away in his pocket and took out a wallet with an identification card in it; picture, thumbprint and the rest. It looked genuine. So did he.

I said, "I guess we ought to talk, huh?"

He took off his cap before coming in. If I'd had a doormat I think he would have wiped his shoes, too. Carefully. He was that kind.

I knew quite a bit about Interpol. The warrant, which looked legal as far as it went, was signed by a French judge, and France had about as much jurisdiction over me in Tangier as it would have had in Tokyo.

The guy stood there holding his silly cap, politely and patiently waiting for me to come along quietly. While I was hesitating, his cap dropped from his fingers, his eyes froze and glazed, his mouth fell open. Boda had come down from the roof...

The LAST MATCH

by David Dodge

A HARD CASE CRIME NOVEL

A HARD CASE CRIME BOOK
(HCC-025)
October 2006

Published by

Dorchester Publishing Co., Inc.
200 Madison Avenue
New York, NY 10016

in collaboration with Winterfall LLC

*This book is a work of fiction. Names, characters, places, and
incidents either are the products of the author's imagination or
are used fictitiously, and any resemblance to actual events or
persons, living or dead, is entirely coincidental.*

ISBN 0-8439-5596-1
ISBN-13 978-0-8439-5596-5

Printed in the United States of America

Visit us on the web at www.HardCaseCrime.com

THE LAST MATCH

Chapter One

The guy who was waiting for me in my room merely wanted to blow my head off, that's all. To teach me a lesson, as it turned out. He used a little short-barreled revolver, a thirty-two I think it was, but he didn't know how to hold it to keep the barrel from flipping up every time he pulled the trigger. The kick of the shots lifted the bullets over my head or over my shoulder or somewhere else that wasn't into me. He got off three of them before I could do anything about it.

There's something to be said for combat training even if there's nothing at all to say for the rest of the schooling they give you in the U.S. Army. After you've been bounced hard enough and often enough by experts because you're not reacting fast enough, your reflexes tend to sharpen up. And when you're scared silly by a gun going blam, blam, blam in your face they get even sharper. Given a window to jump out of I'd have been gone with the wind like a soaring rocket. But the guy stood between me and the escape in that direction, and in the other direction I had just trapped myself by closing a hotel-room door behind me before putting on the lights so he could see to pot me. In the circumstances there wasn't much to do except throw my room key in his face and go for his ankles before he fired number four.

It worked. He was small, middle-aged, nothing much

to handle. I took the gun away from him and sat on his chest. He began to cry.

He looked and was dressed like an American. I thought I might have seen him someplace before. He didn't have the kind of face to remember. After my heart had eased back down my throat to where it belonged, I said, "What did you want to go and do that for?"

"Mildred," he blubbered, the tears puddling in his eyes. "Sh-she's going to l-leave me, and I l-l-love her."

"Who's Mildred?" I shook the live shells out of the revolver to put them in my pocket where they wouldn't kill anybody.

"Don't you dare mock me, damn you!" He was both indignant and tearful at the same time, but more indignant than tearful.

"No, honest. I don't know any Mildreds."

"You're a liar!"

"All right, I'm a liar. I still don't know any Mildreds. If I let you up, will you please tell me what it's all about without pulling a knife?"

He gulped. It sounded affirmative. "But you're still a liar."

"I conceded that. I still don't know any Mildreds."

I gave him a hand to pull him to his feet. He said automatically, "Thank you." I said, "You're welcome. Here's your pistol. It isn't loaded."

"Thank you," he said again. He was a polite little murderer, I must say.

The cops were there within a few minutes after the shooting. The hotel was one of the best in Cannes, on the Croisette, and there were always a couple of *flics* out in front to keep the crowds moving whenever somebody important checked in, like a movie star. Before they hauled him away I made another attempt to find out what it was all about. All I could get from him was that Mildred had said she no longer loved him and was going to leave him. It was all my fault. So he had decided to shoot me, to retain her love. Simple.

Even simpler was the fact that I really didn't know any Mildreds. I checked up on the guy while the cops had him—they took the pistol away, fined him and turned him loose three days later—and learned that he was registered at the hotel with his wife. MacCullin, their name was. The *concierge* pointed the wife out to me, a so-so number with orange hair and a figure that had seen better days.

I did, too, know her, although not by name. We had been fellow guests at a party somewhere, Eden Roc I think it was, where everybody had had more than enough to drink. Mildred and I ended up in a garden for fun and games under the stars. Nothing serious came of it; a spell of catch-as-catch-can wrestling, heavy breathing, shared lipstick, that was it. The garden was too crowded with other wrestlers for anything more. I may have told her, I probably did tell her as anyone but a cad would tell a lady he's been grappling with, that I would love a return bout in more sheltered circumstances, but that was the end of it. I didn't ask if she had a husband, she didn't volunteer the information, nobody jealous came looking for her. Now she had fingered me to him for reasons of her own I didn't want to know about.

When MacCullin came out of hock and returned to the hotel I got him alone and bent his ear.

"Mac, pal," I said. "Listen. I don't know what's with your wife, but there's nothing between us. I've never even spoken to her. Honest."

"You're a liar. She told me—"

"Hear me and read me. I don't care what she told you, there's nothing in it. I give you my solemn word of honor. If that isn't enough for you, figure it out for yourself. Would I be playing around with your wife in the same hotel where I've got a woman of my own? She's mad crazy jealous of me, and if I even looked at another doll she'd cut me right off at the pockets. I'd have to go to work. You wouldn't want that to happen to a pal, would you?"

"You're not living together," he said suspiciously. "Not in your room you're not. I looked around."

"She has to maintain appearances." I gave him the old man-to-man eye. "You know how it is, an older woman and a young guy like me. Your must have seen us together; a nice looking lady, dresses well, maybe a bit on the plumpish side—"

"I thought she was your mother."

"And you were going to shoot the boy of a nice lady like that? Shame on you!"

"I wasn't really trying to shoot you," he said lamely. "I just wanted to scare you."

"You scared me. Don't do it again, please, buddy, huh? You're going to have to pay for the bulletholes, too, you know."

"I won't do it again. I really thought she was your mother. I'm sorry."

We shook hands and had a drink on it in the bar. I looked at myself in the mirror over the back bar and wondered if I'd do better without a profile.

One of the curses of my formative years was an overdose of prettiness. It is mine no more, thank God, age and a receding hairline being as erosive as they are, but mention of this early failing is necessary because of what it did to my youth. As a child I was a lady-killer at the age of six. Women loved my mop of brown curls, my brown calf's eyes with the long curly lashes they all envied me for, my cute button nose, all the rest. (The cute nose got unbuttoned in later years, but even that didn't change things much.) With the cunning of the deceptive little bastard I was I learned to capitalize on these assets, and did so at every opportunity. My parents should have drowned me, but didn't.

As an adolescent I was an unmitigated young prick, like most adolescents, but a prick with charm I had cultivated since childhood. Girls were easy for me, including other guys' girls. This led to trouble from time to time with one of the other guys, who would feel justified in trying to beat on me. I was big enough to beat back, bigger than the average, so I didn't take as many lickings as I was entitled to. In college I began to grow up some, learn different values, but the twig had been bent and the tree was so inclined. Women, including other guys' wives, were as easy for me as girls had been. I even developed a talent for slickering husbands out of beating on me when they should have been beating on me. I became, in short, a college-trained con man; amateur skill, but with all the qualifi-

cations to turn professional at any time. Two years of
compulsory servitude in the army only deferred my
eventual blossoming in the full flower of fulfillment;
first, briefly, as a gigolo, later an off-and-on jailbird, in
time and with experience as a hustler, bunco steerer
and peddler of phony gold bricks.

All this is less by way of *mea culpa* than to explain
how and why things happened as they did. When I had
finished my two years of army service, during which I
perfected various techniques for violating the rules
against fraternizing with the cooperative *fräuleins* of
West Germany, I took my discharge there, got a passport in Frankfurt and bummed my way around
Europe on the cheap while my severance pay lasted. I
ended up on the French Riviera because I had heard
you could sleep comfortably on the beaches there
even in wintertime. (You can't.) My cash was about
finished.

In Monte Carlo I decided to turn it back into a
bankroll by investing it in *le jeu de craps-game*. I'd
done all right with dice in the army and during the
summers I worked as a roustabout for carnie shows,
but a house game is not the same as bouncing the
bones on a blanket. Monte Carlo's *jeu de craps-game*
chewed me up and spat me out, bloodless, in about
half an hour. I didn't even have cigarette money left,
or bus fare to get out of town.

That didn't bother me much. I had tapped out
before without dying of it. I was young, healthy, able-
bodied. Something would turn up. I went out into the
casino gardens overlooking the Mediterranean, hoping
to find a long cigarette butt. (Casinos are too fast

about replacing used ashtrays with clean ashtrays, I
suppose for fear that a smoldering butt may burn the
green felt.) A lady who had been watching the game—
and me, as I was aware—followed me out.

The shores of the south of France are littered with a
flotsam of lonely women, cast up there by divorce,
widowhood, dissatisfaction with the availabilities, other
reasons. They are Americans or British, in large part,
and they all have a fair amount of money; enough to
run with the company they keep. You can see half a
dozen of them around the roulette tables in any casino
on an average night. Because they are both rich and
lonely they are fair game for the kind of guy who is on
the make for a moneyed mama. I wasn't one of these,
and I'm pretty sure the lady knew it. She may have had
some idea that I was going to blow my brains out, as in
those stories you read, mostly fiction, about desperate
gamblers broken on the wicked wheels of Monaco.
She came over to where I was sitting on a bench
looking despondent only because I was casing the
ground around the bench for usable butts, my head
and shoulders down.

"You lost all your money, didn't you?" she said.

I said, "Yes, ma'am. Although it wasn't much to lose."

"You needn't keep your chin up for me, poor boy. I
know how you must feel. Here."

She had opened her purse while she was talking.
She took out a thick wad of *mille* notes—this was in
the days of the old franc, when French money had big
figures on it although not much more buying power
than it has today—and shoved it at me. "Take it. I won
it this afternoon."

"You can lose it just as easy tomorrow afternoon, ma'am. Thanks all the same."

"Take it," she insisted. "Only promise me you won't gamble with it."

I couldn't read her at all. Here's this dame, middle-aged, not good-looking, not bad-looking, a motherly type, well dressed, obviously in the bucks, pushing money at me she'd won gambling but didn't want me to gamble with. I said, "Lady, thanks very much. I appreciate your offer, but I can't take your money. Even if I did, I'd gamble with it."

"Don't talk back to me, boy," she said. "I'm old enough to be your mother." And damned if she didn't drop the wad of bills in my lap and start back toward the casino.

I had to go after her. In those days I had principles; a few, anyway. She flatly refused to take the money back. I could call it a loan, if I wanted to, but I had to keep it. And no gambling.

So what do you do around a gambling casino if you can't gamble? It ended with her taking me home in a car she had rented for the day to her hotel in Cannes, there to install me in a room of my own and buy me the best dinner I had eaten in Europe, with a bottle of *Gewürtztraminer* that must have set her back at least ten bucks. She said she was celebrating her birthday.

"Although I'm not going to tell you which one," she said girlishly. "So don't ask me."

"The twenty-first, I'll bet," I said. "They wouldn't let you into the casino if you were any younger. I'm sorry I didn't know about it sooner. I'd have bought you a present. With your money."

"Oh, please. Let's not talk about money." She put her hand over mine on the table. "Dear boy. You've made me very happy today."

Like that, I was a gigolo. See how things can creep up on you when you're not looking?

Her name was Mrs. Emmaline Stokes; a widow. She wasn't crazy mad jealous of me at all, just motherly. As a matter of fact she was kind of proud of me because the girls gave me the eye all the time. We never slept together. At first I thought that was what she wanted of me, but when I made a few exploratory passes she reacted as if I had suggested incest. She was lonely, she was rich, she liked having a good-looking young man paying attention to her. Particularly a young man whose language she could understand. It didn't matter that I was more of the age and temperament to be interested in the fifty thousand cute *poupettes* of all sizes, shapes, colors and nationalities bulging their bikinis all the way from Menton to St. Tropez, not to mention a somewhat smaller group untrammeled by bikinis or anything else who congregated in an open-house nudist rookery on the *Île du Levant*. Emmaline dear was satisfied with me as an acceptable escort, and wanted nothing more. She bought me the wardrobe I needed, evening clothes, an expensive wristwatch, a gold cigarette case, other things, and supplied me with the money to take her places. She never required an accounting, or questioned expenditures, or embarrassed either of us by making me ask for money when I ran out. She was a kind, generous woman, and I liked her. Ours was the relationship of a Boy Scout helping a nice little old lady across the street to the gambling hell.

Then I met Nemesis. It wasn't her real name, but I
didn't know her real name when she first pointed the
accusing finger of retribution at me, and I got to think
of her that way before I knew anything about her.

I was sunning myself on the beach in front of the
Martinez, Emmaline dear's hotel in Cannes. She had
gone back to the hotel to call on Uncle John, as she put
it with maidenly modesty. I was lying on my back with
my eyes closed when I became aware that a shadow
had fallen on my face. I opened my eyes and looked up
at this girl, woman—she was about my age, in the mid-
twenties—looking down at me. She wore a rubber
bathing-cap with the ear-tabs turned up so she could
hear, a bathing suit on the conservative side by local
standards, and she was easy to look at. Nothing to
make a man leap to his feet and lunge, but all right.

"Hello, Curlilocks," she said. "Where's your mother?"

She had a British accent to spread on a crumpet. It
was a kind of hoity-toity drawl that sounded as if she
were inwardly amused about something secret.

"If you mean the lady whose company I'm keeping,
she isn't my mother. She went where ladies can't send
someone else to go for them. She'll be back in a few
minutes."

"I was afraid of that." She smiled at me, and I must
say she had lovely teeth. A lot of Englishwomen don't.
"Is that your natural hair, or do you do it up in curlers?"

"I give myself home permanents," I said. "I'm one
of the Toni Twins."

I didn't know why she was giving me the needle, but
after two years under a tough top sergeant I was cal-
lused to needling. She didn't bother me too much.

"I'll wager you curl the hair on your chest, too."

"As anyone can see at a glance. Now push off and go pester someone else, will you? I'm sleeping."

I closed my eyes. She said, in the same hoity-toity drawl, "You contemptible little spiv!"

I opened my eyes again, wondering, What the hell? I'd never seen her before, to recognize. She might have been around, but she wasn't the type to catch my eye easily.

"What's a spiv?" I asked her.

"You are. A wretched spiv."

With that she walked down to the water, fixed her ear-tabs, fastened her chin-strap, dived in and swam out to a float anchored off the beach. She swam easily and well, a kind of inwardly amused drawl although of course I mean crawl.

About then Emmaline dear came back from Uncle John's place and plopped down on the sand beside me.

"Who's the girl you were talking to?" she asked, with no particular curiosity.

"I don't know. I never saw her before. I'd just as soon never see her again, too."

"Why?"

"She called me a wretched spiv."

"A spiv?"

"A spiv."

"Well, I don't think that was very nice of her, whatever it means." She patted my hand comfortingly where it lay on the sand. "*Dear* boy."

I found out what a spiv was from Cedric, the Martinez' head bartender. He was British. According to him, spivs were originally by-products of World War II, when England was on short rations for everything and black-marketeering was big business. Spiv was the name for a black marketeer. When black markets went out, spivs moved into other lines of business the way mobsters in the U.S.A. went into other lines of business when Prohibition was repealed. Spiv came to mean any kind of grifter at all, although usually with an overtone of small-time attached. A peanut-pincher, as they say around the carnie lots. A cheap chiseler, in effect.

That hurt my feelings. It's bad enough when a strange female you've never seen before walks up to you out of nowhere and accuses you of curling your hair, but to call you a cheap chiseler as well is too much even for army calluses. She rankled on me every time I thought of her, which was too often. I took to looking for her whenever Emmaline dear and I were out on the town. Often I saw her around; gambling indifferently or dancing with some guy at one of the *boîtes*—her escorts tended not to last long, two or three or four evenings at the most before a new one took over—or sunning on the beach, most often alone. She saw me too. But she never gave any sign of recognition or, what was even more rankling, interest. Damn the woman, what did she think she was made of, anyway? Marble?

Then Emmaline dear had to go back to Pawtucket or wherever it was. Something was cooking with her investments. I think she would have liked to take me *avec*, as the French say, but she still had family living at the old homestead. To come back from wicked, wicked France with a gigolo half her age would not have been the thing at all. She cried in a motherly way when we parted, promised to write and slipped me a check for a thousand dollars U.S. You couldn't go far on the Côte d'Azur with a thousand bucks even in those days, but you could eat for a while. While I was still eating I began to toy with the idea of moving in on Nemesis as a new den-mother. She was a challenge as well as a ranklement.

Her name was Reggie Forbes-Jones. The Honorable Regina Forbes-Jones, to give it full treatment. The Honorable meant there was a title in the family. Her father was an earl or something of the kind. She never talked much about him, or the fact that her family was loaded. I found out these things on my own, through Cedric and others. She was British by birth and inclination, but spent six months or more of each year on the Côte d'Azur partly to escape England's foul winters, partly to avoid high British taxes on her respectable private take-home. She was fairly tall, had an attractive face and figure without being a howling beauty or a sexpot, dressed with a lot more *chic* than most Englishwomen I have known and could freeze you as stiff as an icicle with the haughtiest look ever cast down an aristocratic nose at a commoner. I'd seen her put a frost good enough for a daiquiri on Josef, *maître d'hotel* at the Carlton in Cannes for twenty years, a man who had been absorbing the evil eye from kings, queens and Greek multi-millionaires for decades without turning a hair. She was patrician no end, and she let you know about it without telling you so in so many words.

Aside from all this, she obviously had money, she

wasn't ugly, she wasn't too old and she needed taking down a notch or two. One afternoon I fired the opening shot across her bows where she was sunning herself on the beach, alone as usual.

She lay on her stomach, her eyes closed, her shoulder-straps unfastened, her brown skin gleaming with tanning oil. She had a nice smooth back and shoulders.

I lay down beside her, unobtrusively.

"Why am I a wretched spiv?" I asked the ear nearest me.

She opened her eyes to give me a cool, unenthusiastic look of appraisal.

"Because it's in your nature to be a wretched spiv, probably," she said. Actually it came out more like 'prob'ly', and she slurred over syllables in many other words the way upperclass British do, but I'm not going to try to do her phonetically. "Now that you know, you may leave."

"It's a public beach. If I molest you, you can always call the police."

"A gentleman would not make it necessary for a lady to call the police to free herself from his unwelcome presence."

"I'm not a gentleman. I'm a wretched spiv, remember? Would you like me to oil your back? All the grease seems to have been rendered out of you."

"If you move a finger in my direction I'll have you arrested."

Our conversation continued along those lines for the next few days. During that time I learned why she had developed such a low opinion of me. It was because I had been Emmaline dear's pretty boy, taking her money and stringing her along by pretending that I loved her. She was convinced that I had been sharing Emmaline dear's bed. I couldn't persuade her otherwise. She would not believe that our relationship had been what it really was, a kind of amiable companionship; nourished by Emmaline dear's bank account, as I was readily willing to admit, but with no real harm to it or her. In her view I remained a contemptible little spiv (six inches taller and about sixty pounds heavier than she was) as well as a few other things she didn't like. She had a tongue like a riding crop, and she used it.

I hung on, took my whipping, ate crow and fought back. Although she did truly turn out to be the finger of Nemesis in the end, in a paradoxical way it was she who pushed me into a life of crime, bless her. I might even have suffered the indignity of a steady nine-to-five job if she hadn't been so tough to crack. But the more she cuffed me around and showed her contempt for what she thought I was, the more determined I became to force the moat, smash the portcullis and invade the baronial castle of the Honorable Regina Forbes-Jones. I thought I just might be able to bring it off. As much as she lashed at me with her riding-crop and however scornful she might be of my morals, behavior and ways of life, she was interested in me as a person. Otherwise there was no reason for her to have picked me as a whipping-boy from among the crowd of other gigolos steering their *poulets* around Cannes, or for letting anyone as loathsome as I was hang around her even on a public beach. It stood to reason. And what mere woman could resist old Charming

Charlie when he really got down to it and went to work on her?

She could, by God. She wouldn't yield an inch.

"If anywhere in your nefarious spiv's head you have any faint hope of diddling me as you diddled that silly old fool who was keeping you," she told me one day, "give it up. You're wasting your charm on barren soil."

She wasn't the type to bandy vulgar words with *canaille*. 'Diddle,' to her, meant to swindle, nothing more. I said, "Whatever gave you the idea that I might want to diddle you?"

"The oily way you keep trying to ingratiate yourself speaks for itself."

"I'm not trying to ingratiate myself. I enjoy your company. Your subtly witty conversation sends me."

She sniffed. "I fail to find yours in any way amusing. Do you prefer my company to that of—those, for example?"

'—those, for example,' with another, unexpressed, sniff of disapproval, were a couple of bonbons wiggling down the beach in elaborate ignorance of the attention they were getting from the boys. Both were young, cute, stacked like the proverbial brick outbuilding and wearing as little as they could get by with even in Cannes. On the make for a pickup.

"Of course I do," I said. "Otherwise I'd be with them instead of you, wouldn't I?"

"Not bloody likely."

"Why not bloody likely?"

"Because I have money and they don't. Come off it. Do you think I'm simple?"

"I think you're simply scrumptious."

"Oh, do go away, please! You bore me."

It wasn't until I'd been taking my lumps from her for a couple of weeks that I began to see what made her as thorny as she was, and why she was going to be tougher to take than I thought. It wasn't just me she was lashing out at. I've already said she never talked much about herself, but a successful bunco-steerer has to be a good psychologist as well as the other things. Inside her aloof patrician shell Reggie was a sad and lonely girl. Her trouble was too much money. I never knew the details of her upbringing and family background, but somewhere along the line she'd been heavily indoctrinated with the idea that the world was full of men like me, out to take her. She had looks, youth, intelligence, poise, pedigree and at least a normal woman's wish to be loved for herself alone by a member of the opposite sex. Her fortune, and the further fortune that was to come her way when her old man died, cursed her. No matter how honest the devotion might be in a man's eyes when he looked at her, she saw, or suspected, dollar signs in them. I mean pound sterling signs, of course, but the idea is the same. Her money poisoned her outlook on life.

And of course the Côte d'Azur was the worst of all possible places to look for a cure for her kind of illness. It's a natural gathering ground for grafters, grifters, chiselers, hustlers, flimflam artists, fortune hunters, sharpshooters, bunco-men, fakes, phonies and hocus-pocus operators of one kind or another. Those who haven't the *grisbi* are there to get it from those who have. Some of the most successful getters in the business are the smooth, handsome, charming, cultivated,

clean-cut, attractive, highly eligible no-good playboy
bums whose only ambition is to marry or otherwise get
next to a woman with a potful of money and live happily forever afterward at her expense. (Never mind
about me and Emmaline dear. That was only temporary.) It was the reason Reggie's boyfriends always
faded so quick. The more charming and attentive they
were, the less faith she had in their sincerity.

You might ask, Why the hell didn't the poor little
rich girl give her money to the Salvation Army and
find true love in the arms of the nearest shoe clerk?
The answer is, I don't know. Maybe she'd tried something of the kind and found that it didn't work either.
But from disliking her and wanting to do her down I
began to feel sorry for her. Hers was not a baronial
castle to invade and overthrow, but a dungeon to be
breached.

I won't say her money didn't interest me. Money
has always interested me, whoever owns it. But that's
all I'm going to say about Reggie's riches except that I
never got any of them to keep. With Reggie herself,
paradoxical though it may sound, I had an inside track.
She knew I was a crook, a spiv and a hustler, therefore
had no doubts about what I was after. Her defenses
against me were established, tested and firm; so firm
that she could tolerate my trying to bore through
them. I never bored too hard or too persistently. She'd
have taken my insolent peasant hide off in strips if
I had.

She never used my name. Sometimes I was Curly or
Curlilocks, more often, You, there, or, Oh, it's you

again, or some other term of affection. In return I took
to calling her Hon, which she detested. Not Hon as in
honey but Hon. as in Honorable, only with the "H"
sounded instead of silent.

Once she asked me how I had found out she was an
Honorable, since she had never mentioned it. I told
her I had done research on her.

"Why?" she asked sharply. She reacted to something like that the way a barnyard chicken does to the
shadow of a hawk wheeling overhead.

"Oh, I thought we might be related somewhere
along the line. My grandmother was a Forbes."

"Never fear," she said, looking down her aristocratic
nose. 'Nevah feeyah' is more like it. I know I promised
not to try to reproduce her accent, but a lot of her
frosty flavor is lost without it.

"Still, wouldn't it be neighborly if we turned out to
be distant cousins or something, Hon?"

"It would be unbearable. And stop calling me Hon.
I've spoken to you about it before."

"Yes, ma'am."

"And stop saying Yes, ma'am! You sound like a
schoolboy."

"I used to be one, ma'am. Before they drafted me."

"What did you do in school? Rob lockers?"

You know how it goes. Love talk.

Then, by God, perseverance, pluck and American
grit began to show signs of paying off. I'd never tried
to speak to her anywhere except on the beach, and
then only when she was alone. I had a feeling I'd be
pushing too far too fast if I presumed upon our

acquaintanceship to try to mingle socially without invitation. The time wasn't yet ripe for that, and anyway our paths didn't cross much off the beach. We traveled in different circles since I had moved from the Martinez to a cheap *pension* where the food was good. But one day while we were on the sand throwing the usual barbs into each other a *chasseur* came down from the hotel with a telegram for her. When she had read it she said in a tone of great annoyance, "Oh, *dash* it! How perfectly bloody!"

"Blue blood, no doubt," I said with courteous interest. "Somebody in the family?"

It didn't even rate a comeback, so I knew something fairly serious had happened. I suppose it really was fairly serious from her viewpoint. She had been stood up on a date; like any common shopgirl, as she might have put it. What was worse, the date was for the following evening and the occasion was the biggest social bust-out of the year on the Côte d'Azur: the charity ball at the Summer Sporting Club in Monte Carlo annually presided over by Prince Rainier and his lady-of-the-moment. (This was a year or so before Grace.) Everybody who was anybody in the Riviera rat-race was going; the ladies in their special-occasion diamonds, not the ordinary wash-day icing, with gowns created for the occasion; the men flashing all the decorations, medals, royal orders, crosses, bangers, gongs, ribbons and other chest ornamentation they were entitled to wear and some they were not. Admission was by princely command, champagne corks were said to pop like machine-gun fire, the dancing went on until dawn or later, and if you weren't with it when the starting trumpets went ta-ra-ra-ta-ra you were socially extinct. Non-attendance meant either that you didn't have the money to throw in the pot with the Onassises and the Niarchoses and the Benitez-Rexachs when the poorhouse plate was passed, or that you were *persona non grata* around Monaco.

I didn't learn all the details there on the beach, of course. The Hon. Reggie wasn't the type to break down and spill her troubles to a peasant in public. But she had her invitation and her new gown—it had cost a real bundle, as was obvious when I saw her in it—and she was hard up for an escort. Boyfriends she had plenty of, although she would never have called them that. Guys who had taken her out, would do it again if she gave them the chance, but would prefer to take her in. She couldn't stoop to a last-minute call for rescue in that direction, nor appeal to a gentleman of her class if there had been any around. There weren't. There wasn't anyone around she could turn to in a last-minute emergency. Except little old contemptible me.

So I got the nod, along with an icy lecture on behavior, manners, how to clean my nails and a few other niceties. I still had the evening clothes Emmaline dear bought me, not yet having reached the point where I would have to hock them to eat. Reggie had an elegant black-and-chrome Mercedes-Benz she didn't use very much. She gave me a wad of franc notes with which to hire a chauffeur for the evening and meet other expenses. ("I'll expect a strict accounting, mind you." "Yes, ma'am." "And if you say yes, ma'am, to me once again this evening, I'll scream!" "It won't be necessary to scream, ma'am. I'll call you Reggie, Hon.") We took off for the doings, after I had gallantly presented her with an expensive corsage I bought with her money. I thought she would appreciate the gesture when she found it on the expense account.

Chapter Two

It was quite a gala, the charity ball. I don't know how much the poor benefited from it, but I had a hell of a time. I looked and felt sharp in Emmaline dear's dinner clothes, the champagne was plentiful and good, the food was superb, the music was the kind I liked to dance to, and Reggie knew the moves. I'm strictly a club-fighter on the dance floor. With another stumble-bum, I stumble too. With a good dancer, I'm a lot better. Reggie was thistledown on her feet, and she never made a misstep. She presented me to some other women she knew at the party and I danced with them while she danced with other men who came up to ask her. She didn't have to sit any of the dances out unless she wanted to, and I was kept circulating. But dancing with the other dolls wasn't like dancing with Reggie. It was an odd thing. She was just as cool, as remote and withdrawn from me as ever, and yet somehow, when she was in my arms, she seemed to—well, fit there. She made me feel big and strong and chivalrous. I wanted to *do* something for her, damn it. The poor little rich girl was such a sad sack inside her dungeon, she made me sad for her. All that money, and no fun.

Part of it was the champagne, of course. But not all of it. For one crazy moment, out there with her on the dance floor, holding her in my arms, I thought of sticking my lips against her ear and telling her the old three-word tale that hooks so many of them. It would have been pure con, the worst possible gesture I could have made, but I considered it. Very briefly. I considered a lot of other approaches less briefly while we danced. Nothing sensible came to me.

We drank quite a lot. It was good champagne, as noted. Along about two or three in the morning she wanted a breath of fresh air, so we went out into the gardens overlooking the sea. There was a big moon, stars, the scent of flowers, a nice setting. Other couples were there enjoying it, too, but they weren't in our laps. We leaned against a balustrade hanging over a cliff and smoked a cigarette.

While I was trying to think of something pleasant and harmless to say, she said thoughtfully, "Curlilocks, d'y'know, you could really make something of yourself, if you tried."

"Yes, ma'am," I said.

She didn't notice it. She said, "You have looks, intelligence, a good bit of personal charm, a fine body— you should be ashamed of yourself."

"I am," I said. "I truly am. All those things working for me, and no sex appeal."

"I suppose you have even that, for a certain type of woman. Obviously you have. I think it's a good part of your trouble, actually. Women have always made things too easy for you. What you need is the challenge of adversity. It would strengthen your character."

"If you say so, ma'am. You're paying the check."

In the moonlight she managed to look down her nose at me, although it's difficult to do when you're half a foot shorter than the person you're looking down on. "You should be ashamed of that, too."

"I am," I said. "And if I weren't, you'd sure arrange to make me feel that way, wouldn't you? Let's go in and drink up some more of your money."

She really made me sore. Here I'd been thinking all evening of ways to do something nice for her, and all she wanted to do was throw darts.

It was around four A.M. when I took her back to her hotel. The chauffeur had been hired for the night, but I paid him off, told him to park the car and blow. My *pension* was within walking distance. Then I took Reggie to her room, said good night, thanked her for a lovely evening at her door and was ready to trundle off to beddy-bye when she said crossly, "Oh, come in, do! It's still early."

I should have backed off and run for the fire escape right there. But I was tired, full of champagne and slow on the uptake. Also, as she had said, women had always made it too easy for me. I'd been invited into ladies' bedrooms before then and come out of them without serious scarring. I didn't think for a minute that she was inviting me in for the reason some ladies invite gentlemen into their bedrooms at 4 A.M. If I had just clung to that conviction, which was one hundred percent correct, I'd have been better off.

It wasn't a room but a suite, and elegant. A little balcony outside the windows of the sitting room overlooked the Croisette, with the empty beach and sea beyond. The big moon was farther over now, on the declining side, and spread a glittering moontrack across the water. The night was quiet, warm, and peaceful. A night for love, you might say, although I didn't say it. Not even when she came to stand beside me where

I was leaning on the rail of the balcony looking at the moon.

She brought two *fines* with her. Damn fine *fines* they were, too, as I could tell by smelling mine when she handed it to me.

"A nightcap," she said. "At the end of a pleasant evening."

"*A la vôtre*," I said, and put mine away at a gulp. It's not the way to drink a true *fine*, which calls for sipping, but it is the way to drink a toast.

I suppose the slug of good brandy on top of all the good wine could have made me a little foolhardy. That, and the moon, and the Mediterranean night, and the faint sweet lavender scent she wore, and the fact that I had been holding her in my arms most of the evening without argument while thinking chivalrous thoughts. I don't remember having any further thoughts, chivalrous or otherwise, there on the balcony. I can't even remember what happened to the brandy glasses, when I reached once again to take the Honorable Regina Forbes-Jones around the waist and pull her toward me with a gentle tug. She came easily and gracefully, unresisting, and I held her in my arms as I had held her at the ball. Only we weren't dancing now. We were looking at each other's face and eyes in the moonlight. I for one liked what I saw, all of a sudden. It must have been the booze.

I didn't say anything. There wasn't anything I knew how to say. When I kissed her she still didn't resist. She didn't kiss me back, but she didn't bite a chunk out of my lip, as she might have, or put up a struggle. She held still until I let her go. Then—wham!

It wasn't any ladylike slap, either. She doubled her fist and let me have it right on the doorbell. I had my mouth half open. I think I was going to try to say something then of what I felt for her, and the punch made me bite my tongue. It also lit up the night sky for a moment with more than a normal number of stars. When my ears stopped ringing she was saying icily, "—common little guttersnipe! If you ever have the temerity to touch me again I'll see you in jail!"

I was beginning to understand what she meant by the challenge of adversity. I took my sore tongue, my sore jaw and my shattered illusions out of there without any further encouragement from her. She had a nice right-hand punch. I don't know about her left. I never put myself in a position where she could hit me with it.

After that I didn't see her for a while. I was engaged with some entrepreneurs in making a score. This was back in 1955, when Tangier still functioned as an international free port, before Morocco took it over. You could buy any kind of action you wanted in Tangier in those days; women, boys, dope, booze, free-market money both real and counterfeit, gold, contraband diamonds, anything else portable. There were no import duties, no taxes, no trade restrictions of any kind and not too much policing by the Belgian *flics* who were supposed to keep order around town. Americans, like other nationals of the governing powers, had extra-territorial rights, too. If you did get into trouble with the law in Tangier—it was pretty hard to do, but it could be done—the judge of your case was one of your fellow-countrymen, usually your own consul. Normally he'd pass sentence by telling you to haul ass out of town before nightfall and not come back. It was a nice setup all round, if you didn't get stabbed in a back alley for your pocket-money. That could happen, too.

One of the best buys in Tangier then was American cigarettes. A pack sold for the equivalent of about fifty cents U.S. on the black market in France and Italy. In case lots on the dock in Tangier you could buy the same pack for about eight cents. Since it was a run of only three days and three nights in a reasonably fast boat from Tangier to the French coast, a lot of smuggling went on. Much of the contraband was landed southeast of Marseille, where the shoreline is cut by dozens of little *calanques*, narrow inlets big enough to harbor a good-sized power boat where it won't attract too much attention. I had a chance to ship aboard one of the *contrabandiers* as a deckhand and, if I wanted to invest my own money and take my own risks, become one of the minor partners in the venture. For services rendered, like swabbing the decks and heaving the trade goods.

I heard about it from Jean-Pierre, a friend of mine who had been a sous-bartender at the Martinez until Cedric caught him watering the Scotch to make up for what he was pilfering. He had connections, including the kind necessary to convert Emmaline dear's thousand dollar check into francs at the black market rate. He hadn't clipped me too badly on the deal, so I knew he was fairly honest, for a crook. He thought, or hoped, that a wealthy playboy like me could be persuaded to spring the necessary investment and cut him in for a piece because he was such a sweet fellow. He was *décavé*, as they say. Flat. Stony.

"*Figure-toi*," he said, over a beer he had persuaded me to buy him. He spoke better English than I did French, but I preferred to practice my French whenever possible. Since I was putting out for the beer, he obliged me. The dollars-and-cents figures are my own translation of what he said in francs, to make it easier to follow. "*Figure-toi*. With a thousand dollars we buy twenty cases, twelve thousand packs. At retail, that's six thousand dollars, five thousand clear profit. Even if we wholesale them to get our money back fast, we can get thirty-five cents a pack easy. Let's see, wait a minute, that works out at—"

"You wait a minute," I said. "What's all this about 'we' and 'our money'? What are *you* planning to put up?"

"Every sou I have in the world." He looked hurt. I suppose the way he had looked when they caught him watering the Scotch.

"How much is that?"

"Three hundred francs."

Three hundred francs was then, at the old rate, worth something less than seventy-five cents American. I said, "What did you have in mind for the profits from my thousand dollars and your three hundred francs? Something like a fifty-fifty split?"

"Certainly not. I concede that you should have more than half. Say seventy-five twenty-five? I have to do the cooking aboard the boat."

"Say nine hundred and ninety-nine to one if you serve soup the same way you serve whiskey. Anyway, I haven't got anything like a thousand dollars left. I've been living on it for a couple of months now. Let's start over again."

As it worked out, I was able to get up a good part of the thousand by cashing in the gold cigarette case, the wristwatch and the wardrobe Emmaline dear had bought me, including my elegant evening clothes (still with stray bits of confetti in the pockets as a reminder of the charity ball and Reggie's character-strengthening adversity). It left me stripped down to pretty much the assets I had on my back, but with those big profits to come on the investment I wasn't worried. Jean-Pierre begged, borrowed or embezzled enough to sweeten his share of the pot a bit, and we went aboard the cigarette-runner in Marseille harbor.

It was a converted British navy cutter with a souped-up engine and a false name that Jean-Pierre and I had to paint over its rightful registry as soon as we were at sea. Its captain was a hard-case Corsican who went by the name of Le Sanglier. A *sanglier* is a wild boar, of which both Corsica and Sardinia still have respectable populations. They are among the most dangerous, ugly and single-minded killers in existence if you challenge them. Some sportsmen choose to do so with a lance and a pal standing backup with a rifle in case the lance misses. A *sanglier* will not only rip your guts out with his tusks if he can get them into you, he will eat your guts afterward for lunch. To look at, this one was no exception. All he lacked was the tusks sticking up out of his lower jaw. He had been away three times for murder, according to Jean-Pierre.

The mate—I guess you could call him that since

he was the one who yelled at Jean-Pierre and me to
get off our *culs* whenever anything had to be done
aboard the cutter—was another Corsican, a relatively
benevolent type who called himself La Planche; The
Plank. He had only been away for murder once, which
made him something of a sissy. All the *gangstaires*
and hard characters doing business on the Côte d'Azur
were Corsicans, great boys for a nice friendly vendetta
with their pals when they weren't knocking off other
people. The Boar and The Plank were typical speci-
mens. They were the ship's complement except for
Jean-Pierre, me and the engineer, who liked engines
better than he liked people and mostly stayed below
playing with his toys. If he had a name or nickname
I never knew it, although I suppose the French cops
did.

We put out of Marseille, stopped briefly at Barcelona
for some reason that took The Boar ashore for a while
but was none of my business and did not make me
nosy. I am never nosy in any way about the doings of
tough *mecs* like The Boar and The Plank. Two days
and three nights later we put in at Gibraltar to fuel up
for business. We shipped what seemed to me like an
over-large deckload of high-test gasoline, in drums, as
well as topping up the cutter's fuel tanks. I was still
keeping my nose strictly to myself, but The Plank
bought a couple of bottles of something while we were
at Gib, and while he didn't offer to share with his hard-
working crew it made him talkative enough to explain
why we needed all the extra *essence*.

"Can't always find it in Tangier," he said. "Then
you're in trouble. The Spaniards, dirty bastards, they

run customs patrols out of Ceuta. As if they owned the Mediterranean. Even when you're beyond the territorial limit, they come after you. With machine guns, no less. There are also pirates who cruise around looking for honest *commerçants*, to steal their goods. Even a good fast boat like this one, it can't outrun a bullet, and they always aim for the fuel tanks, to cripple you. What we do is, we rig an auxiliary feed-line and pump for each engine so we can tap into a drum right away if we're hit, *tu piges*? That way, we know we can keep moving. In this business, you keep moving or you're out of this business."

He laughed at his own wit and had a pull at his bottle, not offering it around.

"Jean-Pierre kind of forgot to mention the bit about the shooting," I said. "Does anyone ever get killed?"

"Oh, now and then, now and then. There's no need for it, though. Not if you stow your cargo right."

He didn't volunteer any further explanation, so I didn't ask for one. But I found out what he meant when we tied up in the *darse* at Tangier, where the dockside warehouses are, and began to heave cases of American cigarettes aboard.

The Boar must have been heading up some kind of a syndicate operation, or else he had knocked off a bank lately. Jean-Pierre and I lugged cartons until our tongues were dragging and still they kept coming, wheeled out of the warehouse to dockside on a hand-truck and dumped there for us to load by hand. I lost count of the number of tons of tobacco we sweated aboard the cutter, but The Boar didn't, not for a moment. Neither did the warehouse checker. Not at

$60 a case, cash and carry. The trouble was, they didn't check their tallies with each other until the loading was finished. At that point The Boar's count was two cases short of the warehouse checker's count.

Cash and carry in this kind of trading means cash down first, on the barrelhead, carry only after the money has been counted. Any other kind of arrangement would mean quick bankruptcy for the sellers, dealing as they are with crooks and *gangstaires* who would think nothing of loading up and taking off without payment if they could get away with it. According to the checker, The Boar had received the merchandise he had paid for, and that was that. According to The Boar, he still had two cases coming. Difference of opinion. Clash of wills. Argument. Not for long, though.

The Boar had an odd expressionless voice, without much inflection. I think one of his Corsican *amici* had tried to cut his throat but succeeded only in damaging his vocal cords. In a later year I saw this happen in Brazil, where a guy pushed a bamboo pig-sticker three inches into another guy's throat during a fight without doing much more damage than a tracheotomy. An inch to either side of the gullet he'd have caught an artery or a major vein. The Boar had a scar where it would have happened to him, and his odd voice might have been the result of scar tissue on his larynx. He never raised it or strained it in any way. He didn't need to.

The warehouse checker was reasonable about it, and patient enough, but a Frenchman himself and therefore a pighead. He said, "Observe, *mon vieux*. I am paid a wage because I know how to count. I have checked goods out of this warehouse for fifteen years to earn my wage. I do not look at the girls' tits when I should be minding my business, nor count that which does not pass before my eyes. If you wish you may unload the boat and we will count again." (I felt my spine go at that.) "Otherwise the transaction has been completed. *C'est fini. Bon soir et bon voyage*."

"Two more cases," The Boar said in his funny voice, although by "funny" I don't mean in any way comical. He never joked, laughed, smiled or showed any visible sign of enjoyment that I ever noticed. He may have done so while he was killing people.

"I don't make mistakes," he said. "Other people make mistakes."

He was standing on the cutter's deck, the warehouseman on the wharf. The tide was so low, and the cutter so heavily laden, that The Boar's head was about at the level of the warehouseman's knees. He talked to them, or maybe to the guy's feet, not bothering to crane his neck until the warehouseman said impatiently, "*Dis donc*, don't be a stubborn fool, man. You have the *mégots* you paid for—"

The Boar looked up then. I couldn't see his face. I was standing behind him. But just the reflection of it, so to speak, in the warehouseman's eyes was enough to scare me at second-hand. The warehouseman stopped talking with his mouth open, looking sick. In the same dead, expressionless voice The Boar said, "Nobody cheats The Boar."

That was the end of the debate. He jerked his thumb at Jean-Pierre and me, motioning us up onto the wharf.

We went where the thumb indicated, up on the wharf
and into the warehouse. The checker kind of tottered
along after us. Jean-Pierre and I had each picked up
another case of cigarettes and were on our way back to
the cutter before he caught up with us. If he saw us or
the cigarettes go by, all he registered was a No Sale.
He still looked sick, as if he had taken a good stiff kick
in the balls.

The Plank showed us how he wanted the stuff stored,
most of it as deck-load stacked and lashed and covered
with a tarpaulin to make head-high breastworks around
the wheelhouse except for such peepholes as were
necessary to navigation; another breastwork around
the high-test drums, another along both thwarts building up at the stern to higher than waist level. He knew
his job, The Plank did. When Jean-Pierre and I finally
collapsed of bone-weary fatigue after personally trans-
ferring the contents of one whole warehouse to the
cutter, we were able to poop out behind the security of
the prettiest fortification you ever saw sandbagged
with Lucky Strikes, Camels, Chesterfields and other
popular carcinogens. A spray of machine-gun fire
wouldn't do the merchandise any great good, but the
tobacco would still be there and saleable, even if
shredded, and the slugs weren't going to come through
the thickness of a double tier of tight-packed cigarette
cartons nearly a yard through. I felt some better about
making the run for home and mother when I realized
what we had constructed for ourselves.

We got out of Tangier that night around 1 A.M.,
winding up easily as we went across the bay. The Boar
had the heavily laden cutter doing twenty knots or

better by the time we cleared the end of the breakwater. He had sensibly picked a moonless night for the
enterprise, counting on speed and darkness for insurance, and ran without lights as soon as we were in
open sea. The cutter's engines were finely tuned,
well-balanced and well-muffled, first-class power
plants. The Boar was no fool when it came to business,
or looking out for *Numéro Un*.

We had to run the Straits of Gibraltar at their nar-
rowest point, about ten miles or so west of Ceuta and
the Rock, and the Spaniards had patrols working out
of both sides, Algeciras as well as Ceuta. Their boats
weren't as fast as The Boar's cutter, couldn't touch
it in a stern chase. Bullets could, as The Plank had
remarked. It was something to think about, although
of course not seriously with all those fine fortifications
around us and all those well-nourished horses thrum-
ming away below-deck.

I don't know where territorial limits end and the
high seas begin in the Straits. I think they must be
international waters open to all shipping, and I don't
think Spain legally had any right to patrol them as it
did in those days. As a matter of international law,
about which I don't know too much, it seems to me
that the mere fact of a load of a few tons of tax-free
cigarettes legally bought and paid for aboard a boat is
no basis by itself for persecuting the boat's owners
and/or operators before they have done anything to
justify persecution. Like maybe smuggling the stuff
ashore where they shouldn't. Anybody who tries
to relieve them of their lawful cargo by force and
violence before that happens is no better than a

Communist or a lousy hijacker, in my opinion. There we were, peacefully humming along through the night minding our own business and molesting nobody when force and violence burst at us without warning out of the nearby dark in the shape of a bright stitching of machine-gun fire laid squarely across the cutter's bow. At the same instant the beam of a powerful searchlight snapped on to catch us in its glare, and a voice began yelling through a bullhorn warning us in three languages to heave to before they blew us out of the water. Some more of that adversity Reggie had been sure would make a man of me had just taken a hand in the strengthening process.

Chapter Three

As The Plank explained later, his voice trembling with honest indignation, the dirty *salauds* had cheated us by not following the rules. The Boar had been threading the channel of the Straits by instinct, the seat of his pants and the positions of the running lights of other craft within sight—including, The Plank said, what they both were pretty sure were Spanish patrol boats safely off to port and starboard. But the *salauds* also had another boat out, running dark as we were but undoubtedly with some kind of apparatus aboard that enabled them to pick us up and track us in the dark. A *cochon's* trick, in The Plank's words. The Boar, who was already getting just about everything out of the engines they had to give, jammed the throttles wide open, put the wheel over and went away from the searchlight, dodging and weaving the cutter as if it were a polo pony. He really knew how to handle that boat. But the cops aboard the other craft knew how to handle themselves, too. The searchlight beam stayed with us. Machine-gun slugs began to thud rhythmically into the cutter's hull and stern breastworks of pure Virginia burley.

Jean-Pierre and I were on deck when the fireworks started. We were still pooped from heaving the inventory but recovering nicely with a bottle I had bought in Tangier. We did not propose to share it with The Plank or anyone else, and we had gone aft to commune with

it by ourselves. By good luck we were sitting behind
the stern fortification figuring our profits, our heads
well below the line of fire, when the serious shooting
began. The Boar and The Plank were both in the
wheelhouse behind their own bulwarks, and the high-
test had its own protection, so there was no great
damage on deck. The Spaniards were not, in spite of
their promise, trying to blow us out of the water, as
they could have done easily enough with any kind of
deck-gun. They wanted the cutter and its load, not
prisoners or corpses they would have to account for.
But they kept machine-guns chattering at us, and I
could feel the cigarette cartons at my back jerk, flinch
and wince, or thought I could, as the slugs went into
them.

Actually there were more holes in the hull than in
the merchandise when we made an inspection the
next day, possibly because the guys with the firepower had been trying to puncture the fuel tanks more
than they had been trying to puncture us. But at the
time it seem like an awful lot of lead all homing in on
me, and while my mind kept telling me, *You're perfectly safe, you're perfectly safe, you know they can't
come through all that tobacco,* my cold stomach and
the back of my cold neck and the rest of cold cowering
me cringing there in the scuppers said, *Pal, you have
had it.*

It didn't last for long, only about five hundred years
before we pulled away out of range. During it all Jean-
Pierre was as calm and collected as the calmest combat
veteran you ever saw. He didn't cringe and whimper
and try to dig himself into a deck-seam the way I was

doing. He took it all without turning a hair. In fact he was so cool and unperturbed and unmoving when I finally straightened up and wiped my clammy brow that for a moment I thought a slug had got him.

Nevah feeyah, as the Honorable Reggie would have said. He'd merely fainted; passed out cold at the sound of the opening shots. I brought him around with a couple of belts from the bottle, after first taking a couple myself for my nerves.

After that it was clear sailing, fine weather and no particular sweat. We still had to keep a lookout for hijackers, but during the day we could outrun anything that showed on the horizon, and at night pirates would have had to have some pretty elaborate equipment to pick us up in the dark without lights. They'd have to catch us after that, too. It wouldn't be easy in the open sea where The Boar had plenty of maneuvering room and all those horses under him. Just to be on the safe side, however, he or The Plank, whoever was at the wheel—they stood watch and watch—would stop the motors every now and then during the night to listen for anything on the water nearby. Nothing ever got close to us.

As we drew closer to home base, both The Boar and The Plank, solid businessmen with a strong sense of responsibility to their own welfare, began visibly to relax and take it easy. The Boar, in what was for him practically a moment of benevolence, told Jean-Pierre and me we could smoke a *mégot*.

"One of your own, not mine," he said. Pockmarks on his pig face and little cold black eyes like Corsican goat droppings didn't help him look any more big-hearted than he meant to be. "One, not two. And stay the hell away from the high-test while you're smoking it."

Jean-Pierre and I said, "Yes, sir," in chorus, grateful for small favors. Until then, the rule had been strictly *défense de fumer* at all times on deck since Gib, although both The Boar and The Plank smoked in the wheelhouse. We hadn't been invited to join their club, and we didn't try to form a clandestine club of our own. Dealing with *durs* like those guys, you do not risk your life for the sake of a quick puff. We each had one *mégot*, not two, and stayed the hell away from the high-test while we were smoking it.

Even the sourpuss engineer, who only came topside for meals and whose usual response to a friendly Hello was, "*Merde, alors*," began to act less grumpy than usual. I couldn't read the reactions, and it bothered me. As far as I could see, the trickiest and most risky part of the operation, the actual smuggling of the goods ashore, was still ahead of us. I asked Jean-Pierre what he thought, if maybe somebody had something up his sleeve for us, but he didn't think so. Neither did I, really. Our piddling twenty cases didn't even qualify as worth thieving alongside the load the cutter was carrying, and as fall guys for something big we just weren't believable. We finally got The Plank to tell us the reason for all the sweetness and light aboard the cutter as we went into the last leg of the trip.

It was easy. The fix was in.

"Not a thing to worry about, *mes potes*," he said. "Ours is truly a piece of cake. Two of Nice's best are with us in the *assiette au beurre*, right up to their *délicieuses*. They are to supervise the shore operations."

"*Sergots?*" Jean-Pierre said unbelievingly.

The Plank grinned.

"*Motards*, no less. We'll truck the stuff away under escort."

You have to *piger* the argot used in Marseille's *milieu*, underworld, to understand exactly what they were talking about. I didn't *piger* all of it, but I got enough. Two motorcycle cops from Nice, moon-lighting I suppose on their spare time, were involved in the smuggling up to their whatnots. They would presumably be ready, willing and able to take care of any necessary little details ashore like misdirecting their Marseille colleagues to the wrong *calanque* during the landing operations if anything of the kind became necessary. They would also be on hand in all their uniformed majesty to ride shotgun on our convoy of contraband when we drove it into Marseille, after loading it into the trucks that would be waiting for us at the *calanque*. It was a sweet set-up.

"I think we might even fly the tricolor from the leading truck, to lend distinction to our passage," The Plank said. "*Allons enfants de la patrie, le jour de gloire est arrivé.*"

He went forward humming *La Marseillaise*.

I began to relax after that. Everything was lovely. Not the least of the loveliness was the fact that every-body involved in the operation would be anxious to move the stuff out of the *calanque* and get it rolling as quickly as possible. Jean-Pierre and I would not have to unload the whole cargo without help, as we had loaded it. In fact—enjoying another of my own *mégots* which The Boar had generously allowed me to consume—I felt rich, lucky and euphoric.

Talk about adversity. As they say in the funny papers—POW!

We arrived off the French coast in the middle of the night, hanging well offshore still without lights while The Boar talked briefly on the cutter's radiophone. French territorial jurisdiction extends twenty kilometers into the Mediterranean. You're legally a *contrabandiste* the moment you take untaxed cigarettes, booze or anything else across the twenty-kilometer line. As such you are subject to the full penalties of the law, which are horrid. The state confiscates not only your cigarettes, if that is what you are smuggling—they are then sold by *Régie Nationale*, the French National Tobacco Monopoly, for its own profit—but also your boat, your equipment, your shirt, whatever else you have in your possession and your freedom while the *juge d'instruction* decides what to do with you. Everything else involved in the venture, for example the trucks and small boats waiting to move the loot from the landing ground, is also forfeited, and fines are assessed based on the value of the gross take. Of course you never have anything left to pay the fines with, but still the loss of all those valuables must be painful to those who lose them.

The Boar took no chances. He stood off well outside the twenty-kilometer limit until he was ready to go, about three A.M. Then he went in hard and fast; lights out, throttles open, straight as a homing pigeon to the haven of the agreed-upon *calanque* and the warm welcoming arms of the Marseille cops waiting for us there.

Looking back, I suppose there was something mildly humorous about the beef that arose later between the Marseille police, who confiscated the motorcycles of the two *motards* along with the other loot, and the Nice police, who owned the machines and wanted them back. The humor of it didn't strike me for a long time. Before we went into the *calanque* The Boar signaled ashore with a blinker, got the right blinks back and pulled the cutter up as pretty as you please exactly where the *flics* were ready to jump aboard. They had guns and flashlights poked in our faces before the motors had even been cut.

Guns and flashlights in my face didn't scare me half as much as I would have been scared if I had been the guy who sold out The Boar. When they put the bracelets on him he asked one question only, in his expressionless way: "Who did it to me?"

"*Ferme ta gueule!*" one of the *flics* said, cracking him on the chin with an elbow. It's a trick French cops have, useful when they've got a gun in one hand and a flashlight in the other. They can keep both pointed at you and knock you down at the same time. This one didn't knock The Boar down, but he got the message. His *gueule* stayed strictly *fermée* from then on. He wasn't the type to talk much when talking served no purpose.

The engineer said "*Merde alors*" in a resigned way when they handcuffed him. I didn't say anything. All of a sudden I had forgotten how to speak French. Jean-Pierre babbled a lot without saying much. The

Plank was the only one of us who attained any real eloquence.

That was when the five of us were loaded into a truck that already held the rest of the catch, including the two *motards*. The Plank tried to go for them, cuffs and all, but caught a bang on the ear from one of the cops in the truck with us that knocked him over. Not down, just over. The truck was too full for him to go down all the way; just to his knees. Kneeling there, in an attitude of reverent prayer, his hands more or less clasped before him by the stricture of the handcuffs, he called the *motards crottes de chameaux, fils de putains*, and assorted kinds of *merde* and *espèces de cons morbides* as well as a number of other colorful names which I would rather not translate even if I could speak French. The *motards* shrugged, lifting their hands to show their own bracelets. The Plank finally ran out of air to curse them with. I wondered if maybe they were the double-crossers The Boar had asked about, wearing the cuffs and taking the ride in the truck with the rest of us to prove that they, too, were innocent victims. If so, I hope they never went back into police work again, unless it was in an armored car.

They threw us in the *violon* in Marseille. I had been smart enough not to bring my passport or any other documentation on the expedition, just in case. My identity papers, army discharge and the rest, were safe back in the *pension* in Cannes. Since I couldn't speak two words of French I had time to think up what I was going to say in English before an interpreter showed up.

"What's your name?" was the first question.

"Phineas T. Barnum."

"Where do you live?"

"The Bronx, New York, U.S.A."

"What street address?"

"Three thirty-three and a third Joe Doakes Boulevard."

"What's your business? When you're not smuggling cigarettes?"

"I wasn't smuggling cigarettes. I'm a simple, honest tourist—"

"What's your business when you're not smuggling cigarettes?"

"I just got out of the army. Before that I sold Bibles."

"You what?"

"I sold Bibles. In a Bible store. The Bronx Biblical Basement."

"Where's your passport?"

"It was stolen from me in Tangier. So were my money, baggage and everything else I owned. That's why I had to work my way to France on what I thought would be a yacht until I discovered to my horror, surprise and despair that—"

"Throw him back in the tank." The *flic* who was feeding questions in French to the interpreter to relay in English yawned, nodding to another *flic* to show me back to my suite. "The *juge d'instruction* will enjoy talking to this one."

In France they do not have trial by jury, habeas corpus, Bills of Rights or any of those effete refinements. The law is based on the Code Napoléon, which says in effect that you are guilty until judged innocent. The judging in the initial stages of a criminal investigation is done by what they call a *juge d'instruction*. He looks at the facts of the crime, he looks at the available evidence, he looks at you, he ponders, he concludes. While he's concluding, you stay in the *violon* for as long as it takes, perhaps years if he can't make up his mind easily. No bail. Sometimes he decides you're innocent and turns you loose, say after you've been on ice for two years. You don't get a refund of the two years, but you've been exonerated. Justice has triumphed. Sometimes, after the same two years, the *juge* decides that you're guilty two years worth and turns you loose. You've served the same time as the innocent guy, but that's because you were guilty, see? Justice has triumphed again. Sometimes the *juge* thinks you're guilty more than two years worth. In that case he keeps you in escrow for as much longer as he thinks you have coming to you, or turns you over to a formal court for trial on the basis of his findings and recommendations.

Les juges, I am told, are mostly fair. But they are also practical Frenchmen, and the practicalities in the cases of The Boar, The Plank and Merde Alors were their pressing needs to get back to work at their trade, namely gangsterism, if they were ever going to contribute their bit to *la patrie* and the French National Treasury. I don't think anyone ever believed for a minute that they would pay one sou of the huge fines they owed, or a centime in income tax, anything like that. What they were expected to do, what they probably did as soon as they were released, was stick up a bank or a jewelry store for enough loot to buy another boat, if they couldn't pinch one, and a new cargo of contraband. Sooner or later, maybe not the first time or the second time they tried it, the cops would get them again with another big windfall. And so on, without waste of *le juge's* time or taxpayers' money on free board and room for a trio of Corsican hoods. They were out of the *violon* and on their way back to their jobs within a week. Trusties, kind of, you might say. Everyone had a lot of confidence that they would be back.

Jean-Pierre and I were different. The *juge* didn't think we would necessarily be back if we were turned loose. We didn't have what it took to be real *gang-staires*. If he had known the Honorable Regina's favorite word he'd have described us as a couple of spivs. He never questioned us together, and we never got to see much of each other in the *violon*, but I knew he was pumping Jean-Pierre at the same time and along the same lines as he was me because he knew things that only Jean-Pierre could have, I mean would have, told him.

One afternoon while we were going through one of our Q-and-A sessions and I was having my usual stumbling difficulty in figuring out what his questions meant as filtered through the interpreter's indifferent English, he said casually, "I'm thinking of letting your friend go."

I got that on the interpreter's first try. I said, "That's good to hear, sir. When do we get out?"

"I said, your friend. Not you. You'll be with us for a while yet."

The uncomprehending look on my face was genuine enough when I heard that, first in French and then in English. (Incidentally, there is nothing like a stretch in jail where nobody else speaks your language to sharpen your knowledge of what is being spoken around you. I recommend the experience without reservation to anyone really in earnest about becoming a linguist. After a few weeks in the *violon* my French was as fluent and polished as that of any waterfront pickpocket in Marseille. I also came out with a fair working vocabulary of alley Arabic from a couple of Algerians who were doing time for a smash-and-grab.) "I don't understand, sir. Jean-Pierre is just as—I mean to say, I'm just as innocent as he is. Why discriminate against me?"

"I've learned all I need to know from him. In your case, it's rather more difficult. Because of the language difficulty, you understand." He cocked an eyebrow at me. "What a pity you speak no French, eh?"

He was a shrewd old boy, and a decent fellow. I think he kind of liked me, in a disapproving way. I'm pretty sure he would have liked to disapprove of me less than he did. I thought, what the hell. Before the interpreter could translate his last comment, I said, "*Pas un seul mot.*"

The *juge* chuckled.

"I thought so," he said, and told the interpreter, who looked shocked at what must have seemed to him pretty close to contempt of court, that he could leave. "Now would you like to tell me anything you have failed to tell me so far? Anything of the truth, that is to say."

"I'd guess you have it all from Jean-Pierre already, sir."

He nodded. "I think so. Jean-Pierre does not have your native intelligence. It is the main reason I am letting him go. I can only empty his dull mind, not reason with it. Yours I hope to be able to reach and influence. Do you realize the risks you assume, the dangers you are exposing yourself to, when you associate with cut-throat criminals like Le Sanglier and La Planche?"

"I think so, sir."

"I think not."

He went on to give me a father lecture on the evils of forming bad acquaintances. He didn't put it on a legal plane or appeal to my sense of Christian morality. I'll say that for him. He simply set out to scare the hell out of me, and did. In a way he, too, had a hand in nudging me into a life of crime, I mean the kind of life of crime I chose, because he sure nudged me away from further intimate association with Corsican hoods. The Boar had been put away for three murders and The Plank for one, as Jean-Pierre had said. But each had several unscored kills to his credit, known kills but without enough evidence left behind for conviction, plus a large number of probables. They killed business competitors, vendetta rivals, bank clerks who tried to kick off an alarm, innocent bystanders, all with equal indifference, as if they were mosquitoes. Human life, the *juge* said, meant nothing to them because they were not themselves human. They lived like jungle beasts. They would die like beasts when a stronger beast attacked them.

"As you can die simply by becoming known as an

associate of either man," he warned me. "To become a
friend of Le Sanglier or La Planche is to make blood
enemies of all his enemies, of which each has hun-
dreds. Do you know why they were betrayed in the
calanque?"

"No, sir. Do you?"

"I do not. Neither do they. I suspect it was done
for vendetta, in the hope that they would be killed,
nothing more. No reward for the betrayal has been
claimed or paid. Only France benefited from it in
a material way. But some day, somehow, either Le
Sanglier or La Planche or both will learn the identity
of their betrayer, and then he will die more or less
horribly depending on how much time they have to
spare for him. If they and their friends and the people
suspected of perhaps being their friends are not all
brutally murdered first. Am I making an impression
on you?"

"You are indeed, sir." I wasn't giving him any
blague, either. I could practically feel those machine-
gun slugs thumping into me instead of the cigarette
cartons. Jerk, flinch, wince. "I give you my word I will
associate with no more Corsican gangsters. Not voluntarily, that is."

He smiled gently.

"I have yet to know what your word is worth," he
said. "Or the extent of the reservation you have in
mind when you qualify your promise to voluntary association with Corsican gangsters. You may go now."

He pushed the button to call the cop who took me
back and forth to my cage.

"When will I be released, sir?"

"When I make up my mind that you are ready for release."

Two days later he made up his mind. Better to say, Reggie made it up for him.

He had me brought up again for what I thought would be another round of Q-and-A. When the cop delivered me, backed out and closed the door to leave us alone as was customary, we weren't alone. The Honorable Regina was with us, looking down her patrician nose at me with even greater lack of regard than usual.

"Hello, sweetheart," I said. "How nice to see you. What are you in for?"

I almost added, "Soliciting?" but refrained out of inherent gentlemanliness. I didn't care what the *juge* thought, or what her reaction would be. I wasn't in the mood for chivalrous thoughts. The last I had held toward her had won me a sore tongue and a smart crack on the boko. Besides, I had my own kind of dungeon to get out of, without worrying too much about hers.

It appeared, however, that my situation had changed, not entirely for the better. The *juge* said, "Lady Forbes-Jones has persuaded me to release you in her custody."

I didn't say anything. I couldn't think of anything to say.

The *juge* went on. "I am placing you on probation to her for three months. You will do what she asks of you. At the end of that time, if you have broken no more laws and her report on your behavior is favorable, there will be no further restriction on your actions. Other than the normal restraints of the law, of course."

I said, "What constitutes favorable behavior?"

"Lady Forbes-Jones will be the judge of that. I will be the judge of the fairness of her report. You are free to leave now. With Lady Forbes-Jones."

"I'd rather stay here. I like it here."

"You have no option." The *juge* bowed courteously to Reggie. "Good day, Lady Forbes-Jones. I am sure the young man will benefit from your interest in his welfare."

"He will." Her stubborn British jaw was set like the blade of a bulldozer. "He will indeed. Nevah feeyah."

We went out to the Mercedes-Benz, which was parked in front of the *violon*. On the way I said, "What's with the Lady Forbes-Jones jazz? You're no lady."

I was hoping she'd take it the wrong way. Instead, she said frostily, "The deception occasionally serves a purpose. I do not use it as a device to cheat people. Get in the front seat."

I got in the front seat. There was a black chauffeur's cap on the seat beside me, no chauffeur. She said, still frostily, "Put on the cap."

I put on the cap. It fit well enough.

She said, "Get behind the wheel. Start the motor. Drive to Cannes."

I said, "Hey, wait a minute, what—"

"Do as you are told. Drive. There will be no further discussion."

"The hell there'll be no further discussion! What do you think you've bought yourself? A trained poodle?"

"A chauffeur. Drive."

"No, ma'am." I took the cap off and put it on the seat where it had been. "I appreciate your kindness, but no dice."

"You are on parole to me. What I report of your behavior during the next three months will determine whether you go back to jail or not, and for how long. Drive."

"No, ma'am. I didn't give my parole to anybody. You and the *juge* cooked this up without consulting me. I told him, I'm telling you, I'd rather go back to jail. Anyway, I don't have a *permis de travail*. Goodbye. It's been real cozy knowing you."

I opened the door to get out of the car. She said, still with the same frost in her voice, "Get back behind the wheel. Put on the cap. Drive. A *permis de travail* is not necessary for the employment I have in mind. After you have started the motor I shall explain why you are going to do exactly what I tell you to do, without discussion or opposition."

Something about the way she said it persuaded me that she had me by *les délicieuses*, as The Plank might have put it. I did what she said. She explained what she had said she was going to explain. There was no further discussion.

The Honorable Regina, a habitual reader of French papers like *Nice-Matin*, had seen a report of the happenings in the *calanque*. From it she surmised, with her usual tendency to believe the worst and in view of my disappearance from the Cannes scene a few days earlier, that I might be the American lad involved in

the affair who spoke no French, had given his name as
P.T. Barnum of the Bronx and was then sitting it out in
the Marseille slammer. For my own good, as she said,
but in my opinion more to tenderize me for what was
to follow, she had let me marinate in there for a few
weeks; not, however, without first hunting out my *pension* and there pinching all my papers by conning an
easily conned landlady into believing she was an old
family friend. She had my passport, army discharge,
everything. With those in her grip, she had me, too.
Right where it hurt.

I could have gone to law about it, probably. She
had no right to sequester my identification papers,
whatever other authority the *juge* had given her. But
going to law against somebody who can have *you*
sequestered as easily as not for an indefinite period
seems kind of shortsighted. I decided not to make an
issue of the papers, although I didn't like not having
them. I couldn't legitimately leave the country, move
around freely within it, register at a hotel, collect on a
postal or telegraphic money order, cash a traveler's
check anywhere I wasn't known even if I'd had traveler's checks to cash—in short, I was cooked, canned
and encased. I no longer had my wristwatch, my gold
cigarette case or my snappy wardrobe. Nothing but a
black chauffeur's cap—hers—and my remaining personal attire: a pair of dungarees, a pair of rope-soled
espadrilles, a denim shirt and an army field jacket.

"You'll have to buy yourself a decent suit," she said,
when she had finished dealing out the rest of the cold
deck. "Black. I'll give you the money for it. Also black

shoes, a black tie and a white shirt. On second thought, you're not to be trusted with money. Charge the goods and have the bill sent to me."

"Shouldn't I have a black *boutonnière* to go with the rest of the mourner's outfit? If you'll give me an advance on my salary, I'd just as soon buy my own clothes."

"What salary?"

"I thought you made it fairly clear that I have been inducted into service as your chauffeur."

"I do not recall that mention was made of a salary. Were you to be paid a salary you would of course need a *permis de travail*. You have said you are without one."

"Oh," I said. "Yes. I see. Am I going to be allowed to eat during the next three months, or just think about it?"

"I shall continue to pay your board at your *pension*. I have already paid a month in advance."

"When you stole my papers in a friendly way, no doubt. What about a cigarette now and then, or a *pastis*?"

She didn't answer right away. I drove, twisting over a little in the seat to get a look at her face in the rearview mirror. She was looking out the window at the scenery, which was remarkably pretty even if I hadn't been attuned to it by a stretch in the icebox; a typical poplar-lined French country road through green wheatfields with the blood-crimson splashes of *coquelicots*. Flanders poppies, among the green, the bright blue cloudless sky of Provence over all.

Her face, it seemed to me, looked less grim than it had when she was chivvying me into the car, although grim enough. Grim, and in a way, sad. Without taking her eyes from the view she said, "Curly, do you remember my words about your need for the strengthening effects of adversity?"

"Yes, ma'am. Not the words, exactly, but the viciousness with which they were spoken."

"Whether you choose to believe it or not, I have your best interests at heart. I want you to be something you are not and will never be without direction."

"Yes, ma'am. They used to feed us the same line in the army."

"You have potentialities which I hope to see realized, some day. Meanwhile, stop saying Yes, ma'am. I am not going to speak to you about it again. You may say Yes, madame or No, madame, whichever is appropriate."

I said, "Yes, madame," resisting an urge to tell her she was better qualified to be a madam than a lady. I figured the next ninety days were going to be rough enough on the rock pile without making them any tougher for myself with wisecracks.

Chapter Four

How right I was.

When I bought the suit and other stuff she had told me to get, I added to the list a few further essentials like underpants, socks, an extra shirt, handkerchiefs; the necessaries, nothing more. No wristwatches, no gold cigarette cases. She didn't rack me up when the bill came in, so I figured she was maybe going to be reasonably reasonable about cigarette money and such. Nevah feeyah. For more than a month I literally didn't have a centime in my, I mean her, pants pockets; no way of picking up a centime on the side the way she kept my nose to the handlebars, and nothing to hock. She didn't use the Mercedes-Benz much during the day, but she insisted that it be kept clean, shined and polished at all times. It took a lot of massage. The car was a fine piece of machinery; gasoline-engine powered, not one of those rattly Diesel jobs they were putting on the European market at the same time. I fiddled around with the motor of this one until I had it tuned as fine as Merde Alors' twins on the cutter. It helped occupy my time, not too unpleasantly.

The bad hours were when she went out on the town with one of her quick-turnover boyfriends. I'd have to wait around maybe five or six hours outside some casino with no cigarettes, no *apéritif* money, no coffee money and no nonsense about knocking off and coming back later, James. I did the full stretch every time, listening to the fun and games going on inside the casino, wishing for a smoke and meditating on the strengthening effects of adversity. Sometimes I could bum a *mégot* or a cup of *jus de chaussettes* from one of the other galley-slaves waiting for his boss, but not too often. French chauffeurs, like other people, are not inclined to lay out for coffee and cigarettes regularly to a guy who doesn't lay out once in a while in his turn.

I spent many a bare and empty evening that way while she lived the gay, carefree life of the glamorous Riviera with some of the most obvious fortune-hunting phonies you could find even in that part of the world. They were real prize packages, most of the guys who took her out. I learned a few tricks of the trade just by observing where they went wrong with Reggie. Not that any of them was ever right with Reggie, but they kept getting wronger and wronger the longer they worked at it. All of them were so convinced of their own irresistibility to females that her imperviousness to their magnetic charms and overwhelming sex appeal drove them ape. Sooner or later they would make the mistake of a heavy pass, often enough in the car.

Those were my only moments of enjoyment. I'd hear Reggie's fine right hand whistle into action, the crack of her fist on the guy's chin, his grunt of surprise and pain. Then I would say respectfully, over my shoulder, "Does madame wish me to hurl the crumb-bum into the street?" She'd say, as cool as ever, "I'll let you know if I need assistance," and that would usually be the end of it. They rarely invited a second pop on the button. I knew why, too.

I had to move in only twice. Both times the guys
had had too much to drink. One was a Belgian, easy to
handle; a nothing. I pulled him out of the car, kicked
his ass and told him to piss off while he was able to.
The other was Italian and a gutter-fighter. He'd been
around. When I pulled him out of the car he let me do
all the work without argument until he got his feet on
the ground, then belted me on the back of the neck
with his locked hands and brought his knee up as my
face went down to meet it. His knee got me smack on
the chin. It was my own fault for thinking he was going
to be a soft touch, like the Belgian. The knee in the
chin stiffened me, but at that it was a lot better than
a knee in the nose. He'd have flattened it like a
squashed tomato.

I woke up on the ground with my head in Reggie's
lap and a *flic* shining a flashlight on us. He thought I
was drunk and had made a pass at Reggie myself. Her
dress was torn at the shoulder. We got him straightened out after a while. Reggie said she didn't want to
bring charges, and declined to give the guy's name.
The *flic* shrugged, helped me up, found my uniform
cap, asked if I was in shape to drive, shooed away a
small crowd that had gathered in the street and went
his way. Reggie and I went ours.

My head ached like hell, and I felt cheap. The guy
had handled me too easily. Reggie may have sensed
something of my feeling, because after I'd been driving
for a while she said, "I'm sorry he hurt you, Curly."

That made me feel a whole lot no better. I went on
driving. A while later she said, "Thank you for trying to
help," and a moment after that, "But I did say I'd ask

for help if I needed it, and I didn't ask. I can take care of myself."

"What were you going to do, let the clown strip you naked before you were ready to yell?" She, the headache and the cheap feeling all combined to make me mad.

"Don't be impertinent!"

"*I'm* impertinent for taking a knee in the face from a guy who's trying to rape you? Madame, if I may say so without disrespect, you are without doubt—"

"I don't want to hear your view about my actions! Please attend to your driving."

I thought she sounded a good bit more independent and sure of herself than she really was. Back there on the ground, when I had woken up with my head in her lap and the *flic's* light shining on us, her face had been white and scared. She had looked lost, abandoned, bereft; I don't know how to say it exactly. It was one time I saw her with her defenses down. Just a quick glimpse into the dungeon before the gates closed again.

I'd been her bond-servant for about five weeks, on good behavior all the time, when I was approached by a smooth character in a leather jacket like those worn by the *motards* who had been in the sneezer with me in Marseille. I was standing my usual evening watch outside a *boîte* in Juan-les-Pins, hungry for a cigarette and a cup of coffee. It was a cold night, with a colder drizzle coming down. Sitting in the car to keep warm, I saw this guy park a big Jaguar and get out. Without any hesitation he came over to the Mercedes-Benz to offer me a cigarette.

I thought he was another chauffeur at first, until I tasted the cigarette. It was American; the two hundred and fifty franc kind. Chauffeurs smoke Gitanes, or Gauloises Bleus.

"Keep the pack," he said, speaking with a strong Niçois accent. "Go for a drink?"

"Of what?" He definitely wasn't any chauffeur.

"Coffee with cognac."

There wasn't a thing in the world right then I wanted more than a coffee-cognac to go with that good American cigarette. Still, ministering angels who climb out of big Jags bearing gifts like those are objects of suspicion to people with suspicious minds. I said, "What's the rest of it?"

"Can I get in the car? I'm getting wet out here."

"If your mind is on a stickup, *pote*, forget it. The car is too conspicuous, and I'm too flat."

He grinned. His teeth flashed white in the light from the *boîte's* marquee. Good bouncy jazz was coming from inside. Reggie and her guy would be occupied for a while yet.

"No stickup," he said. "Just a simple little swindle."

"How simple?"

"Your part, very simple. A piece of cake. Let me get in the car while my pants are still dry." His leather coat was beginning to glisten with the moisture on it.

"If you're figuring to swindle my boss, unh-unh. She's too sharp."

"Not your boss. A real easy mark. Do you want the drink or don't you?"

"Get in the car," I said. "But be ready to blow the minute I give you the nod. My boss has a prejudice against crooks. And leave the bottle behind when you leave."

It was good coffee-cognac, very warming to the stomach. So was the prospect of picking up a bit of *braise*, dishonestly or otherwise. As I have pointed out before now, it was Reggie's cruel and inhuman treatment that forced me into a life of crime. Otherwise, who knows? I might have become a bishop.

The *mec* in the leather jacket was too cagey to tell me any more than he had to, that first meeting. He played his tickets as close to his chest as he could, like any other cautious hustler. Later he had to show more of his hand to bring me into the game. The first night, all I learned was what I told him I would have to know if we were to go any further; his name, his track record and how come he had picked me out of the grab-bag. The answers to those questions were satisfactory enough. They had to be, and he knew it.

He was a cashiered cop, a Niçois, name of Albert Bernard. He had been busted off the force for embezzlement of police funds. I don't suggest that all Niçois cops are crooks, just the one I happened to know. He and some pals had got hold of a pigeon and had been plucking him for more than a year. But their gimmicks were wearing thin, and they wanted to set up a new one using an American. I was the American they had in mind, for a piece of the action. The two *motards*, pals of Bernard's, had vouched for my dishonesty, good appearance and willingness to participate in a *fricfrac* if it was crooked enough. Bernard and I made a deal; tentative at first, firm when I knew more about what I was doing.

The de Lille du Rocher swindle got so much publicity when it was exposed that I can write about it now as if I saw the whole picture while I was involved in it. Actually I never did. I guess nobody ever saw the whole picture as it really was, unless it was Bernard. The truth was so incredible that it got distorted in the re-telling, like a juicy bit of scandal full of belly laughs and incredulities; so fantastic that it made headlines not only in France but all over the world. It was written up in *Paris-Match* and several other European periodicals as well as the American issue of *Reader's Digest*. Later it was turned into a TV production by one of the U.S. national networks. Each reporting was a little different from the other, in its details. The substance of the flim-flam, my part in it anyway, was always reported with reasonable accuracy. Except for my right name. That part nobody found out to tell, and I was long gone when the *pot aux roses* was *découvert*, as the French newspapers had it.

Monsieur le Marquis Alain de Lille du Rocher was a pigeon beyond invention. If he hadn't been real he would have been unimaginable. The disclosure of the way he had been repeatedly buncoed over a period of more than a year won him no sympathy, only howls of laughter at his unbelievable credulity. After the first few days of the trial of Bernard and the other crooks who had milked him he never showed up in court again, but went into hiding with Madame la Marquise. He was a man of about forty; very wealthy by inheritance, very simple by nature, and very fearful of the Red Menace. In his view, Communism was a far greater threat than hellfire and damnation. Those might cost him his eternal soul and condemn him to perpetual torment, but the Communists menaced his moneybags, a matter of far greater importance to him. He was very greedy as well as the other things.

One of the people who overheard his anxious and repeated whinnies about the Communist menace was ex-cop Bernard. Bernard still had his cop's uniform and an impressive chestful of war ribbons, some of which may have been legitimate. He passed himself off to M. le Marquis as Inspector Bernard of the Sûreté Nationale or some such official body. With no effort at all, M. l'Inspecteur sold M. le Marquis a gold brick that was made not of gold but of uranium, much more valuable than gold, and far, far more useful in the constant fight that *la belle France* and other powers were waging against the Communist threat.

As Bernard told the tale, the Powers were stockpiling an arsenal on the south side of the Pyrenees for use against the fearful possibility—nay, probability— that the Red hordes would overrun western Europe and the north side of the mountains and have to be fought back from the bastion of Spain. Generalissimo Francisco Franco, Defender of the Faith, was prepared to pay forty thousand dollars for the uranium brick, which Germany was equally prepared to sell to France for only twenty-five thousand dollars. (Approximate dollar equivalents of old French francs here. So many millions and billions of those were involved that the figures lose meaning.) Unhappily the French national treasury was fresh out of francs, *pour le moment seulement, vous comprenez?* Would not M. le Marquis, as a patriotic Frenchman and dedicated anti-Commie, like

to step into the gap with the twenty-five in cash, accept
delivery of the uranium as his security, drive it to the
Spanish border and there meet with the Spanish emissaries who would pay him the forty for his precious
package, C.O.D. Old *pote* Inspector Bernard would
arrange all the details.

M. le Marquis was fairly slobbering with eagerness
to cooperate before Bernard had even finished sinking
the gaff. It took him only a day or two to raise the
twenty-five thousand. For the money he got a hefty
lead box marked, in red, *Danger! Ne Pas Ouvrir!* He
and the marquise, who was a dutiful wife and went
along with her husband on most things, drove the box
to St. Jean-de-Luz, near Biarritz, and there waited
four days for the Spanish emissaries to appear. They
might have been waiting still had not Bernard, who
had been keeping an eye on them through a confed-
erate to be sure they did not open the box prematurely
or otherwise discover that it was full of genuine Mediterranean beach sand, decided that M. le Marquis
would hold still for another trimming. He tolled them
back to the Côte d'Azur to hide the uranium in the
garden of the Marquis' villa on the Cap d'Antibes until
Soviet agents, who had prevented the rendezvous at
St. Jean-de-Luz and were on the trail of the lead
balloon for themselves, could be sidetracked. He
then sold M. le Marquis another, larger, package of
uranium. For $75,000. With the same tale.

"I don't believe it," I told Bernard, when he had got
that far along with the story. "You're conning me now.
Nobody can be that dumb."

"I didn't believe it myself," he confessed. "My

original idea was simply to take him for the twenty-five big ones and fade before he woke up. But then the boob sat there at St. Jean-de-Luz for four days and nights without even feeling the gaff, and when I pulled on the line he came so trustingly I didn't have the heart not to try to pop him again. He practically wept with gratitude when I let him have the second box of sand. He hocked his wife's jewels to get up the *grisbi* that time."

"He can't have much left, then. What do you need me for? I don't get it."

"It keeps coming in. He has a fat regular monthly income from investments. I've been letting him pay in installments for a third package of uranium and a couple of containers of heavy water, you know the stuff they use to make atom bombs with?" Bernard grinned, his teeth very white in his swarthy good-looking Niçois face. "It was heavy, all right. I loaded the containers myself. But now he's getting restless. He wants to see some of the profits before he invests further. That's where you come in."

"I have a feeling it's where I ought to get out. But go on with the tale. I'm still listening, for the time being."

What he wanted of me was my clean-cut American front and a dash of good old-fashioned American razzle-dazzle. He knew quite a lot about me and my situation; that I was on probation to Reggie, that she kept me on a tight leash both financially and in other ways, that my evenings were occupied by her comings and goings and my mornings by the regular groomings I was required to give the Mercedes-Benz. He also knew that she almost never used the car during the day, and that I was mostly free in the afternoons if you can call it freedom when you have nothing to spend but your time, and no one to spend it on. Reggie had warned me not to try to pick up, or let myself be picked up by, anything in any way, shape or form female. Or else. But she hadn't said a word about not letting myself be approached by a crooked ex-cop with big ideas.

"I think he's probably got half a million or so, maybe more, that he can get his hands on in a pinch," Bernard said. "That's what I'm after now. The works, all at once. As much as we can get of it, anyway. All you have to do is persuade him to liquidate his investments and turn the money over to you."

"That's all, eh?"

"I tell you, it will be a breeze. I've got it all worked out. The chump will fall all over you."

"And after him the cops, no doubt. Assuming that I'm interested in taking part, as I'm pretty sure I'm not, what's in it for me?"

He was a hard bargainer. He claimed that there were four others besides himself to be cut in on the take, although I never met any of them. Furthermore, the gang had heavy working expenses to come off the top, so forth and so on, ho hum. All that beach sand and heavy Mediterranean seawater must have cost them a pretty penny, as I pointed out during the negotiations. But we finally agreed on a percentage, a pitch and an advance; the first cash I'd had in my pocket since spending my all for cigarettes in Tangier. It was an odd feeling, to have a bit of *pognon* in the *poche* once again. I liked it. That it was crooked money didn't bother me a bit.

The pitch was simple enough, provided the pigeon was as simple as he had been made to sound. Bernard promised to produce an outfit of decent clothes, American clothes, and a set of fake papers to identify me as an agent of the U.S. Atomic Energy Commission. After that M. l'Inspecteur Bernard of the Sûreté Nationale would present me to M. le Marquis, very hush-hush and off the record. Behind locked doors and closed blinds where we could not be overheard by lurking Soviet spies I would tell M. le Marquis that we—meaning the AEC—had heard of his noble efforts single-handedly to contain the flood of Communism in Europe. We wanted to congratulate him for his public-mindedness, patriotism and selfless dedication to a worthy cause. However, I was the bearer of what might prove to be disturbing news to M. le Marquis. The AEC was now in control of an entirely new type of bomb involving the fission-fusion of the hydrogen atom. (Fission-fusion was my own invention. It had a fine scientific ring.) The new bomb was so incredibly more powerful than the old uranium firecracker that the old one was now obsolete. Generalissimo Franco, the customer M. le Marquis was counting on to take his packages off his hands after so many unhappy delays, was even then, like the French government, negotiating with the AEC for the new super-weapon. It was highly improbable that the Generalissimo would now be inclined to purchase M. le Marquis' private stockpile as well even if the Spanish national treasury could stand the burden of the further expenditure on top of the high cost of the super-bomb. In the circumstances, it looked very much as if M. le Marquis might

be going to have to eat his expensive collection.
M. l'Inspecteur shared my regret but was equally
helpless to do anything about M. le Marquis' predica-
ment. Unless, of course, hem, hem, I couldn't say for
sure, but it was barely possible—

Bernard and I rehearsed the whole pitch until we
had it down cold. The gaff was to go in only after M. le
Mark had been allowed to bleed in agony for a few
minutes, although if he held still for it even then he
was a bigger chump than I had been promised. I
would suggest that the AEC just might possibly be
persuaded to take his inventory off his hands for what
he had invested in it. M. le Marquis would receive a
dollar credit for this amount with the U.S. Treasury,
and would be free to negotiate as he chose with
Generalissimo Franco for the credit. As so shrewd a
businessman as M. le Marquis surely knew, Spain was
not a rich country, nor was its currency highly regarded
on world markets. To acquire the large number of
dollars necessary for the super-bomb purchase, the
Generalissimo would necessarily have to buy dollars
wherever he could find dollars and at whatever price
he was required to pay for them. As M. le Marquis
would further easily perceive—

Bernard was to weigh in here with indignant objections on behalf of *la belle France*. His country was also
negotiating for the super-bomb, also stood in need of
dollars, and also suffered from a weak and unstable
currency. Surely a patriot like M. le Marquis would not
turn his back on his own *patrie* to do business with a
lousy *nigaud* like Franco when he could profitably sell

his dollars right there at home. M. l'Inspecteur would personally guarantee a far better price in francs; a return of at least fifty percent on M. le Marquis' entire investment.

Bernard was to get quite worked up about the possibility that the marquis might do business with Franco when *la belle France* needed the dollars so badly. If the marquis had the brains to point out that it had been Bernard's suggestion that he do business with Franco in the first place, we would both assure him that the existence of the super-bomb had changed things drastically. Europe could now be successfully defended against Communism on *both* sides of the Pyrenees—if enough money could be raised to arm both sides of the Pyrenees with the new super-weapon.

The gaff went in there; slick, smooth and easy. M. le Marquis didn't have to have the brains to figure that if he could command a guarantee of fifty percent profit on the money he had already sunk in his patriotic ventures why couldn't he get the same fifty percent on a further, larger amount? I would plant the idea in his bird brain by suggesting that, in view of his faithful, unremitting and lonely defense of Europe against the Menace while the AEC was tardily getting around to fusion-fission (or was it fission-fusion? He wouldn't remember either), the U.S. Treasury might, just possibly might, permit him to make additional investments in dollar credits which he could also sell to his beloved *patrie* at a profit. No doubt M. l'Inspecteur would also personally guarantee the same return on those?

M. l'Inspecteur would indeed, unhesitatingly and unequivocally. He would further personally guarantee, on his *parole d'honneur*, that M. le Marquis would receive not only a fifty percent return on his money but the Légion d'Honneur; not the mere ribbon of a lousy Chevalier, either, but the *médaille* of a full Officier. Perhaps, even—although this, regrettably, M. l'Inspecteur could not personally guarantee—perhaps even the *baton* of a *Maréchal*! With a public kiss of gratitude from *M. le Président de la République! Liberté, Égalité, Fraternité* and cost-plus patriotism, with the elegant chords of *La Marseillaise* thundering in the background.

"The boob will be wetting his pants with eagerness before we finish," Bernard said. "You hold back a little at the end to keep him hanging on the hook. While I'm throwing in the iron-clad guarantees you keep saying that you can't promise anything absolutely definite, you can speak for the AEC but you don't have authority to speak for the Treasury. You *think* they'll play along, you're pretty sure they can be persuaded, but you'll have to send off a couple of cables to make absolutely certain. You don't want to raise M. le Marquis' hopes too high prematurely, see? But you're pretty sure it will work out as you've said it might work out, and you'll let him know in three or four days."

"It might be a good idea for me to suggest that I'm confident enough about it to ask you to start making preparations to take his collection of playthings down to Marseille, where they can be loaded aboard an American ship. We'll need a heavy guard, complete secrecy, not a word to anybody about anything—"

"Right. Right. You're thinking like a pro already. We'll make him swear to keep his lip buttoned, even to his wife. And not a word from either of us to suggest that it might be a good idea for him to start liquidating his other investments so as to have the *braise* ready to turn over to you when you come back with the glad news from Washington. He'll think of that himself. His mind works that way. He'll want to start drawing that fifty percent just as fast as he can."

I said, "You really think he's dumb enough to believe he can take francs out of a bank, buy dollars with them, sell the dollars back for francs again and make fifty percent on the deal?"

He laughed.

"*Mon gars*," he said. "The pigeon is greedy. And the greedier you get, the dumber it makes you."

He spoke a profound truth. He just failed to realize how profound it was.

Finding the right kind of American clothes for an AEC man presented a small problem that held us up for a couple of days. Plenty of American men's clothes were wandering around the Côte that any good strong-arm could liberate any night, but most were either too sporty-looking, or formal wear. One evening during the period we were marking time while Bernard's friends cased the field, Reggie wanted to be driven to Monte Carlo.

It wasn't unusual. What was unusual, she was alone when I picked her up at the hotel. No guy. I figured we'd gather him up somewhere along the way, but no, she had no escort that evening unless he was waiting for her in Monte Carlo, and besides she wasn't the type of girl to go out with characters who didn't call for her at her own door. Mine not to reason why, or volunteer small talk about things that were none of my business. I pointed the Mercedes-Benz in the right direction and drove.

When we were coming into Nice she said, "Take the Grande Corniche, please."

I said, "Yes, madame," and took the Grande Corniche. It's not the fastest road between Nice and Monaco, but it offers the most spectacular scenery. During the day you can see all the way over into Italy, the hills of Corsica as well if the day is clear. At night you look down on the sparkling lights of Cap Ferrat, Beaulieu, Villefranche, Eze, and, if the American Sixth Fleet happens to be in the roadstead at Villefranche, a whole bunch of brightly lit-up battle wagons looking like toy boats far below. At any hour of the day or night the Grande Corniche gives you your money's worth of view. The trouble is, if you let your mind wander from your driving to the spectacular scenery you're as liable as not to end up participating in the scenery, and it's a long way down. The Grande Corniche is that kind of a road. I kept my attention focused on my driving and left the enjoyment of the view to the Honorable Regina.

We never got to Monaco, although we had a fine view of the lights of the whole principality spread out below us when, nearing La Turbie, Reggie said, "Can you pull off the road here, Curly?"

"Not here, madame. There's no room. A bit farther on, I think."

"As soon as you can, then."

I said, "Yes, madame," thinking, What gives? Even if she *did* have to make a hurried trip into the bushes, she'd have strangled first before letting me know she was *pressée*. Whatever else might be on her mind, she wasn't *pressée* for the bushes. Maybe she just wanted to look at the moon. It wasn't as full or as spectacular as it had been on the night she busted me on her balcony, but it was pretty spectacular. Maybe she wanted to bust me again, for exercise.

I pulled off the road and parked as soon as I could manage it. After we'd sat there for a while she said, "Turn off the lights, please."

"I have to leave at least the *veilleuses* burning, madame. It's the law."

"And you're always law-abiding, aren't you?"

It was a crack, and yet it wasn't a crack. She sounded more depressed than sarcastic. I switched off everything but the *veilleuses* and offered no comeback.

After a while she said, "Would you like a cigarette?"

"I've given up smoking." I hadn't, but the hell with it. I'd smoke my own cigarettes on my own time, not hers. She was a little late with the handouts.

She lit a cigarette. When it would have been about half-smoked she said abruptly, "You can't believe that I'm doing this for you own good, can you? That I don't hate you, or wish you ill?"

I said nothing to that, either. She said, still depressed, not in temper, "I asked you a question."

"You also told me on another occasion that you did not want to hear my views about your actions."

"I want to hear them now."

"I'd rather not express them."

I could hear her sigh. I thought she started to say something more, but changed her mind. I said, "But if madame wishes, I'll be glad to tell her of my experiences in the army."

She was an intelligent girl; more than intelligent enough to know I wasn't talking to hear the enchanting sound of my own voice. She listened, smoking quietly.

I said, "I served two years in the United States Army. Not voluntarily. I was drafted. I had a tough regular Army sergeant who made a point of being hard on us draftees. I think he was the toughest sergeant in the whole army. He gave us extra pack drill, extra calisthenics, extra field drill, extra everything he could load on to us. He kept saying it was for our own good. To make soldiers of us lousy civilians."

"Curly, I—"

"Please, madame. There's not much more to the story. I never complained. Anybody who did complain suffered for it. He called them whiners, conscript crybabies, other things, and thought up extra extras especially for them. I took all he could hand out for two years, because I had no choice. Then, when I got my discharge and had all my clearances, my civilian clothes on me again, I called him out of a bar where he was having a beer with his pals, all regular army sergeants, and while they stood around and watched, madame, I beat the hell out of him. With my fists. For his own good. So he would be able to appreciate the viewpoint of us lousy civilians. But I didn't hate him, or wish him ill."

I could hear the lid of the ashtray in the seat-arm

where she was sitting open and close. Nothing more, until she said, in the same depressed tone, "Take me back to the hotel, please."

"Yes, madame. Shall I return by way of the Moyenne Corniche?"

"I don't care. Any way you like."

"Thank you, madame."

I drove her back to the hotel. No conversation *en route*.

The next day, I think it was, I got my American clothes. I wasn't going to give Reggie any remote chance of seeing me in them, any more than Bernard gave the Nice cops a chance to catch him in the uniform he had been cashiered out of. We met by agreement in Antibes, where he had taken a room at a convenient distance from the marquis' villa on the Cap. He had already got my false papers; where, he didn't say and I didn't ask, any more than I had asked where my new wardrobe came from. The papers, like the clothes, looked pretty good. We climbed into his big Jag and set out for the field of enterprise.

The marquis was a slight, extremely good-looking man, snappily dressed in tailor-made sport clothes, clearly vain of his appearance and so gullible that he didn't even want to look at my phony identification. It was enough that his good friend M. l'Inspecteur vouched for me. After all, if he couldn't trust M. l'Inspecteur and M. l'Inspecteur's judgment, whom could he trust? Bernard and I both agreed with the implication, but also we both insisted that I be allowed to produce my bona fides for his inspection. Soviet spies had been known to pretend to be what they were not, as we were sure M. le Marquis was aware. A man could not be too careful. He immediately got a hunted look, as if he was about to peer fearfully over his shoulder, and said he certainly was aware of such things. But he was so vain that he wouldn't admit he didn't understand what my false credentials said when he tried to read their English wording.

The marquise was somewhat sharper, I suspected, although not much sharper. Not if she had let her husband hock her jewels to pay for his second sandbox. I didn't offer to show her my papers. I had a feeling she would have sneered at them because they weren't written in French. She was the haughty type; as vain, I thought, of the title she had acquired by marriage as the marquis was of his good looks, expensive wardrobe and handsome villa. I'd like to have seen Reggie put the marquise down, just for the hell of it. She wasn't any better-looking than she was *sympathique*, either. I found that odd. With his looks, title, money and the rest, the marquis should have rated a French beauty queen at least. But his wife's looks were none of my concern. Only his money.

She wasn't invited to join our little conference group. The marquis made it pretty clear that we men could get along without her while we talked business. We really did get together to talk in a locked room with drawn blinds, as Bernard had said we would. So Soviet agents could not read our lips through binoculars, as he explained to me with proper solemnity. Bernard had a special gadget he carried around to detect bugging, hidden tape recorders, secret television lenses and other sensors in a room before it was used for confidential conversation. It was an ordinary voltmeter hooked up to a flashlight battery with an inconspicuous button he could press when he wanted it to "detect." He checked the room out carefully with it, showing us how he got readings from legitimate telephone wires, a TV set and the like but nothing that wasn't strictly as it should be. The marquis took it all in like a kid watching a cops-and-robbers movie. Then we got down to *nos moutons*.

The pitch went over beautifully. M. le Mark reacted exactly as he was supposed to. He showed self-satisfied gratification at words of praise and appreciation from the AEC, dawning horror when he sensed the import of my news about the fusion-fission bomb; trembling shock followed by sustained agony when he saw his money going, going, gone down the drain; pathetic eagerness to believe, believe, that I might, just possibly might, be able to save it for him, perhaps not with the profit on top he had hoped for but at least without that awful loss; all-consuming, poorly concealed greed at the prospect of turning an even larger profit than he had dreamed of; finally, the puffed gratification of a selfish bastard at the thought of the great big public honor that would come to him simply for making that great big profit for himself at his country's expense. It was a real pleasure to do dirty business with a cheap son of a bitch like M. le Marquis.

I told Bernard as much after we got away from the villa. He said, "Pigeons or pricks, what's the difference? They all bleed the same kind of cash." He was a great one for philosophical remarks.

We stalled for three days. The wait made me jumpy.

It was my first big con. Little cons, the kind you learn in the Army, do nothing to prepare you for the big time. I hadn't yet learned that a properly gaffed mark worries a lot more about missing his big money-making opportunity than you do about his slipping the hook. That's why a pro never hurries the grab, or pushes too hard on the gaff once it's in. The longer you can wait after the gaffing to make the grab—within reason, of course, and with an eye on the exits—the less suspicious the sucker. Obviously if you *were* a crook, you'd be reaching for his pocketbook at the first possible opportunity. But let him linger, doubt, worry, have time to calculate his potential profits, hear a suggestion or two that the deal isn't going to come off after all, sorry, pal, tough luck all around—brother, he'll hand you his money with tears of gratitude in his eyes when you give him the chance.

Bernard knew all this. I didn't. I thought we were taking unnecessary chances. I got snappy with my nice landlady, talked back to Reggie a couple of times when I shouldn't have, built up a lot of tension. Reggie was a lot more tolerant of me than she had to be, although I didn't realize it at the time. When I was just about as jittery as I could get, Bernard at last decided it was time.

Harnessing up in his Antibes hideout, we went back to the villa. I had faked a very nice cable from Washington—in code, to deceive Soviet spies—saying that the AEC and the U.S. Treasury, in view of M. le Marquis' long, sustained and continuing dedication to The Cause, had decided after great deliberation to go along with my recommendations. In a word, he was In. Up to and far beyond his *délicieuses*. I took with me a translation of the cable, in French, to gladden his greedy Gallic heart.

When Bernard pulled the Jag up in front of the villa and we had got out, we heard screaming coming from inside the house.

"What the hell is that?" I said. I was still jittery.

Bernard shrugged. "*Je m'en fous*. Maybe he's beating up his broad. Business before pleasure, in all events. Let's go."

A pretty but nervous *bonne* opened the door when we rang the bell. The screaming continued. Two women appeared to be screaming at each other in counter-point. The *bonne* wasn't sure whether she should let us in or not, but Bernard didn't give her a chance to stand in the way of the Sûreté Nationale. He swept her aside with a wave of his hand and marched in. I followed him, jittering. The screaming did nothing for my nerves. And we were moving toward it, rather than away.

It wasn't two women. It was the marquis and the marquise, yelling at each other. Of the two, his voice was the shriller and more fishwifely.

"Camel!" he was screaming, his face red with fury. "Cow! Vixen! Slut! Stupid beast! Species of a diseased bitch! I demand that you obey me!"

"I spit on your demands!" she screamed right back. "Fool! Imbecile! Species of a retarded ignoramus! You lack even the sense to know when you have been *foutu*! Never in a thousand years! It is my money, my *dot*, and you may not touch it!"

"Idiot!" he howled right back. "Sow! Whore! Dis-respectful woman! What of your marriage vows!"

She told him what he could do with her marriage

vows. For a marquise, she had a good command of
the *argot*.

They hadn't yet noticed our arrival. They were too
preoccupied with each other. I had a feeling that
an unobtrusive withdrawal was indicated for us, the
sooner the better. I had taken Bernard by the arm to
whisper the suggestion in his ear when Madame la
Marquise caught sight of us in the doorway.

"Aha!" she yelled, turning her attention to us. "So
you have come for more blood! Vultures! Scavengers!
Thieves! Jackals! Swine! Swindlers! Monsters!"

"Madame—" Bernard began smoothly.

It was the first, last and only word either of us said
for some time. Boiled down to pure venom, the gist of
what she had to tell us was that she had been saving
up what she had to say (to Bernard—I got the benefit
of what splashed off him) for over a year, ever since
her husband had hocked her jewels. She had known
even then that we were vultures, scavengers, thieves,
etc., etc., etc., but had bowed to her husband's wishes
like the good French wife she was—

"Liar!" her husband howled. "*Intransigeante!*
Stubborn witch! Unnatural woman!"

"Simpleton!" she yelled back, not diverting her
attention from us but taking a crack at him in passing
more or less the way a polo player takes a crack at the
ball as he rides past it at full gallop. "Gull! Booby!
Jobard! Listen to me well, messieurs—"

We listened to her. I would just as soon have turned
and run long before she finished, but Bernard stood
solidly between her and me without moving. I will
say for him, he had nerve. Too much nerve and not

enough judgment was his trouble, I guess. I listened to her tell him, as clearly and bluntly as anybody was ever told anything, that he was not going to get another centime out of the marquis if he worked at it until doomsday. All the money they had left was hers, her *dot*, and her husband could not touch it without her written consent. And that he would never, never, never receive, we could assure ourselves.

All the time she was ticking us off the marquis kept screaming an obbligato of insults, curses, demands, even tearful pleas before he gave up. I mean he actually cried, big tears of self-pity because she was depriving him of all the goodies he had been promised. Bernard paid no attention to him at all, his wife only enough to call him a contemptuous name or two or three now and then. I never realized how rich the French language is in invective until I listened to Madame la Marquise de Lille du Rocher name her husband for what he was and phony Inspecteur Bernard for what he was without interrupting or repeating herself for the best part of ten minutes. Apparently, she hadn't made up her mind where I stood, except in a general way. I hoped she would never get around to specifics.

When she had said all she had to say, Bernard gave her a slight military bow. He had been standing at stiff attention all the time she was lacing into him. I hid as much of myself as possible behind his back. The marquis sniffled and wiped his nose, too crushed to fight any further.

"Have you quite finished, madame?" Bernard asked coolly.

She matched him manner for manner, now that she had finished blowing her buttons. Once more the haughty marquise, she said, "That depends on you, monsieur. If you leave this house now, never to bother me or my husband again, then I have finished. What you have already stolen from us is not too much to pay to keep my husband's incredible stupidity from public knowledge. But if you ever molest us again in any way, then no, monsieur. I have not finished with you by any means."

Bernard bowed again, turned on his heel and motioned me to precede him from the villa.

"I regret that it was necessary for you to witness this disgraceful scene, monsieur," he said. "Please do not believe that all Frenchwomen are viragos."

As a parting shot, it fizzled. The marquise said, "Or that all Frenchmen are scoundrels and thieves, monsieur. Or fools."

The marquis snuffled on, a broken reed.

I was sweating like a pig by the time we got back to the Jag. The day wasn't hot, either. When Bernard had started up and we were safely clear of the villa, I mopped my wet face and neck.

"*Merde alors*," I said shakily. "At least we're safely out of it."

"Safely out of what?" Bernard said. "That woman is completely crazy. I've got to see a lawyer."

"You've got to see a *what*?"

"A lawyer. I never heard of a Frenchwoman having control of her *dot*. It's her husband's, to do with as he likes. Otherwise why would a man marry a hag like that, eh?"

"You mean—you can't mean—my God, man, you aren't still going to try to *get* it, are you?"

He looked at me briefly, coldly, unsmiling, then back at the road. The Jag purred along smoothly. Not as smoothly as Reggie's Mercedes-Benz, but smoothly enough. Like a jail door closing, say.

"We are still going to get it," he said, slightly emphasizing the 'we.' "Tomorrow I will contemplate a new strategy to aid Monsieur le Marquis in his valiant struggle against the Communist threat. Today we have lost a battle, not the war."

He didn't know it, but he had just lost something else, too. Me.

He really did have four others working with him on the swindle, as he had said. They were tried with him when the roof fell in. I read about it in the papers, from a safe distance.

Chapter Five

Another thing about Tangier in the bad old days. You didn't need papers to get in. So many different national powers shared the administration of the international zone without sharing each other's police powers that nobody bothered to keep track of the fleet of small craft that ran in and out of the bay without lights on moonless nights. Aboard one of those, you didn't even have to know your own name.

I went to see Jean-Pierre. He had a new job watering scotch in a bar in Juan-les-Pins. So that he wouldn't see how *pressé* I was to leave France in a hurry, I let him think I had dropped in for old time's sake and a spot of chitchat. When we had compared notes and lied to each other for a while about this and that, I said, "The Boar back in business?"

"The Boar is never out of business. He just switches his bets."

"What's he betting on now? Cigarettes again?"

Jean-Pierre's eyes flickered here and there around the bar before he answered the question. "Keep it to yourself. *La hache*."

That's what I thought he said, at first. I didn't get it. *La hache*, the axe or hatchet, has no meaning in the argot that I knew of. Then I realized that what he had actually said was *la H*. Meaning the big H. Meaning Heroin. Meaning keep it to yourself, *pote*. He was a horse's ass even to talk about it. But he couldn't resist talking when he had someone interested listening to him, and I was interested. I even bought him drinks to keep him going.

Back in the fifties a kilogram of pure heroin could be had for around $2,500 in Marseille. It was worth more like $11,000 or $12,000 in the New York whole-sale market, a whole lot more than that retail when it had been cut a few times. The morphine base came from the Middle East, mostly from Turkey and Iran, and was processed in a number of small factories in and near Marseille; in stores, waterfront warehouses, factories, barns, everywhere. It still is. Heroin-making might be called Marseille's cottage industry. The col-orful Corsican peasants who brought so much of the glamour to the glamorous Riviera during its post-war years have always been up to their ears in the traffic, naturally. So also, from time to time, have been cuddly young airline stewardesses who smuggled the stuff into the U.S. in their girdles and brassieres, seafaring men who brought it in in their sea-bags, honest tax-payers and tourists who hid it in toothpowder cans, bath powder boxes, medicine jars, cameras, hollow heels, or carried it taped to their bodies or even care-fully packaged for insertion into their bodies. 'Carefully' in the preceding sentence means with extreme care, because if you have a substantial container of pure heroin concealed in your rectum or vagina and the container ruptures, you are going to die in a hurry although perhaps not in as much of a hurry as you might wish for. For all its risks the traffic has always been big in Marseille, and profitable.

According to Jean-Pierre, The Boar had made him-

self a stake to get started in the H-trade by pulling off
a couple of *crimes américains*. *Le crime américain* is
what the French call kidnapping in honor of American ingenuity and adaptability in perfecting if not
inventing the snatch. The Boar's methods were very
simple, requiring neither confederates nor a division
of the *grisbi*. He would grab the man he wanted, tie
him to a chair and apply enough uninterrupted unre-
strained brutality to break his victim's resistance. The
victim would thereafter cooperate in whatever steps
were necessary to place his liquid assets in The Boar's
hands, and be released with a warning not to identify
his kidnapper to the police or he would die. One of
the victims at least had failed to heed the warning.
He had died. Half a dozen Corsicans had taken an
oath that The Boar had been playing *pétanque* with
them at the time of the murder as well as at the time
of the snatch, and he had got off. Since he picked
other *gangstaires* like himself to extort from, the
cops couldn't have been more unconcerned unless
all the hoods in the south of France, Corsican and
non-Corsican, had chosen up sides and wiped each
other out.

I said, "What about The Plank?"

"He copped it during a jewelry-store job in Nice.
Four or five months ago."

"Stiff?"

"As a plank."

Jean-Pierre thought that was pretty funny, although
he stopped grinning when I said, "Did he or The Boar
ever catch up with the *mec* who shopped us in the
calanque?"

"Not that I know of. I'd have heard about it if they had."

"I'll bet The Boar gets him sooner or later. I wouldn't want to be around to get splashed by the blood when he does."

"Neither would I."

A customer began rapping on the bar for service about then. When Jean-Pierre had waited on him and come back, I said, "Anybody else you know running cigarettes these days?"

I thought I had slipped it into the conversation casually enough, but he gave me a sharp look, smelling money. "Why?"

"Oh, I've got another thousand dollars or so looking for work. Provided it's nice safe work, of course."

He wouldn't cooperate until I'd promised him ten percent of the profit. With that settled, he sent me to Merde Alors, who had a job on a boat then tied up in Antibes harbor. Merde Alors was as grumbly as ever, but he passed me along to a pal on a *contrabandier* that was about to take off for Tangier.

I got a job aboard her by swearing I knew all there was to know about cigarette-buying. The captain questioned me a bit, but he didn't know beans about it himself and I gave him all the right answers, at least as far as he knew. He said, Veddy well, I could work my way. He was British. The boat was a pretty white yacht with two masts; a ketch, I think, nautically speaking, but with enough auxiliary power to move her when the wind failed. She wasn't in the same class with The Boar's cutter, because she couldn't have out-raced a Spanish patrol-boat or a pirate with a two-day head

start. Her captain didn't seem to think anything like
that would be necessary. Whether he was the boat's
owner or just borrowing it in the owner's absence I
never knew, but what he seemed to have in mind was
taking her into Tangier under her own name and registry, loading her up with cigarettes and sailing her
back to France without let or hindrance from anybody.
I was glad I wasn't planning to go back with him.

Packing wasn't going to be a problem. I could get
everything I owned into a small bag and cram Reggie's
mourner's outfit in on top. I figured that pinching the
suit made up in part for her theft of my papers. I also
had the equivalent of a little less than a hundred dollars in francs from Bernard's advance. Where he was
headed, he wouldn't be needing it.

He didn't call on me for help with the new scheme
for the marquis before the yacht sailed. If he had, I'd
have got out of it some way. I carried out my usual
Reggie-routines right up until H-hour of D-day. Just
before we pushed off, I dropped my resignation in
the mail.

It read:

Dear Hon. —

   *Sorry to have to take off so abruptly, but I never
gave my parole to you or the juge, remember?
Please try to believe, for your own happiness, that
all men are not as contemptible as your ever
untrustworthy —*

                              Spiv

Then I went aboard the yacht.
We trudged across the Mediterranean, mostly under

sail, until we raised the Algerian coast five days later, then turned westward for Tangier. The captain didn't even put into Gib to fuel up, not that fueling up would have done him any good. He was a real pigeon. I don't know what happened to him and the yacht. When we docked at the *darse* in Tangier and I had helped him secure the mooring lines, I went below to get my bag, walked down the gangplank and started off.

The captain was on deck. "Hoy!" he called after me. "Where the devil do you think you're going?"

"Your guess is as good as mine," I called back. "Thanks for the ride."

Well, His eye is on the sparrow, as they say, and when He isn't too occupied with the sparrow's affairs I know He watches me. Within ten days I had acquired a job and a blonde *poupette* named Boda, a Dane. I got them both from the same guy. He was an American; Jim something or other. I forget what the something or other was, and Boda said she never knew. She was that kind of *poupette*.

The way it happened, the first thing I did after getting off the yacht was to go to the U.S. legation down in the medina and apply for a passport. I said that mine had been stolen from me, the truth. But I had memorized the number and date of issue, those being the two things you have to know about a passport when you are asked unless you want to consult it every time you check in at a European hotel or border crossing, and of course I remembered my army serial number as well as the date of my discharge in Germany. They could check on me easily enough. They said they would get right on it. However, for various reasons it might be some time before a new passport could be issued. I said that time was what I had a whole lot more of than money, left my address and went away.

Most of Tangier, south and east of the *darse* and its warehouses, is fronted by a fine, white, wide curving beach. Because the beach is in the bay and protected in large part by the breakwater it hasn't much to offer in the way of surf. But it's a fine place to paddle around, sun yourself and watch the coming-out parties. In Morocco, which was then and still is now to an extent a French protectorate (read Tangier for Morocco here, since they should have been and were in time integrated), at least half of the women you see in the street are Moslem. They dress universally in a long enveloping blue-gray hooded *haik*, with a *litham*, face-veil, concealing the lower part of the face; everything hidden from view but the eyes and the upper part of the nose. They remind you of a Pullman sleeper after the berths have been made up for the night, all curtains except for the eyes peering at you through the slits. The color of the curtains doesn't vary much, although the quality of the material going into them may, and you can sometimes guess something, not much, about the wearer's social status by her shoes if you catch a glimpse of them under the draperies. But walking toward one of those animated duffle-bags on the street you can't tell from thirty feet out if she's one of the Sultan's wives out for a stroll or a *poule* who will pitch at you as you pass with, " *'Allo, bébé.* Feefty dirhams, eh?"

Guessing the quality of the goods beneath the draperies is even more difficult, although provocative in its way. When one of the bundles came down to the beach to swim or sun itself, as happened with fair frequency, it drew the attention of all eyes as soon as it stepped on the sand. The *litham* always came off first, and was carefully furled. Next, the hood of the *haik* would be thrown back, so you could have a look at the face. Then, as the world watched and waited with bated breath, the duffle-bag would bend over, grab the bottom hem of itself and lift the curtain on the final act. It was something of a striptease, something like the unveiling of a monument. What usually emerged from under the yardgoods, on the beach that is, was not much. Moroccan women tend toward dumpiness and spread, a combination without eye-appeal even when wrapped in the French bikinis many of them wore when they got down that far. Besides, when you have cased the whole Côte d'Azur on the half-shell during the summer season, you are inclined to be a bit choosy about what you elect to look at. I was saving my eyesight for something worth the effort.

When it came, it was well worth the wait. The French say, *Il faut de toutes sortes pour faire un monde*, and that's what populated the *laissez-vivre monde* of Tangier back in the good old bad days; *toutes sortes*. Rich men, poor men, beggarmen, thieves and, naturally, a fair population of swindlers. I was still an apprentice, and on my uppers besides, but there were pros working in and out of Tangier who could have sold the White House to the President of the United

States for cash. You had to keep your guard up at all times, even on your uppers, because you never knew how or when you were going to be roped.

One morning I was sitting on the beach feeling depressed and downtrodden because I was almost out of money and faced the dreary prospect of going to work if I wanted to continue eating. At the same time I felt pleased with myself because of a newspaper squib I had seen that morning reporting the arrest, in Antibes, of a gang of *escrocs* headed by one Albert Bernard, *ancien agent de police*. As he had said, the greedier you get, the dumber it makes you. While I was congratulating myself on my own superior intelligence for having pulled out before it was too late, Boda rose on my horizon. For the time being I lost all interest in other things.

She was wearing a kind of loose beach-robe when I first saw her. I think the cops must have made it a condition of her stay in Tangier that she keep the robe on until she was actually on the beach. If she had let it drop from her on the esplanade of the Avenue d'Espagne the way she let it drop as soon as she reached the sand below the esplanade, traffic would have backed up for miles. I vaguely remember some guy appearing out of the shimmer of her penumbra to pick up the robe where she dropped it, but then he disappeared back into the penumbra again and was lost from view.

Everything else was lost from view while Boda filled your eyeballs. To say of her that she was corn-silk blonde, blue-eyed and beautiful is like saying of the star-filled heavens that they are cute. She was breathtaking, awe-inspiring, as flawless a piece of sculptured Danish pastry as has ever been perpetrated. She was also fairly big for a girl, I mean tall. Maybe five-nine or thereabouts, a hundred and forty incredibly well arranged pounds. She carried herself like an empress, if you can imagine a blonde, blue-eyed empress tanned a rich golden honey color all over.

I say 'all over' because even before I saw her all over, Boda in a bikini gave the impression of stark nudity. As a matter of fact she was the nakedest woman I ever saw even when fully clothed. Wearing two skimpy pieces of fabric that barely contained what they were supposed to contain, she was unbelievable. The word 'contain' isn't exactly accurate as I have used it here. 'Restrain' doesn't say it a lot better. She didn't require restraint in any direction, only appreciation. 'Detain' is close but still not precise. Ordinary words didn't apply with precision to Boda.

Later, when she got to be mine and I had reached the point where I could look somewhere else than at her, I used to watch the people on the beach when she walked along it. It was like watching the audience at a well-fought tennis match in slow motion. All the heads simultaneously turning left as the ball goes in that direction, simultaneously right as it comes back, you've seen it? Not only the heads of the *mecs* on the beach but of their *poupettes*, too. All of them trying to poison her with their eyes because she had so much more of everything than one woman is entitled to. I don't think she was ever more than vaguely aware of the effect she had, either on the *mecs* or on the *poupettes*. If she was, it didn't matter to her one way or the other. She was like the moon in that, if you'll excuse another celestial simile. If men wanted to worship her or bitches howl at her, it made no difference. She sailed along in her own track regardless.

About the third or fourth morning I had been a member of the slow motion tennis-game gallery as she passed, the guy who trailed along to pick up her robe emerged from her penumbra and came over to where I was lying on the sand.

"Hi," he said, squatting on his heels and picking up a handful of sand to dribble through his fingers. He was as recognizably American as peanut butter and jelly. "My name's Jim something or other."

"Hiya, Jim," I said. "Some people call me Curly."

"Yeah," he said, with no interest at all in what people called me. "I've seen you watching my girl."

"Your girl?"

His use of the possessive pronoun to apply to a phenomenon like the honey-colored atomic bomb shocked me. It seemed kind of sacrilegious, in a way. But there could be no question about whom he meant. There was only one girl immediately visible to the masculine eye. She was lying in the sun, flat on her back with her eyes closed. 'Flat' isn't the right word to describe Boda lying on her back, either. She lay supine, let's say.

"My girl." He moved his head in her direction. "Or hadn't you noticed me? Most guys don't."

"To tell the truth, I haven't paid you much attention. Are you trying to make something out of something, or something? Sure, I've watched her. Anybody who didn't would have to be blind."

"Don't get excited. I'm not trying to make anything out of anything. How would you like to take her over?"

I had to gulp. I couldn't think of anything to say, right off. He didn't look or act like a pimp, and besides who ever heard of anyone pimping for an empress? For that matter, who ever heard of anyone taking over an empress, except maybe an emperor? I finally said something, I forget what it was, while trying to figure what the gaff would be when it came. He had begun to tell his tale, squatting there beside me on the beach drifting sand through his fingers and looking upset.

He had got Boda from a German on Ibiza the same way he was offering her to me, as a free gift. The German had brought her to the island from Denmark for the summer but now had to go elsewhere without her. Reasons not explained, any more than Jim's were for having to go elsewhere without her. The German, apparently a decent enough fellow, seemed to have been fond of Boda and concerned that when he left her she might take up with the wrong kind of guy. Somebody who wouldn't treat her right, might even try to exploit her terrific drawing power at the male box office. He had hand-picked his successor, Jim, from among the availabilities on the island, and told Boda she now had a new boyfriend. There had been no argument from her.

"She isn't stupid or anything," Jim said. "Hell, she speaks four languages. You can't do that and be stupid. But she just doesn't seem to give a damn about thinking for herself, or much of anything else. All she ever wants to do is lie in the sun, eat, drink, sleep and make out. She never says much, she never gets mad, she gives no trouble and she does whatever she's told without backtalk. That's why I'm worried about her." He threw a handful of sand away. "She's too easy. One of these Ay-rab characters gets hold of her, or any of the other sons of bitches that stink up this place—you see what I mean? I can't just turn her loose and leave her on her own in a dump like Tangier. But I've got to leave."

"So you picked me to take over," I said. "Just from seeing the nobleness of my character shining from my face among all the others here on the beach. I'm underwhelmed."

He tossed another handful of sand away as he stood up.

"I picked you because you're American, you're not queer, you haven't a girl of your own with you and your ass is hanging out a yard," he said unemotionally. "There's a job goes along with her, if you know how to hold a job. But forget it. I'll look around."

The next day, same time, same place, I went over to where he was sitting on the sand beside her. She was lying in the sun with her eyes closed, as usual. Being that close to her made me feel lightheaded. I squatted down in front of Jim and began to drift sand through my fingers as he had done the day before.

"Any pigeons?" I asked.

"What do you care?" he said. "Bugger off. Go get run over. I'm busy."

"About that job with the fringe benefits. Can we talk?"

"Why?"

"I've been giving it some thought. I figured that

since you know my ass is hanging out you can't be trying to screw me for something I haven't got. You're trying to con me into taking some kind of fall for you, but I believe I can be had. On the terms you offered. Can we talk?"

"We can talk," he said. "She doesn't hear anything she isn't told to listen to."

"More and more I believe I can be had. Tell me about the job. About her, I know enough already."

That's the way Boda and I set up housekeeping. Along with her and the job I got the little apartment she and Jim had been sharing on the hill behind the Grand Socco, with three weeks rent paid in advance. There were enough groceries and wine in the place so that with what I had left of my francs we could get by until my first payday. Jim was in a hurry to be on his way to wherever he was going, so I moved in the same day he moved out. He explained to Boda how it was going to be with us from then on. She listened to what he had to say, smiled her big slow beautiful smile at us both, kissed him goodbye, kissed me hello—it made my ears vibrate like twin tuning-forks, at least they felt that way—and that was it. What man and crazy fortune hath brought together let no creep cast the first stone at. While it lasted I made her happy, and she made me happy, and no harm was done to anyone.

The job was writing come-on letters, ropers, to American suckers who had taken the first bait of the American and French Bank of Tangier. The A. & F. B. was a bucket-shop operation that eventually folded its tents like the two Ay-rabs who ran it and quietly stole away with other people's assets worth around

$4,000,000 when Morocco took over Tangier in 1956.
Until that time bucket-shop operations were as unre-
stricted as other expressions of individual enterprise
like prostitution, counterfeiting, dope-peddling and
cigarette smuggling. I wrote my persuasive prose on
a letterhead that showed a large impressive stone
building vaguely resembling a Federal mint or other
reliable institution, its roof topped by a forest of flag-
poles bearing the flags of various countries including
the Stars and Stripes prominently displayed front and
center. If the johns who got the letters chose to believe
that the A. & F. B. operated out of a building like that,
nobody held them back. The actual store was two
dingy rooms of a three-story walkup on a side street
off the Rue de la Liberté.

What the bank, if I may use the term loosely, did for
its living was advertise in various periodicals here and
there around the world the advantages of investment
in Tangier. The ads offered a selected group of favored
prospects the highest interest rates in the world,
"safety-security," freedom from income tax and other
benefits. That none of the pitch was in any way true is
neither here nor there. Many of the eager inquiries
from the selected list of prospects who read the ads
came from the U. S. of A., which in my experience has
a larger saturation of easy marks per square acre than
any other country in the world. Perhaps this is so
because Americans tend to believe what they see in
print until it's proved to be demonstrably false, whereas
Europeans among others know damn well it's all a
pack of lies even when it's proved to be demonstrably
true. My job, as an American knowing the American

language and American ways of thought, was to compose convincing follow-up letters individually tailored to gaff the marks who had written in. The Ay-rabs spoke Arabic, French and Spanish, as everyone does in Tangier except tourists, and fair English. Their English just didn't have that old homespun apple-pie sincerity to grab the American sucker. Mine did, as I found out with modest pleasure at the discovery of a new talent. I wrote letters that would have drawn blood from a turnip without making it unhappy.

It was piecework, paid inadequately but in cash by the letter rather than nine-to-five rates. Boda and I had plenty of time to spend together on the beach and in the sack. I mention this only to try to give some insight into her character. She was as magnificently animal in her appetites as she was magnificent to behold, and wholly content with life if those appetites were satisfied. Very much like a large beautiful golden cat.

Her simplicity of purpose and desire in life often complicated the lives of other people. We had a *fatima*—it's what you call a *bonne à tout faire* in Morocco—named Kadoosh working for us. Kadoosh came to work in the morning in the usual Pullman-sleeper curtaining, top to bottom. Under the layer of draperies, which she removed on the job, she wore several other layers including long pink bloomers down to her ankles and a kind of elbow-length sweatshirt. Stripped down that way, you could see her face, neck and arms up to here. That was her whole display. Boda, on the other hand, was inclined to shed what little she wore in public, never more than slacks and a pullover over the bikini, as soon as she came into the apartment. Thereafter she'd go empress-ing around the place naked except for her slippers. Jim had warned me about this, and that they'd lost a couple of *fatimas* who couldn't take it. On his advice, I adapted to a schedule by which Boda and I went to the beach in the morning. We came back to the apartment only in the afternoon when Kadoosh had finished her chores, re-curtained herself and gone home. After lunch Boda would sun herself again, minus the slippers now, in a kind of screened-off cubicle Jim had put together for her on the roof of the apartment house, while I got down to business writing letters to the suckers.

I did all my work at home; partly because I never felt comfortable anywhere I couldn't keep an eye on Boda at all times. Stupid she may not have been, but she was certainly simple. Or maybe I mean guileless. If I had left her alone in the apartment and a shifty-eyed character wearing handcuffs and an Oregon boot with a prison uniform had knocked on the door with word that I had told him to take her and everything else moveable in the apartment away with him that moment, the only question she might have asked would be, "Should I put some clothes on first?" But the situation presented no real difficulty. Jim had left me an old Spanish typewriter that worked fairly well, and the Ay-rabs didn't care where I worked as long as I delivered clean copy.

A difficulty with the small apartment when I was trying to get some work done was Boda herself. I'd be pounding away at the mill, grinding out my immortal prose for our daily cakes and ale. She'd come down

from the roof in the robe I made her wear coming and
going so she wouldn't burn the neighborhood down.
As soon as got inside she'd drop the robe to the floor
the way she dropped it on the beach, then stand there.
Not saying a word, as quiet as a mouse. Merely pro-
jecting herself at me like a high-powered laser beam
until I could take it no longer. Human flesh and blood
were not made to withstand Boda.

I'd look up from the mill and say, surprised, "Oh,
hello. I didn't know you were here. I mean there."

"I don't want to disturb you, Carly."

I never knew whether she couldn't pronounce Curly
right or thought my name was Carl, but no matter. The
typewriter keys would be starting to melt just from the
effect of the current flowing between us.

"Oh, you're not, you're not! Believe me, dear. I'm
just a little sweaty from overwork."

"What are you working at, Carly?"

"Well, right now what I'm doing seems kind of non-
productive, but what I started out to do was bake a
batch of cheese biscuits."

"You did not. You were writing a letter."

"Oh, I was not either."

"You were, too."

And so on, until I surrendered. She always won.
Sooner or later, mostly sooner. I would spring out from
behind the melting typewriter to grab myself an armful
of naked toasty-brown honey-dipped sun-warm blonde
empress, and no Caesar ever grabbed a finer one. Not
that I'm going to go into the intimacies of my sex life,
now or at a later date. But shacking with Boda was a
pleasant experience while it lasted. Four golden enjoy-

able months before Nemesis caught up with me and I had to take foot in hand once again.

I was beginning to lay up a fair hoard of savings from the job. At the legation they said things were moving along satisfactorily as far as they knew, and that they expected to be able to issue the new passport within a couple of weeks or thereabouts. I had a larger than average swatch of sucker letters to write, so I persuaded, ordered, Boda to leave me alone at least until four-thirty before ruining my day in her usual manner. I told her if she'd let me be long enough to get the letters finished I'd take her on a vacation from her wearing life of eating, drinking, sleeping, making love and lying in the sun. She thought that sounded nice, and fudged only a little now and then on the four-thirty whistle.

I rented a car from a Frenchman who ran a garage on the Rue Victor Hugo as a front to move hot iron. All his cars were hot, but only on the European continent where they had been heisted. Not in Tangier. They'd be hot again as soon as he'd smuggled them into Morocco. As long as they wore Tangier plates and their papers weren't examined too closely, they were reasonably legitimate. The one I got was the least expensive in the store, an old Citroën *teuf-teuf* that rattled a lot but seemed to run all right. Boda and I threw a few things into it and took off down the coast for Rabat, Casablanca and Marrakech, to see some of the country.

It was a good time of year for Marrakech; late spring, before the hot weather that would turn the interior of Morocco into a fireless cooker. We rolled along merrily until we were about fifty kilometers from Marrakech. At that point the *teuf-teuf* began to show signs of acute senility. It was burning far too much gas, overheating badly and giving out with knock-bang-clank-whoosh instead of its familiar reassuring *teuf-teuf*. I nursed it, prayed to it, whispered words of love to it, at last brought it into town dying on its feet but game to the finish. The whole top half of the motor had burned up; valves, valve stems, plugs, gaskets, even the cylinder head. Everything above the block.

The mechanic who tore it down looked at the wreckage, slapped his forehead with the flat of his hand and said something filthy in Arabic. The new cylinder head, valves and most of the rest had to be ordered from Rabat. It meant at least a week of waiting, more probably two weeks or even longer. I didn't dare go back to Tangier without the *teuf-teuf* because then I would have to buy it at the hot-iron dealer's price. Or else, *pote*. He had friends. I couldn't afford his friends. Neither could I afford to keep Boda with me in even the cheapest hotel for two weeks or more on the money I had budgeted for the trip, and I didn't want to let her go back to Tangier alone because I was afraid some Ay-rab would get her. But I had to send her back to Tangier because if we both stayed away twenty-four hours longer than I had told the *fatima* we would, she would conclude we had both been killed (*mektoob*, it is written) and start dismantling the apartment to hock the pieces. All in all it was a rum go, as the British say.

I finally screwed up the courage to put her on a plane by herself. There was a once-a-week flight direct to Tangier, Allah be praised. She wouldn't have to make any dangerous transfers or hang around airports in the public eye. I made her take off all her makeup and promise me not put it on again until I got home. Then I made her hide all her corn-silk hair under a *babouchka* and promise not to take it off until she got home. Then I bought her a cheap *kaftan* to put on over the slacks and sweater she wore, and made her promise not to take *that* off until she got home. Her slacks and *pullovaire* weren't particularly snug or provocative, because she never dressed to tease. She didn't have to. She was provocative enough even in the *kaftan*, which covered her like a tent from wrists and ankles to the neck. I was scared silly for her when I pinned what money I could spare inside her underpants before taking her out to the airport to turn her over to the airplane stewardess.

"My sister is kind of simple upstairs," I told the stewardess. "Also she has fits when strange men speak to her. She's very shy. Please take care of her for me. Put her in a seat with something motherly, deaf, dumb and blind, if you can."

"Don't give your sister another thought, *mon beau*," the stewardess said. She was a pleasant little French number. "I'll see that she gets there. But why worry about one sister when there are so many of us?"

She tipped me a wink and took over after I had kissed sister on the brow in a brotherly fashion. I took the opportunity to whisper "You stay in the apartment and do what I've told you until I get home or I'll whack your behind until it glows like a red-hot stove. You hear?"

"Yes, Carly," she said. "Must I keep my clothes on even in the apartment?"

"At all times. Night and day. Don't go up on the roof, and don't open the door to anyone but Kadoosh. Let her do the shopping for you."

"Yes, Carly."

My heart broke when the plane took off. I knew I'd never see her again. She was foredoomed. Poor, poor kid. *Mektoob*.

Chapter Six

After that I could only wait for the new parts to come up from Rabat. While I waited I spent a lot of time at the table of an outdoor café on the edge of the Djemaa El Fna, watching the action. *Djemaa El Fna* means Place of the Dead, but in fact it's the liveliest place in Marrakech, if not in Morocco; an enormous square, four acres of it, in which something is going on every hour of the twenty-four, seven days a week. It's a four-teen-ring circus night and day, with acrobats, tumblers and clowns, magicians, medicine men, fire-eaters, story-tellers, snake charmers, dancing bears, muscle men, contortionists, water sellers peddling their wares in brass cups filled from dripping swollen goatskins, hashish peddlers selling theirs in squares of sweet candy, whores peddling theirs in the usual packaging —you name the merchandise, it's odds on the Djemaa El Fna offers it for sale. On the far side of the square, away from the modern city of hotels, tourists and wide French boulevards, the world of the *souks* begins; a rabbit-warren of markets, shops and stores where you can buy whatever isn't for sale in the Djemaa El Fna. Marrakech is quite a town, full of color, charm and odd smells. Winston Churchill used to go there winters to paint. Other people go there to enjoy the Arabian Nights flavor of the place. There are also a few others who go there for the same reason they go anyplace else, to con somebody out of a fast buck.

One afternoon I was sitting at my usual table, drinking beer and making a meal out of cheap *kimiyah*, a kind of not-so-free lunch, when one of the café's crooked waiters tried to gyp an American tourist on the check. All Moroccan waiters gyp all American tourists on their checks as a matter of course, and normally get away with it. American tourists, generally speaking, are not only easy marks but unable to fight back properly in French or Arabic. One language or the other is all the waiters of Marrakech choose to speak when an argument starts. This particular tourist had a French doll with him, and she cut the waiter up but good. In French. The *bagarre* started behind my back, so the first I saw of the tourist and his girl was when I turned around in my chair to see who was applying the fire and brimstone to the *garçon*.

Michelle, as her name turned out to be, had just finished calling the waiter a *sale cochon* and a *filou*. She was stirred up. When she wasn't stirred up she was as sweet and nice and attractive as whipped cream on strawberries. Not particularly pretty. You wouldn't have been able to see her within a mile of the Honorable Regina, or eighteen miles of Boda. Her nose was a bit too big, for one thing. But she had a Frenchwoman's talent for making the most of her good points while minimizing the bad ones, and her overall impact was of a cute, moderately sexy, attractive young woman, *très, très française* and in every way on the up and up. Which she was. It made it easier for her boyfriend or husband or whatever he was and me to use her as a roper when we got into action. As we did before long.

During the chewing out at the café her boyfriend or husband or whatever he was stood by looking like the biggest cornfed hick ever to come out of Horner's Corners. His name, let's say the name he claimed as his while we were doing business, was Elmer Wiggins. So help me. Phony as it was, it fitted his appearance. You never saw such a rube in your life. All he needed was oatstraw in his hair. He was kind of big and clumsy and shambling, with big hands and feet, guileless cow's eyes, clothes that didn't quite fit across the shoulders or cover his big wrists, pants a mite too short—oh, he was a work of art. Michelle didn't have any idea of the kind of killer shark she was tied up with, or that he and his equally crooked business associate (me) were using her in the bunco we pulled off. She was truly innocent, as naive as she was nice. She loved the big jerk, and I think he loved her, too, in his own way. But he was the kind of jerk who couldn't help using her any more than he could help conning people. Of course, I used her, too, but then she wasn't my girl. (Did I still have a girl, or had the Ay-rab wolves already gotten her? I agonized a lot about that, and often found myself communing with Allah, since I was on his territory. Please, Allah. Keep her safe until I get there. Lay off the *mektoob* business and give her a break. Please.)

During the *bagarre* at the café the waiter gave Michelle some rough backtalk in Arabic, which she didn't understand and I did. Mine had sharpened considerably during my time in Tangier. I moved in and gave the waiter a piece of his own back by telling him he was a *manyuk* and an *akrout*. The first meant he sold himself to other men, the second that he pimped for his sister on the side. Then I called the owner of the place and chewed him for permitting his waiters to use coarse language to the customers. I made it loud enough so everyone in the joint and most of the tourists in the Djemaa El Fna could hear me. They wouldn't understand the words but they'd get the music. The upshot of the whole business was that Michelle, Elmer and I ended up at the same table drinking beer and nibbling *kimiyah* together. Elmer stuck me for the beer with the Thirteen Match game.

"Oh, 'e is so lucky wiz zis game, I 'ate 'eem!" said Michelle, gazing at the big apple knocker with adoration in her eyes. "I can nevaire win 'eem, not one time! Please win 'eem for me, m'sieur."

She didn't mean the game by " 'eem," but Elmer. She used 'win' to mean 'beat,' and hashed up her English in other ways, all cute. Her accent was cute, too. Everything about her was cute except maybe her nose, and Elmer. He was as ham-handed and clumsy as he was crooked.

The Thirteen Match game, if you have never played it, is one of the simplest and most effective swindles in existence. The mark can't ever win unless you want him to. You throw thirteen matches, thirteen toothpicks, thirteen beans, thirteen of anything you have available on the table. Then you and the john take turns extracting one, two or three matches from the pile at a time, each player's free option each pick. The aim is not to take that last match or toothpick or whatever. That's the aim of the game, I mean. The *first* aim, if you want to be sure of winning, is to make sure the john takes the first draw. After that he's dead.

Whatever he draws, one, two or three, you take the
reciprocal to make a total of four each time. As long as
you do that, and start with a multiple of four plus one,
it could be five or five million and one, it works out the
same. As anyone can figure out by stopping to use his
knob for three seconds. The sucker is inevitably going
to be stuck with the old maid at the end. You let him
win now and then (as Elmer was too dumb to do) so he
won't catch on to how mechanical it all is, and you go
first half of the time while you're breaking the boob
in so he won't read the importance of the first draw.
But when money is down, you generously give him
first pick. That's all there is to it except banking the
proceeds.

I let him stick me to see if, having taken me for a
lousy four or five dirhams, he'd try to sell me the
Djemaa El Fna. Maybe it does take one to know one,
but I had Elmer taped in a hurry. He just didn't get
any fun out of life unless he was screwing somebody,
even if only for four or five dirhams. We got together
to do business as naturally as two buzzards gravitate to
the same carcass.

What we worked out was pretty smooth, and very
nearly legitimate. Elmer was a crossroads operator
at heart, a skin-'em-quick-and-blow-along man. He
lacked subtlety. I held out for the more professional
sell he finally agreed to. It was a good example of the
artistic con that leaves the marks grateful to you for
doing them a favor and you in a position where the
speedy getaway is not necessary. The safety measures
cost us part of the take, but they were worth it in my
opinion. Elmer's opinions didn't count.

Except in summer, Marrakech is usually full of American tourists holding heavy fat books of traveler's checks. Many of them stay at the big old Mamounia Hotel where Winnie used to hang out in his day. We put cute little Michelle in a bikini, took her over to the Mamounia pool, exposed her to the eye and let nature take its course. The Daddies loved her oo-la-la accent as much as they loved the rest of her. The Mommies kind of got their noses out of joint at first, but she was such a natural charmer that pretty soon she had the Mommies on her side too. I have to add, immodestly but for the record, that I helped more than some with the Mommies after Michelle roped the Daddies. She and I made a good team, although she didn't know she was a part of it. Elmer just kind of hulked around looking like one hundred percent American green corn.

We sold camel-caravan trips to far-off romantic dreamy Timbuctoo; one way by camel, that is, return trip by air, four nights and five days at the Timbuctoo end thrown in. Price for the package, one thousand U.S. rasbuckniks or acceptable equivalent, cash down. No credit cards. Who doesn't want to see glamorous far-off dreamy romantic Timbuctoo, particularly if he or she is the kind of adventurous citizen who already has made it as far as glamorous far-off dreamy romantic Marrakech from Weehawken, N.J.? The fact that Timbuctoo is a mangy flea-ridden mudwalled Nothingsville approximately as far from Marrakech as Brussels is from Madrid meant nothing. We didn't have to bring that up. (Have you ever tried riding a stinking *camel* as far as from Madrid to Brussels, fifty-two uninterrupted days perched aboard your ship of the desert, without a single place along the way to have a hot bath?) We also kind of failed to invite the attention to the gimmick in which the gaff was hidden, down there in the fine print. I insisted that we draw up a formal contract, simple but clear and binding, so that there could be no question of bad faith afterward and maybe complaints filed with the legation in Tangier before I got my new passport.

The gaff was a proviso that if, by reason of war, riot, rebellion, civil disturbance or other Act of God we, the parties of the first part, were unable to get the camel caravan moving in the right direction within a certain period, then we the parties of the first part were obliged—get the wording?—without further charge to the parties of the second part to arrange for the transportation of said parties of the second part to as well as from Timbuctoo by air; a round-trip which, by the shortest route via Casablanca and Bamoko in Mali, cost around $400. The whole package, including the agreed upon hotel accommodations and the rest of it, wouldn't amount to $500, and that amount would be reduced by the cut of commissions I planned to jack out to the travel agent who would do all the work of booking the reservations, arranging for the air tickets and the rest of the drudgery.

There never was any remote chance that Elmer and I might be soiling our hands with vulgar travail or a bunch of smelly camels, even by accident. This was back in the days before de Gaulle came to power to lop off what was left of France's colonies, but there was already political unrest and talk of independence among the French colonials of North Africa. Algeria, a good piece of which the camel caravan would have had to traverse to romantic dreamy flea-ridden Timbuctoo, was stewing uneasily if not already red-hot and boiling; a condition which brought the escape clause into effect before the venture ever got off the ground or the camels up off their knees. It made Elmer and me an easy $500-plus clear profit per customer without working up a sweat, bending the law or hurting anybody's feelings.

"We will go, too, *n'est-ce pas, cheri*?" Michelle asked Elmer one afternoon when we were at a café table figuring the arithmetic. "Wiz zee camels?"

"Well, uh, gee, honey," Elmer said, fumbling. "Somebody's got to stay here and run things." He gave me the eye to say, Take me out.

This is what I mean by clumsy. He had no finesse at all. All he had to do was say Yes to make it come true in her mind. The reality didn't matter. That could come later. But the oaf didn't even know how to lie smoothly. He was a disgrace to the profession.

For her benefit, not his, I said, "Of course you'll go, Michelle. I'll stay and carry the ball here. I know the language, the people, the ropes. Elmer doesn't. There's nothing at all to prevent him from going along with the rest of the camels and taking you with him."

"Oh, sank you, Curlee!" Michelle grabbed one of my hands in both of hers. We were on first-name terms and better by then. " 'Ow can I 'elp but love you?" And she gave me a great big sisterly kiss that meant nothing at all except that she was a natural born con-woman herself. Even without knowing it.

With her unwitting help we roped eleven johns and their ladies; gross handle, twenty-two thousand of the best, cash in advance. Some of the suckers were shy about laying it on us ahead of time all at once. Why not half or a third down and the rest C.O.D., something like that? Most of them were retired businessmen who had been around. We said No, we had to put up an advance for a string of camels, guides, tents, equipment, food, booze, hotel reservations, plane-fares, etc., etc. Sorry, sir, but that's the way it has to be. Some of them still balked until their wives took them by the ear and said, Now you listen to me, George Spelvin. The Mommies couldn't bear the thought of that sniffy Mrs. Jones being able to talk about that wonderful trip afterward and them not. Having hooked one Mommy, we hooked them all, and with them the Daddies.

For sweeteners we promised, flatly guaranteed, palm-shaded oases watered by gushing springs every afternoon, a full moon every night, nautch dancers, gourmet cooking, iced champagne, innerspring mattresses, color TV, everything, anything—what the hell, why not, they weren't really going to *go* that way. In the end we had the full twenty-two thousand in our hands, less about $10,000 we had to lay out for the legitimate package they were actually going to find under the Christmas tree come Santa Claus day.

After that there was the small matter of cutting up the melon. We had the money in a lockbox, the lockbox in the safe at the Mamounia under an arrangement by which we had to take it out together or not at all. It was just too bad for the other guy if one of us dropped dead, but on the other hand it was the best possible insurance against a doublecross, or rat poison in somebody's soup. We both had a lot of confidence in our business partner.

"I don't see how I can rightly claim a third for Michelle," Elmer said real generous-like. The yokel couldn't even pronounce her name right. He called her 'Mitchell.' "What she done mostly was lie around in her bathing suit. I tell you what, neighbor, what do you say we cut her in for five bills, then you and me—"

"I tell *you* what, neighbor," I said. "Stop shoveling horseshit for a minute and come out of the barn. I'll put out to buy your doll a new dress and maybe a new bikini, because she's cute and I like her. But that's as far as she rides on this haywagon, so come off it."

"Aw, now look, neighbor—"

"Aw, now look yourself, neighbor. Don't try to bunco a bunco-steerer. It won't work. We split down the middle or not at all, and I can outwait you. The cops aren't looking for *me*."

I didn't know they were looking for him, either, but the chances were better than even.

He aw-now-look-neighbor'ed me some more, but I'd made him reach for the first match and we both knew I had him by the short hairs. Besides, he was anxious to get on with the business of conning me out of my cut after we had split. He was that kind of business associate. After all, if you can bag one john, what's so immoral about bagging another? For my part— well, guess, neighbor. As noted earlier, it takes one to know one.

The money was mostly in dirhams, with a small admixture of dollar scratch. Some of the Daddies had tried to pay off with large leaves out of their books of travelers checks, but travelers checks are hard to convert into the real thing unless they're your own and you have a passport with the right name in it. Also there is the small but significant matter of vigorish, or breakage on the exchange when you convert from one money to another kind of money. We didn't want to assume any unnecessary expenses. So we had collected in cash; as aforesaid, mostly dirhams.

Elmer didn't want dirhams. He meant to blow along fast, after he had conned me, and dirhams would be a handicap to him for several reasons. There was an exchange control on them at the time, prohibiting the export of Moroccan currency from the country. You could always smuggle it, but if you got caught you lost not only the loot but usually your freedom to move about unhampered for a year or two. For another thing, the dirham wasn't too strong outside Morocco. You could trade it for something else in Tangier, but the Tangier price wasn't too favorable if you were after pounds, dollars, something hard like that. Elmer wanted dollars. He could have bought dollar traveler's checks at a fair rate there in Marrakech, but he shied away from that because of the passport business. You're supposed to be able to change a traveler's check anywhere simply by countersigning it in front of the guy who's going to give you the cash for it, but try and do it as a practical matter. They want to see your passport first, match the picture in it with your face, the signature in it with the signature on the check before you go any further. Since Elmer Wiggins was, for the moment, doing business as Elmer Wiggins, with

Michelle as with everyone else, things could get a bit hairy if he had to produce a passport with another name on it. Elmer was in a spot. It left him open to a little counter-bagging.

I made him an offer. I said, "Elmer, neighbor, I tell you what. I'll buy your dirhams. You'll have to make me a price, because I'm not going to do you any favors" (he'd have shied away from me like a startled milk-cow at any hint of generosity), "but I'll take them off your hands for pounds sterling and pay you in cash at a better price than you could get in Tangier or anywhere else. Want to deal?"

He was suspicious, naturally. Right away his instincts made him say, no; no deal. I expected that. But he thought about it—I expected that, too—and he began to see a way he could deal and con me at the same time. I expected *that*.

"Hey, now, neighbor," he said, in his best cornpone drawl. "This here now deal you was talking about. What's in it for you?"

"Money," I said. "What did you think?"

"I thought money," he said. "What kinda money?"

"Vigorish money," I said. "I'm spending dirhams here. I'm going to spend a lot more before I leave here." (I had told him and Michelle about the *teuf-teuf*.) "I have to buy dirhams with other kinds of money. If I buy them from you at a better price than you can sell them to a bank but still get them at a better price than I have to pay the bank—you figure it."

He figured it. He was still suspicious, but it sounded right. Besides, he was counting on cleaning me, of dirhams as well as everything else, before he moved on. He agreed to deal, after some hemming and hawing.

"All right," I said. "We deal. But first I have to dig up five-thousand-odd dollars worth of sterling in Tangier to buy your dirhams, and that's not the kind of cash I ordinarily carry around in my pants. You'll have to let me take my half out of the box."

He balked there. It hurt him to let that kind of money get away, even temporarily. But he had to come around if he wanted to do business, and by then he had his own con adjusted to the new developments.

After we had cut the melon we argued some more about who was going to stand the costs of the Tangier trip. Both of us put up a good fight to show what square-shooters we were. In the end we split it down the middle, as we expected to do from the start. There was only one other small difficulty.

"Druther have dollars," he said. "I don't trust this here now sterling stuff."

I shrugged and said, All right, I'd get him dollars if I could, as many as possible, but pounds sterling were easier to come by in Tangier because of its busy trade, in part legitimate, with Gibraltar. I wouldn't be able to give him as good a price in dollars as I could in pounds. He finally agreed to take pounds. Still suspicious, of course.

"How long you gonna be gone?" he wanted to know.

"Well, let's see. There's only one Tangier flight out of here a week, on Saturday. That's tomorrow. It'll be back a week later. I ought to be back with it if I don't have any trouble finding the money or get knocked over going or coming. Why?"

"I don't want to git to worryin' about you."

"Why would you git to worryin' about me, neighbor?"

"I'm jest a natcheral born worrier, I guess."

"That's sweet of you, but don't go bald worrying about me. I'll be back."

In her own time Michelle got me alone to ask much the same questions. We spoke French whenever Reuben wasn't tuned in, so her accent disappeared while mine, which wasn't as cute as hers, cropped out.

"You will come back, will you not, Curlee?"

"Of course I'll come back. Why wouldn't I come back?"

"Elmaire thinks you may forget."

"What Elmer means is he thinks I'm going to run out and leave him holding the sack." By then she knew that there wasn't going to be any camel caravan, although not that we had planned it that way from the beginning. "There isn't any sack to hold, Michelle. Whatever happens, the money to meet our guarantee is already in the hands of the travel agent. Elmer is clean if he wants to move along tomorrow."

"He doesn't want to leave. He feels a responsibility until the people have made the trip. He thinks you should share the responsibility with him. So do I."

I couldn't very well tell her that Elmer's only sense of responsibility was toward getting my share of the loot away from me. I said, "If I give you my word that I'll be back as soon as I can get back, will you believe me?"

"How could I not?"

"How could you not what?"

"How could I not believe your word?"

"There are dozens of ways you could not believe my

word. There are lots of words not worth believing for three seconds. Mine could be one of them."

She shook her head, smiling. "No, Curlee. You would not lie to me. I know."

For some reason she made me think of Reggie, who was equally positive I couldn't tell the truth. I said, "Damn it, I would too lie to you! I lie to people all the time. Everybody lies to everybody else all the time. The world turns on an axis oiled by lies. Don't be naive."

"I am not naive. You have given me your word that you will come back. You will be back."

"Yes. Certainly. I did. I do. I will. But I'd give you my word just as readily if I weren't coming back, so where does that leave you?"

"With your word. Thank you, Curlee. I'll tell Elmaire he has no need to worry."

She left me defeated.

If Elmer thought his only worry was that I might not come back with my half of the boodle, he could think again. There I was taking all the risks of smuggling the money, losing it to the law and ending up in a smelly Moroccan jail while he sat on his ass with his share in his pocket and his cute doll to keep him company (Boda, Boda, poor innocent child, I would have done anything to save you) while he enjoyed the entertainments of the Djemaa El Fna. You big hayshaker, I thought resentfully as the plane took off, putting me to all this trouble. If it weren't for Michelle I wouldn't even leave you carfare.

My heart was as heavy as lead when the plane put down in Tangier. Even the feel of all that money in my pants didn't help. Boda was lost to me forever, already on her way to Buenos Aires or some Middle Eastern den of depravity if she wasn't locked up in an Arab joint down in the medina where I couldn't find her in a thousand years. Poor, beautiful, simple, harmless, honey-golden Boda. I was darn near in tears when I opened the door to the empty, lifeless apartment—it was long past Kadoosh's quitting time—and found her sitting there in her slacks and sweater. Not doing anything, just sitting there with her hands in her lap. She gave me the great big slow smile, like the sun coming up out of the sea at dawn on a clear still morning.

"Hello," she said. "I've been waiting for you."

"Oh," I said foolishly. "Have you?"

My mind had ceased to function. I had been so completely convinced that she was lost to me forever that I couldn't accept the reality of her presence.

"You told me to."

"So I did."

"Can I take my clothes off now, Carly? I need a bath. It's been three weeks."

"You mean—you mean—you mean—you mean—?"

That's what she meant. I had told her, to be emphatic, to keep her clothes on night and day, except for the *kaftan*, and by God that's what she had done. Night and day for three weeks.

"Except that I changed my underpants a couple of times, Carly," she said. "Was that all right? I didn't think you'd mind if I changed my underpants. I did it in the dark."

She hadn't put on any makeup, either. I had told her not to. Or go up on the roof, or open the door to anyone but Kadoosh, or the other things. She hadn't even once gone out of the apartment. She had obeyed instructions to the letter, sitting there without makeup or a bath or as much as a walk in the street for three whole weeks because that's what she thought I had told her to do. I guess I had, at that. Anyway I was real glad to see her, and greatly relieved. No more about Boda at this point, except that after she had her bath and put on her makeup I took her out for the best dinner sucker-money would buy in Tangier. I bought her a new lipstick, too. It was all she wanted or needed that she didn't have.

I got back to Marrakech one week later, heavier by a lot of pounds. (Get it, neighbor?) I expected to find Elmer at the café near the Djemaa El Fna, chiseling marks with Thirteen Matches. He wasn't there. He and Michelle had had to retire from public view a few days earlier. Daddies and Mommies had been button-holing him in the street wanting to know when the camel caravan would take off for glamorous far-off dreamy romantic Timbuctoo. Since he couldn't very well tell them the caravan was scheduled to leave the day snow fell on the Sahara, he had gone into hiding. I ran him down after first making sure that the round trip air-tickets, hotel vouchers and the rest were all ready at the travel agent's, each in its properly addressed envelope for delivery to the happy travelers the day after we blew town. I also checked to be certain the *teuf-teuf* was in running order. Everything was fine in both departments.

I gave Michelle the dress and bikini I had picked out for her in Tangier, got a sisterly kiss of thanks in return, and generously took her and Hayseed Henry to the Mamounia for dinner. The Mamounia's food is by no means the best in Marrakech, but I had reasons for choosing the hotel. In the gay spirit of the evening I let Elmer stick me for two bottles of champagne with the Thirteenth Match. Even good champagne didn't taste good to him unless he bilked somebody for it. During the course of the evening, at a time when Michelle had excused herself to go to *le petit coin*, we made the dirham-sterling trade.

I sent a waiter out to the desk for a couple of the big hotel envelopes. Elmer pulled out his wad, I pulled out mine, we made the exchange; counting the bills right there on the table under each other's nose so there could be no kickback. Right? Right. Into the envelopes, envelopes into jackets, the whole thing over and done with before Michelle came back with her nose powdered. We were raising our champagne glasses in a congratulatory toast to each other when she arrived.

In the abstraction business every crook has his own M.O. A second-story man climbs porches. A peterman robs peters. A strong-arm clobbers you, a con man cons you. We do not commonly cross over into fields other than our own, although we may vary the M.O. within those fields. Which is to say, if a peterman can open a box by twisting the dial, he is not going to take the trouble to blow it as an artistic effort. Similarly, a bunco man may get into your pockets in any of several ways, but he does not stoop to violence. It is beneath his talents. I knew I had nothing to fear in that respect from Hezekiah Hayloft, although he was plenty big enough to give me a hard time if he had wanted to. He didn't want to. He merely itched to get his hands on that envelope in my jacket to join up with the one already in his own jacket. Thereafter he would fade over the nearest horizon with Michelle, leaving me with my memories and the last match.

The signal came when the yokel volunteered—*volunteered*, mind you—to *pay for* a third bottle of champagne to cap the evening. I allowed as how that was right neighborly of him. The bottle came and was opened. We toasted each other again, toasted Michelle, drank, and the party was over. According to schedule I passed out cold with my face on the tablecloth as a result of too much champagne and the knockout drops he slipped into my glass with all the ham-handed dexterity of a stableboy forking dung. And who do you suppose paid for the third bottle of wine along with everything else when he woke up with a splitting headache several hours later? Right? Right.

I can only guess how he got the envelope out of my pocket under Michelle's slightly oversize but otherwise attractive nose. Maybe she wasn't wholly innocent as I thought she was, although if she fooled me she was a lot too smart to run with Elmer. I suspect that he said something like, Well, golly, gee, honey, looky here, that pore drunk feller has got this here now envelope full of money on him, I guess it would only be neighborly of me to put it in the hotel safe for him before somebody steals it, huh? Anyway, he got it—the envelope in my jacket pocket, that is. Full of dirham green-goods I had prepared earlier to look like the envelope of genuine dirhams he had just given me and which I had carefully inserted into the lining of my jacket through a slit therein, also prepared earlier. I figured he wouldn't take time to examine the dirhams before getting out of town with them. Any more than he would take time to examine the sterling green-goods I had bought him for two shillings on the pound in Tangier. Even if he did, he wouldn't know a real five-pound note from a counterfeit Irish Sweepstakes ticket. As for the dirhams, he wouldn't believe they were phony when somebody told him. Golly gee, hadn't he *seen* me put that there Mamounia envelope into my jacket after watching me stuff if with the genuine dirhams he had just given me in exchange for pounds? It goes without saying that the most important part of a good con is to make sure the mark never suspects he's getting the phonus bolonus when you slip it to him with something as elementary as the old Envelope Switch. The gratifying part is in letting him think he is conning you for it.

I never heard what happened to Elmer when he tried to spend his collection of wallpaper. I hope Michelle didn't get into trouble with him. I had put an envelope of eating money in the package that held the new bikini I had brought her with the dress, so she wouldn't go hungry on my account. Although if she hung around with Elmer long, she'd end up wearing bracelets. I don't mean diamond bracelets.

The *teuf-teuf* behaved reasonably well all the way home. I felt so good, about Boda and the other things, that I hardly winced at the stout bill the Arab mechanic handed me for the repair job. Not then I didn't wince, at least. Not until the hot-iron merchant in Tangier stuck me with the cost of another repair job. The Arab had put in what was needed in the way of "new," i.e. second-hand, valve stems, plugs and things; patched up the old cylinder-head so it would hold together as far as Tangier, spray-painted everything to make it look shiny and clean and sold me the package as new goods imported from Rabat. It was only a little con, of course. Nothing like the nearly ten thousand dollars I brought home, but still a good clean professional job. It goes to show. If you let yourself do business in the other guy's store you're going to end up with his merchandise at his price on his own terms. I sure wouldn't want to let good ole Elmer get me down on the farm at any time in the foreseeable future.

Chapter Seven

The next day I was back pounding away at the mill, grinding out further immortal prose on the financial attractions of Tangier for believers. I didn't need the money anymore, what with the loot I had safely tucked away under the floorboards of the apartment. But the passport had still to come through and the work kept me from worrying too much about Boda.

The time was fast approaching when I would be moving along again, and I couldn't take her with me. I don't mean I didn't want to, necessarily. I couldn't. She had no papers, she had no wish for papers, she didn't know what had happened to the papers with which she had left Denmark, if any. She couldn't remember. Dragging her *avec* would be like dragging a ball and chain, wholly aside from the constant need to beat wolves off her with a club. And I couldn't leave her alone and unsheltered in Tangier, any more than Jim had been able to. I had to figure something, but I wasn't quite ready to look around for my successor. So I typed. Until one afternoon there was a knock on the door.

She was up on the roof, and she knew she was never to come down without her robe on. No immediate problem there. I opened the door.

A respectable looking French bank-clerk type was standing there. He wore an incongruously sporty cloth cap that had been set squarely on his head with a spirit level. It made quite a contrast with the rest of his get-up, strictly from middle-class Clerksville.

"Good afternoon, monsieur," he said politely. "Is this your name?"

He held out some kind of an official-looking document so I could read the name on it. It was mine.

"It might be," I said. "Why?"

"I have a warrant for your arrest. Interpol."

He put the paper carefully away in his pocket and took out a wallet with an identification card in it; picture, thumbprint and the rest. It looked genuine. So did he.

I said, "Well, come in, come in. I guess we ought to talk, huh?"

"Thank you. I think we should." He took off his cap before coming in. If I'd had a doormat I think he would have wiped his shoes, too. Carefully. He was that kind.

We talked. That is, he talked. I listened, thinking hard and fast.

By sheer accident and the chance of having spent some time in escrow with the two *motards* who had on occasion been assigned to Interpol business and had nothing better to do than talk about it, I knew quite a bit about Interpol. More formally, it's *L'Organization Internationale de Police Criminelle*. The O.I.P.C., which has its headquarters in France and to which most civilized and many semi-civilized nations belong not including Russia and her friends, is not a police force in the sense that the F.B.I. is a police force, for example. It has no body of law-enforcement officers, whatever nonsense you may have heard or read about

secret Interpol agents going around nobbling international crooks. The organization's main function is to
receive, correlate and disseminate information about
crooks on behalf of its constituent members. It also
maintains, in France, a central bureau of liaison
through which the police of any contributory country
can make quick contact with the police of another contributory country to ask for a pickup-and-hold; on
Luigi Giovanelli, say, after Luigi has banged a box in
Turino and lammed out for points north, possibly
Switzerland or Austria. But any arrests made because
of Interpol's intervention in a case are made by the
police having proper jurisdiction on the national soil
where the arrest is made, none other. An Interpol
agent can no more make a pinch in Tangier, or anywhere else, than the Red Cross can. Furthermore,
the warrant, which looked legal as far as it went, was
signed by a French judge, and France had about as
much jurisdiction over me in Tangier as it would have
had in Tokyo. I couldn't even be extradited for a little
thing like cigarette smuggling even if I had been guilty
of that, and I'd never been adjudged guilty. In short,
the guy was either a complete phony or running a
bluff.

I thought it was a bluff. His papers looked real, he
looked real. His neat bank-clerk's manner was right
for a guy who probably spent most of his working
day wearing sleeve-protectors while sorting mug-shots
into alphabetical order in steel filing cabinets. That
meant, probably, Reggie's fastidious British fingers
manipulating the shells and pea. When I asked him for
a closer look at the warrant, which he gave me readily,

I was certain of it. I wasn't wanted for the de Lille swindle, just the theft of personal property from the Hon. Regina Forbes-Jones. That lousy graveyard suit, believe it or not. I hadn't even worn it since leaving France.

All these thoughts went through my head a lot faster than I've been able to set them down. The guy stood there holding his silly cap, politely and patiently waiting for me to come along quietly. I didn't know what to do with him. I didn't want to hurt his feelings by telling him to *foutre le camp*. He was too much of a gentleman for that kind of language. While I was hesitating, trying to decide how best to tell him the disappointing truth, a door opened and closed behind us.

His cap dropped from his fingers, his eyes froze and glazed, his mouth fell open, he stopped breathing as he went into instantaneous shock. Boda had come down from the roof. Thanks be to Allah I always insisted on the robe, even though it wasn't exactly what you would call Boda-concealing. Naked, she'd have turned him to stone.

I got a chair under him before his knees buckled. He was beginning to breathe again, shallowly.

"Boda, dear," I said, "this is Mr.—what did you say your name was, sir?"

"What?" He didn't look at me. He couldn't have seen me if he had. He was temporarily blinded.

"Your name. What's your name?"

"My name? Oh, yes. My name. Of course. My name. Uh, Uh? My name, yes."

He didn't know. I said, "Mr. Uh Uh, meet Boda. Boda, sweetheart, go put on some water for tea. Then put on some clothes, lots of clothes. Then stay the hell out of here until I call you."

"Yes, Carly." She gave Mr. Uh Uh one of her slow beautiful smiles and went away.

When she had withdrawn from his line of vision he began slowly to come around, although he looked dazed and drawn for some time afterward. He wouldn't ever have seen anything approximating Boda among his files of mugshots. While he was still semi-conscious I pumped him for the answers to a few vital questions. Not about who had put him up to the bluff, I knew who that was and that she would have paid plenty to buy him. What I wanted to find out were things about himself; his private life, family connections, habits, inclinations and so on. I'm sure he never remembered the questions afterward, or his replies to them.

When I had learned what I wanted to know I went to the kitchen and made tea, bringing it back myself. I was sure if Boda came close enough to him to offer a tea-tray he'd go into shock again. I wanted him reasonably conscious and able to think, a little at least. It's hard, impossible to con a mark while he's unconscious.

The details of what I had in mind aren't important, if they aren't already so obvious as to need no explanation. He never had a chance. Every time he'd show signs of returning rationality I'd expose him to Boda for the necessary length of time to put him under again without putting him out. I thought I'd overdone it the day I let him accompany us to the beach and she, as usual, dropped her robe as soon as we came down off the esplanade. He barely survived the Boda-ray radiations.

I never let him know I had a new passport coming up. I told him I didn't have any papers at all, and wasn't it going to be pretty hard for him to take me back to France without documentation of some kind? Still dazed by Boda in the honey-colored flesh, he let drop that he had my old passport, the one Reggie had pinched. We could leave any time.

It confirmed what I was pretty sure of anyway, that the hand of Nemesis was reaching again. Her instrument of retribution, however, was as malleable as warm goose-grease. I begged him not to say the ugly words. I couldn't bear to face the hideous reality of the moment when I would have to go off to jail leaving poor Boda alone and helpless in a sink of iniquity like Tangier. I had Mr. Uh Uh figured as a regular churchgoer.

He was. When I confessed further that Boda and I weren't married, he was horrified, shocked, aghast. Particularly after I had pointed out that when I was gone she wouldn't have even the dubious protection of a marriage certificate between her and the wolves.

"What?" he said. "You mean that poor child has nowhere to turn? No family, no friends to shelter her, no guardian soul—"

"—no money, and no papers," I finished. "Only me. Nobody in the world else." I sighed unhappily. "I just can't bear to think what's going to happen to her when I'm gone. Poor kid."

"But—but—but—but—"

"Exactly, sir." He sounded just like a toy motorboat. But there was nothing at all phony about his distress and concern. Mr. Uh Uh was a kind man, as well as badly smitten Boda-wise.

After that I had no problems. He was so horrified by the thought that his action in taking me back to France would expose Boda to several fates worse than death that he was about ready to call the whole thing off and go home. I didn't want that to happen—yet. When my new passport came through at last I had a short private talk with Boda.

"Boda, dear," I said. "I have to leave you. This is goodbye. Mr. Uh Uh will remain. He is a good, honest, decent man, unmarried and unburdened by family responsibilities. He doesn't know it yet, but he will take care of you and love and cherish you for the rest of your life if you allow him to do so. Are you with me so far?"

"Yes, Carly. I wish you weren't going away, though."

"So do I. I have no choice. After I have left, Mr. Uh Uh will ask you to go back to France with him. You are to agree. If he asks you to be his *petite amie*, you are to agree to that. I don't think he will. Most probably he will ask you to marry him. You are to agree to that, too. You are to agree to everything he asks you to do, because what he asks you to do will be for your own good and happiness and, I suspect, his as well. Is this all quite clear?"

"Yes, Carly." She did me the signal honor of blinking back the tears that were in her glorious blue eyes. It was more than she had done for Jim or—I hoped—the German on Ibiza. "When are you leaving?"

"Soon. I can't tell you the exact moment. First I have to get from here to Cairo, where I am going. Cairo, in Egypt. Say it after me."

"Cairo, in Egypt."

"Good. When I am gone, not before, I want you to answer any questions Mr. Uh Uh asks you, honestly and to the best of your recollection. That's all. Now kiss me goodbye, because I may not have time to say goodbye when I take off."

"Yes, Carly. But I wish—"

I shut her up in the most effective way I knew. The kiss lasted from about half an hour after Kadoosh's departure until we heard her come in the next morning and begin uncurtaining herself.

The rest of it was cut and dried. I had only to gather up what was under the floorboards, fold the bills into a money-belt I strapped on next to my skin, stick my passport into the coat of my AEC suit and take off for Rabat and points west via the World's Most Experienced Airline. Mr. Uh Uh would know that Boda was too simple and too fine a girl to lie about my going to Cairo. It should divert him long enough for me to confuse my trail in the other direction. I didn't think he would come after me, but if he did I'd just as soon Interpol looked for me in Egypt instead of some place else. I left the mourner's outfit behind so he would have something to show Reggie for the money he would have cost her.

The next few months were uneventful. Duller than ditchwater, to tell the truth. I went back to the U.S., held a job as a bank-teller for a while and quit. Being caged up with all that cash belonging to other people gave me hives. I bought a car with part of the money in the money-belt, a real sporty convertible, but I didn't have a girl to occupy either the front seat or the back seat with me, except now and then. After Boda, girls—

ordinary girls—didn't have quite what it takes. I don't mean to suggest I was ever in love with Boda. Falling in love with Boda would be pretty much like falling in love with a beautiful woman in a moving picture. She just didn't have the emotional depth to appreciate the fact that she was loved, or reciprocate love. I was fond of her, and I wished her well, but that was it. I thought she was probably doing very well with Mr. Uh Uh, as I had arranged it. She had just spoiled lesser girls for me, somehow.

I traveled around the country a lot, searching for something. I didn't know what it was. It wasn't easy money. The marks were so thick and eager at every crossroad they didn't even offer a challenge. This was at a time when the franchise food chains were beginning to boom and spread out—Colonel Sanders Finger-lickin' Fried Chicken, Aunt Jemima Pancakes, those things—and every small-town capitalist in America wanted a slice of the pie in his community. A franchise could return a whole lot of steady money on a relatively small investment. I had a few sets of fake credentials printed up saying I represented several of the most successful chains, and I worked the towns with populations of fifteen to twenty thousand or thereabouts. The chains themselves weren't trying to promote franchises in towns of under twenty-five thousand. They thought that was the minimum necessary for a successful operation. Maybe it was, for them. *I* sold franchises to johns like the village idiot, president and board chairman of the local bank he was, a real shrewd type, who offered me a bribe of a thousand dollars within half an hour after seeing my phony papers. Just to guarantee that he would get preference over the potential competition.

"Cash," he said, with a conspiratorial wink. "No checks."

"That's very generous of you, sir," I said. "But I can't positively guarantee anything. My job is simply to scout the field, select a promising prospect like yourself, accept a deposit as evidence of good faith and forward my recommendation to headquarters. The contracts are all drawn up there. The most I could do for you—"

"Your recommendation is the basis of the contract, ain't it?"

"Normally, yes, sir. But—"

"That's good enough for me, son. Let's make it fifteen hundred, and no arguments. I'll send it over to your hotel in an ahnvelope this afternoon."

He did, too. I left town without even going back to bag him for the deposit he was burning to give me in addition to the bribe. When the marks start sending their money to your hotel in ahnvelopes, there's no flavor in a flim-flam. It's more fun shooting fish in a barrel.

The snappy convertible made me too conspicuous, too easy to track. I got rid of it and traveled by common carrier: planes, trains, buses, taxis. Getting rid of the car gave me a brief inexplicable feeling of relief, as if I had just put down a heavy burden. I didn't understand the feeling at the time and I still don't. But I was restless, footloose, irritable, bad company even for myself. I wanted something I didn't have, without knowing what it was.

One gray Sunday morning I found myself on the
Baltimore waterfront, for no particular reason. Baltimore is a depressing town at best, even when the
weather isn't gloomy, and I had my own private stock
of megrims to keep me company besides. Mooching
along the wharves wrapped in my private cloud of
gloom, I breathed the salt-oil-paint-slush-garbage odor
of the harbor and was suddenly hit with this overwhelming *saudade* for—something. I still didn't know
what the something was but I craved it. I had to have
it. *Saudade* is a Portuguese word I didn't know then
but learned later in the same way I had learned my
first words of Arabic; in the can. The word doesn't
translate exactly, but it's close to nostalgia, homesick-
ness, *mal du pays*, *cafard*, all those except that you can
also have *saudade* for a plate of ham and eggs or a dill
pickle. You can even have *saudade* for nothing in particular, as I had then. What it really was, or may have
been, was a kind of anti-*saudade* for Baltimore and the
pedestrian life I had been leading. I was in a trap and I
wanted out.

There was an old freighter, medium-sized and senes-
cent but clean and well painted, tied up to the wharf
near where I was strolling. She had the Blue Peter
flying and a couple of tugs standing by, ready to go. Her
gangplank was still out and her lines still fast, with men
waiting on the wharf to cast off. Others were on deck
ready to take the lines in. Otherwise no action except
between a couple of guys who looked like they might be
ship's officers. One, wearing a greasy white cap, was
standing at the head of the gangplank yelling up at the
other, on the bridge. The one on the bridge, whose

white cap was dingy rather than greasy, was yelling right back. Between them they were profaning the Sabbath with some of the crispest blasphemy I had heard in a long time. Nobody was around to appreciate them except me and the guys standing by the lines. They looked bored, as if they'd heard it all before.

The guy at the head of the gangplank caught sight of me first.

"Hey, you! On the wharf!" he yelled. "Come over here!"

I said, "Who, me?"

"Who the hell do you think I'm talking to? Myself? Get over here before I come down there and kick your ass for you!"

"Coming, sergeant," I said, forgetting for the moment that I was no longer in the army. The words and music were so familiar. "What did I do wrong?"

"Nothing, yet. You will. Do you want to ship out?"

Coming as it did on the heels of my attack of *saudade*, it caught me with my guard down. I said, "Man, there's nothing I'd rather do more." I didn't mean I was *ready* to ship out; only that, the way I felt, the idea appealed strongly to me.

"Can you oil a triple-expansion engine?"

"Well, I haven't worked at it lately, but given a little time to get my hand in—"

"Shut up! Can you fire a Scotch boiler?"

"Well, I haven't done that either lately. But—"

"Shut up! You can wipe, can't you? Any dumb son of a bitch can wipe."

"I guess I can wipe, then. However—"

"Shut up! Just my luck to draw a goddamn ladyfinger.

How long will it take you to get your gear and your papers?"

"My—?"

"Shut up! That's too long. I'll give you forty-five minutes, not a minute over. If you're not here ready to turn to in forty-five minutes, I'll have your balls for breakfast. Now *move*, goddamn it!"

"Yes, *sir!*"

As soon as I was out of sight of the freighter's deck I moved more slowly, of course. No profaner of the Sabbath in a greasy cap could order me around like that, by golly. Who did he think he was, anyway? (He was the First Assistant Engineer, that's who he was. On a steam freighter the First, if not God below decks, is his Vicar. God is the Chief.) But then I got to thinking, about this and that and the other thing, and I speeded up again. What the hell, why not? At least I'd be going *somewhere*, even if I didn't know where it was. Instead of doomed to Baltimore, MD, on a gloomy Sunday.

I made it back in forty-two minutes flat. Running, but as light as a soap bubble on my feet, buoyed by a wonderful feeling of freedom and escape. I had all my portable possessions in a suitcase, my papers in my pocket. The two guys in the white caps, now joined by another pair, were still yelling dirty words at each other. As soon as I hove in sight they all turned loose on me, piping me aboard with as warm a welcome as I have ever received anywhere. Somebody began yelling orders, winches rattled, lines began coming in, the tugs hooted signals at each other. We were on our way, wherever it might lead. I felt wonderful.

A few initial complications arose in connection with my new employment. It turned out that the First wasn't ordering me to get my passport, vaccination certificate and the other things when he sent me off after my papers. What he meant was my seaman's book, union card and such. He almost went through the ceiling, I mean overhead, when he found out I didn't have any.

"A fink!" he yelled. "A goddamn fink you worked off on me! My God, the unions will strike the ship so hard her seams will open! You scab son of a bitch, if I'd known what was worming its way into my engine-room—"

I cut in to remind him that I hadn't wormed my way into anything; that he'd practically kicked my ass into his engine-room, promising to have my balls for breakfast if I wasn't ready to turn to in forty-five minutes, remember? I said I was sorry I was a fink, but I hadn't realized that I was going to qualify as one. I thought he just wanted some dumb son of a bitch who could wipe. A cool, rational summarizing of the facts.

It didn't tone him down any. But he did go into conspiracy with the captain, and between them they somehow came up with a seaman's book and other documents to prove I was Thomas Polack, a paid-up member in good standing of the Firemen, Wipers, Watertenders and Oilers Union of America. I don't know where the papers came from, or what had happened to the original Thomas Polack, but I signed on under that name. I could have been Thomas A. Edison as far as the union steward aboard the freighter cared. As long as my dues were paid up. They remained paid up during the entire period of my career in the U.S. merchant marine. Two months and four days. Enough for a lifetime, believe me.

Have you ever been a fireman on an oil-burning freighter? The job of night watchman in a Quaker graveyard is mad riotous living by comparison. I made fireman after a week as wiper because the wiper they moved up to replace the fireman they moved up to replace the oiler who jumped ship in Baltimore was too dumb to handle the fire-room by himself. That means pretty God-awful dumb. Everything is under automatic control and self-tending except for a few small chores at the beginning of each watch like cleaning the oil-filters and the burners; maybe twenty minutes work if you drag it out. The rest of the time you do nothing at all except look at pressure gauges every now and then to see that everything is normal. It always is. Four hours on, eight hours off, night and day, seven days a week, from here to eternity; nobody to talk to, no reading material allowed, no portable radios because they wouldn't work inside a ship's steel hull even if you were allowed to have one on watch, which you're not. Solitary confinement. In two months and four days I was stir-crazy.

What saved a part of my sanity was the fact that many of the black gang were South Americans. The ship was headed for the west coast of South America by way of the Canal. After my first few watches in the fire-room I knew I'd be leaving it at the first opportunity. It seemed like a good idea to polish up my Spanish, which was rudimentary; the kind you pick up in Tangier while habitually speaking another couple of

languages more often and more readily. I spent all my
time off-watch trading English lessons—and cigarettes,
when necessary—for Spanish lessons from the off-
watch black gang, all my dead time below making up
new sentences and phrases to learn as soon as I was
topside again. A crash course like that, complete dedication of effort for a couple of uninterrupted months,
is as good as a hitch in the *violon* for results. I spoke
pretty good South American before I ever laid foot on
the South American continent, or even eyes. Good
enough to sucker the simple native with anyway, I was
pretty sure.

I planned first to jump ship in Panama and look
around for action there among the military personnel
in the Zone. (Soldiers aren't too bright or they wouldn't
be soldiers. Not professionals, anyway.) I couldn't make
Panama. We never tied up there. We were either out
in the stream waiting our turn at the Canal or making
the transit all the time. Buena Ventura, the first Pacific
port we hit after that, was hot, sweaty and unpromising
for a man of my achievements; a banana-port. You
can't con a bunch of bananas. The next port, Guayaquil,
was the same only sweatier. I stuck it out as far as
Callao, the end of my career in the merchant marine.
There I did a pierhead jump, came down running for
dry land and, as it turned out, within a whisker of running right into the Peruvian *calabozo*. Not because of
the pierhead jump, and not on account of Nemesis.
From sheer bonehead stupidity.

Chapter Eight

Callao is the most important seaport in Peru. It isn't much of a place in itself, outside of docks, wharves, warehouses, whorehouses and the other incidentals. But the port is only a few miles from Lima, the country's capital and largest city, and a *tranvía* connects the two. You can get up to Lima from Callao in a matter of minutes and disappear in the crowd in less than that. That's what I did. I had to leave behind everything I couldn't wear or stuff in my pockets without looking too obvious when I went ashore. It cost me a suitcase and a few other possessions, but they were a small price to pay for freedom from the black gang; a release to which I was not entitled, strictly speaking, until the ship got back to Baltimore. The First would be yelling for my balls on toast and the captain would hate me because his ship would have to pay a fine for leaving me behind. They had my sympathy, but my servitude no longer. I was free, free, *free!*

Lima held promise, I could sense it right away. Of course I was in the country illegally, without a Peruvian visa in my passport and with no visible means of support, but no matter. I didn't plan to go anyplace where an examination of passports might be called for. As for means of support, mine were what you could call invisible but well tried.

I tied up with a guy, an American, who was trying to make a living out of the Spanish Prisoner bunco but

not doing too well at it. We got together in a bar that
was popular with the resident *gringo* colony. He pan-
handled me for a beer and a sandwich. He was on the
shorts, although not, as I learned in time, as short as all
that. He was saving what money he had for postage.
When he had got around the beer and sandwich he
tried for another handout; a hundred *soles*, pally? I
said I might, just possibly might, hold still for a hundred *sol* bite if he told the right kind of tale for it.

He was a tall, skinny redhead with freckles, name of
Al Schmidt. Smitty. He'd come to Lima the same way I
had, by jumping ship. At heart he was a frustrated
writer, always talking about the great novel he was
going to turn out as soon as he could get down to it. In
the meantime one of his few assets was a typewriter, a
Smith Corona portable. He hadn't hocked it because
he was using it to write come-on letters to a sucker-list
he had acquired in some way he didn't choose to talk
about. All the addresses on it were in the U.S.A.,
mostly in small towns but never two in the same town.
It looked like a good enough list. He just wasn't getting the responses from it he thought he should be
getting.

"Damn it, Curly," he said, after we had felt each
other out long enough to recognize a fellow member
of the brotherhood. "I can't figure it. I ought to be
getting at least a nibble from one in five. I'm not even
pulling one in ten. Or one in fifteen. It's discouraging.
I just can't figure it."

"Let me see the letter," I said.

He showed it to me.

The Spanish Prisoner swindle is an old one. The

original letter was supposed to have been written by a prisoner in a Spanish penitentiary, therefore the name. Any country will do, as long as it's reasonably distant from the marks you send the letter to. Smitty's read something like the following (I'm recreating it here not from memory but because it always reads pretty much the same, subject to local variations):

Dear Sir:

A person who knows you and who has spoken very highly about you has made me entrust you with a very delicate matter on which depends the entire future of my dear daughter as well as my very existence.

I am in prison, sentenced for bankruptcy, and I wish to know if you are willing to help me save the sum of $285,000 U.S. Cy. which I have in bank bills hidden in a secret compartment of a trunk that is now deposited in a customhouse in the United States.

As soon as I send you some undeniable evidence, it will be necessary for you to come here and pay the small expenses incurred in connection with my legal process so the embargo on my suitcases will be lifted. One of these suitcases contains a baggage-check that was given to me at the time of checking my trunk for North America. The trunk contains the sum mentioned above.

To compensate for your trouble I will give you the THIRD PART OF SAID SUM. *My darling daughter, aged 19, a former Miss Peru, will accompany you to North America to assist you in claiming this award.*

Fearing that this letter may not come to your hands, I will not sign my name until I hear from you and then I will entrust you with my whole secret. For the time being I am only signing, "A."

Due to serious reasons of which you will know later, please reply VIA AIR MAIL *or* WIRE. *I beg you to treat this matter with the most absolute reserve and discretion.*

I cannot receive your reply directly in this prison, so in case you accept my proposition, please air mail your letter to a person of my entire trust who will deliver it to me safely and rapidly. This is his name and address:

Juan López
Calle Marañon 14
Lima, Peru

Too obviously a con? It's been worked successfully for over a century, and it will go on working successfully as long as there are people around who are venal, greedy and dumb. Smitty's letter had flaws, several of them. But they could be corrected easily enough, and I had the money he lacked to send copies of the letter out in quantity. There was a score to be made out of it. Several scores, if it was done right.

When I had read the letter, I said, "What's in it for me, if I tell you what's wrong with it?"

"Aw, come on. Look, I'm not even making for cakes. Don't be like that."

"Suppose I tell you what's wrong and guarantee you'll get one in five nibbles if you make the right changes?"

"For that, pally, I'll cut you in on the gravy. When it starts to flow, of course."

"It will flow. Fifty-fifty?"

"Hell, no. I'll give you a quarter."

"Half. I can sit down and write my own letters as easy as not."

"Not without a sucker-list you can't, pally. I'm sitting on that. I'll give you a third."

We settled for a sixty-forty split of all proceeds.

I said, "All right. You write pretty good English for a Peruvian convict, don't you? Not even a split infinitive in the whole thing."

"What's a split infinitive?"

"Never mind what it is. It's a mistake more Americans make than don't make, including the educated ones. Where did you learn your English, señor A?"

"I'm an educated man. That's why I'm in charge of the prison school."

"With unlimited access to a typewriter."

"That's right."

"Same having an American keyboard. I wonder how an American typewriter found its way into a Peruvian prison school?"

"Hey, wait a minute! You can't tell—"

"The hell I can't tell. Spanish-speaking typewriters have an ñ and an accent key. You've had to do 'López' and 'Marañon' by hand. Any banana-head can smell the glue on this piece of flypaper."

"Most suckers wouldn't notice that about the typewriter." He didn't like what I was telling him. It hurt his professional pride.

"A sucker worth conning is a sucker worth conning

well. This whole thing ought to be written in pencil on cheap copy-paper, the kind you find in a prison school. It ought to contain a few, not many, grammatical errors, too. The way it is now, it's too slick, too smooth. You didn't write it. Where did you get it?"

"Never mind where I got it, pally." (I figured he had pinched it and the sucker list from someone else, although I may be doing him an injustice.) "You think you can do better?"

"Certainly I can do better. But the letter I write you will have to be copied by hand in pencil. No more typewriting."

"My God, how many handwritten letters do you think I can put out in a day?"

"Twenty-five, maybe. If you don't have to waste time panhandling. I'll put up for groceries, and I'll work with you. That's fifty letters in all. Wait until we've worked two or three weeks on that schedule, and you'll begin to see results. You're just wasting stamps, sending this thing out."

He grumbled some, dragging his feet. Twenty-five handwritten letters a day was too much like work for his taste. He wasn't a true artist, just a journeyman pigeon-plucker. But he was smart enough to look facts in the eye when they were shoved down his throat, and he came around. I drafted a new letter, adding a few syntactical errors of the kind that might be made by an educated Latin with $285,000 U.S. Cy. in a trunk and a ravishingly beautiful nineteen-year-old daughter. Then I moved in with Smitty—he had plenty of room, although I had to buy my own bed—after stocking his place with food and drink so we wouldn't have to take too much time off for meals. Together we went on the nine-to-five, just as if we were office workers. Yet, somehow, that kind of nine-to-five didn't bore me silly, as an office job would have done. What we were working at was more—constructive, I guess you'd say.

I made one bad mistake. More correctly, I perpetuated in my letter a mistake in Smitty's letter that cooked us. We were probably already cooked before I moved in on the operation. Smitty was Juan López, of course, and the Calle Marañon address was his own. He should have rented a post-office box or used some other address for a mail-drop. I ought to have seen the need for this immediately, and the danger it exposed us to every time we sent out a letter. I didn't even give it a thought. We were sitting ducks when the law moved in on us.

Actually, Smitty was the sitting duck. I got away by luck and because he gave me the chance to do it at some cost to himself. We had been working for ten days or so, grinding away to make our quota of fifty letters a day. Because we had no refrigerator, I usually took time off before lunch to go out and buy the perishables we couldn't keep in the room; eggs, butter, meat, cold beer, that kind of thing. This particular day I was out when the *chontes* hit us. Coming back to the room from the market with my loaded shopping basket I turned a corner and found myself walking squarely into the open arms of La Julia, as a police paddy wagon is affectionately referred to by the crooks of Peru. The doors of the barred cage where La Julia's passengers ride stood wide for me. She didn't have a Welcome mat out, but her message was unmistakable.

On second view, a couple of delayed heartbeats later, I saw that the paddy-wagon was not reaching to embrace me but had been parked in just the right place to receive a guest or guests flung down the two flights of stairs from Smitty's room. I couldn't see if anyone was behind the wheel, but a uniformed cop was resting his pants against a fender while he cleaned his nails. He looked bored and sleepy. He paid no attention to me.

I kept moving in the direction I was pointed. It took a lot of will-power, but one sure way to interest the cop would have been to drop the shopping basket, turn around and run like hell in the other direction, screaming. The urge was strong to do it. I came on, figuring to pass the paddy-wagon with a cheerful nod to the cop, perhaps a gay little whistle if I could get my lips puckered; go on around the corner, dump the groceries and shift into getaway gear as soon as I was out of sight.

Before I got as far as the paddy wagon Smitty came stumbling out on the sidewalk. Wearing *las esposas*, a native Peruvian term for handcuffs, and with the arm on him. A tough-looking Latin character in plain clothes supplied the arm. Another similar tough character followed along behind them.

Smitty's lips were split and bleeding. One eye showed the beginning of a respectable mouse where he had been hit, and his clothes looked as if he had been going around with the cops on the floor. I stopped short. I either had to push my way by him and the two tough characters on the sidewalk, circle out in the street to get by the roadblock or stand there and gawp. I gawped.

It wasn't easy. Smitty hadn't looked my way yet. When he did—but I didn't want to think about that. Or anything else. Like the passport with my picture in it that I had hidden in my mattress upstairs.

About then, Smitty looked my way. He had to look my way because the two hard guys in plain clothes were shoving him toward the door of the cage. When he saw me, he didn't change expression by so much as the flicker of an eye. But he began to balk and hold back, struggling against the superior weight and strength of the two plainclothesmen.

"You can't do this to me!" he yelled. "Lousy spics! I want to see a lawyer! I demand that my embassy be notified! I demand—"

That was as far as he got with his demands. The guy who had the arm on him smashed him hard across the mouth with the back of his free hand. He must have been wearing a ring or rings, because Smitty's lips began to spurt blood like a cut artery.

"Shut up," the guy said, in good American. Top sergeant American. "You'll get a lawyer and hear from your embassy as soon as you give us the name of your buddy. Not before. Get in there."

"I told you, I haven't got a buddy," Smitty said thickly. I think his mouth was bleeding on the inside, too. "I'm on my own."

"*Pendejo. Cojudo.* Liar," the cop said, and smacked him again. Blood sprayed the air between them in a fine mist. "Get in there before I lose my temper."

He gave Smitty a hard shove that slammed him forward into the cage. The cop who had been leaning against the fender cleaning his nails all this time came around to close the door of the cage and lock it. I gawped.

The plainclothesman who had done the smacking said something to his partner in Spanish. I couldn't hear what it was. His partner nodded and went back into the building where Smitty's room was. The tough guy looked at me.

"What do you want?" he said, hard.

I said, "Gee, I don't want anything. I was just looking. What did he do?"

"None of your business. Friend of yours?"

"I've seen him around, in the street. I live over that way." I pointed over that way, swinging my basket of groceries into view so he could see I was a respectable housewife coming home from the market. "What did he do?"

"None of your business. Beat it. Move along."

"Yes, *sir*," I said. "I'm moving."

The paddy-wagon passed me before I reached the corner. Smitty's blood-smeared face looked at me from the barred opening in the top of the cage door. I said, "Thanks, pally. Good luck," as he went by; not saying the words aloud, just mouthing them. If he caught it, I couldn't tell. He was already too far away.

I blew town fast. The evidence in Smitty's room that two people had been living and working there was undeniable, and they had a stakeout on it. Sooner or later they'd find my passport, if they hadn't found it already, and begin stretching nets. I meant to be long gone before that happened. I still had a fair amount of cash in the money-belt, which I never took off except to bathe. That and the clothes I was wearing were my travel outfit.

It was getting to be a normal thing for me not to have a passport. I reasoned that if I could get off a ship without producing identity papers in a Peruvian seaport, I ought to be able to get aboard a ship the same way. The trouble was, the cops were going to find my Thomas Polack seaman's book along with my other papers when they mined the mattress, and that could lead to a stakeout of every port where I might possibly ship out.

Looking back, I realize I was attributing entirely too much importance to myself as a wanted criminal. I must have been pretty small peanuts in the eyes of the Peruvian law; probably too small to bother with for more than a day or two. At the time, I could hear the bloodhounds baying at my heels across the width and breadth of the country. I played it tight and cute. There was one seaport where I was pretty sure they wouldn't look for me. Iquitos.

Iquitos is more of a river-port than a seaport, strictly speaking; twenty-three hundred miles up the Amazon from its mouth, on the jungly eastern side of the Andes. But the river is so big and so deep even that far upstream that ocean-going vessels can and sometimes do go there. Used to, anyway. Iquitos began to die when the Amazon rubber boom collapsed around the beginning of the century, and the town hadn't much commercial or mercantile importance left when I got there. But there was some river traffic between it and Belém on the Atlantic, because there were—and still

are—no roads or trains in the part of the world. Even
today, you either get to Iquitos by river, or you take a
plane. Although why anyone would want to get to
Iquitos unless he was on the lam is something I've
never been able to figure out.

I took the first plane I could get aboard, first sending
up special delivery prayers that the cops hadn't yet
explored the mattress. I wasn't picked up at the airport. In Iquitos I asked around; about ships, and about
the formalities of getting across the border into Brazil.
It appeared that there was none of either on the river,
at the moment. You simply made yourself a raft or a
dugout, got aboard and floated downstream until you
were where you wanted to be; Peru, Colombia or
Brazil, it made no difference. No sweat. Well, sweat,
yes. The Amazon River valley is pretty much of a
steambath all the time, lying as it does within three or
four degrees of the equator over most of its length.
But no problems with the authorities. I was home free.
I thought. Little did I dream of what was to betide,
as the betrayed virgin says in the true-confession
magazines.

I didn't have to whittle my own dugout. Although
there were no ships on the river and none scheduled,
there were a few riverboats. *Jaulas*, they were called
collectively; birdcages. So named because they were
built with an open-work superstructure to allow the
river-breeze to flow freely through them while they
were in motion. They carried freight and a few passengers. Most of the passengers slept in hammocks slung
inside the birdcage so they would get the breeze but
were protected from sudden rainsqualls.

The *jaula* I took passage on, a seventy-year-old woodburner with Parkinson's disease, had a few cabins as well; four in all, each just big enough to hold two cramped bunks, a chair and a small table. I paid extra to have a cabin to myself because its single porthole was screened against mosquitoes, also because the captain said I could put a padlock on the door to protect the supplies I shipped for my own consumption. I had been tipped off that the only drinkable on the boat was filtered river-water, and that meals consisted exclusively of beans, dried fish, fried bananas and manioc-flour tortillas. I took steps to cure the situation on my own behalf, including the installation of the padlock, before the *jaula* pushed off. The padlock is important in view of what came later, or I wouldn't make a point of it.

The trip wasn't at all as bad as I expected it to be. Most of the *jaula's* passengers seemed to be Peruvians or Brazilians on legitimate business. All in all, captain, crew and passengers, we numbered about twenty. That's not counting monkeys, marmosets and parrots, passengers' pets in cages or tied to a stanchion or roaming free, and a four-foot pet alligator belonging to the *sobrecargo*; purser, I guess you'd call him. His name, or nickname, was Buchisapo, meaning a fat river frog. That's what he looked like in a genial way. The captain was a quiet, pleasant man who didn't talk much. The *práctico* or mate was a young fellow who handled the helm most of the way and had little time for anything else but sleeping and eating.

The engineer we saw hardly at all. His engines were so decrepit he had to stay with them night and day

giving them transfusions. The *jaula* had no radio, no
refrigeration, no running water other than what was
available in two washbowls, two showers and two toi-
lets on the after deck; port for ladies, starboard for
gents. The water for these came out of the river, when
the pumps were working. We drank the same water
after it had been passed through a filter to remove the
mud, or boiled up as black coffee to go with the deli-
cious beans, dried fish and the rest.

I of course did better than the other passengers in
this respect, with a case of canned goods and two cases
of beer in my cabin. Even warm beer is better than
warm river water, with or without mud. I figured the
supply would carry me as far as Belém. What I didn't
figure on was Buchisapo and a fellow passenger who
went by the name of Magro. It means 'slim' or 'skinny,'
in Portuguese. Magro was a large, round, good-natured
Brazilian, very dark-skinned; not fat but formidably
large. His hands looked like fielders' mitts. How he
managed to place his great black fingers on the frets
of a guitar I never could make out, but he was a fine
guitarist. He had a high, clear tenor voice that was a
pleasure to listen to, and a large repertory of ballads in
Spanish and Portuguese. He and I and Buchisapo
discovered a mutual interest and a fair capability for
singing barbershop. Neither Buchisapo nor I had
anything like Magro's repertoire of songs, but his fine
tenor was so clear and his enunciation so good that we
could pick up the words just by listening to him sing a
piece solo a few times. The chords fell into place by
themselves. We had a lot of fun with *Noche de Ronda*,
Mano a Mano, *Amor de Mis Amores*, *La Llorona*, *Uma*

Casa Portuguesa, *Coimbra*, others, and we gave a
small pleasure to the rest of the passengers, who used
to gather on the foredeck in the evenings to listen to us
sing. There was nothing much else to do after dark.
The *jaula* did have an electrical system, but the generator was no better than the rest of the machinery and
rarely worked. You couldn't have read much even if
there had been anything aboard to read.

The forward deck was the most comfortable place
to be when the *jaula* was under way, because of the
river-breeze that blew away the mosquitoes and other
bloodsuckers that sneaked aboard as stowaways every
time we tied up to the riverbank to load firewood.
That was usually at least once a day. Everybody who
could manage it stayed up forward, except when a
rainsquall chased them under cover, with the exception of an odd, withdrawn, non-communicative couple
who had one of the other cabins. They kept pretty
much to themselves, a difficult thing to do on a boat
designed for overall togetherness extending to monkeys, marmosets, parrots and a four-foot alligator.

He—the man, not the alligator—looked like a wrongo.
I do not mean to assert that you can tell a wrongo by his
looks, because a lot of wrongos look like investment
bankers and a lot of people who look like wrongos are
not. But this guy had the—aura, I guess you'd say. He
was a little better than medium size, well built, about
forty maybe, with a hard tight mouth that never smiled
or relaxed and as cold a pair of gray-blue eyes as I have
ever looked into. He smoked cheap native cigarettes a
lot, and the way he smoked was wrong, it seemed to
me. He'd hold the cigarette by the butt between his

thumb and forefinger so that it stood up like a stick of
incense in a holder, and he'd look at it with those
freezing fish eyes, staring at the glowing coal as the ash
and smoke were whipped off by the river-breeze, more
than he'd puff on it. Just letting it burn away while he
watched it. It was as if—I don't know what it was as
if. After what came later, it's hard to separate what I
observed from what I imagine I observed. But he gave
me the creeps, and not only because of the cigarette
trick. He was a creepy character.

His woman, according to my first impression, was
about his age although she moved like someone older.
As if she had rheumatism or arthritis or a bad back. (In
time I learned that she was in her early twenties.) She
tended to sit down carefully, too, as if she creaked.
She was American, from her accent the few times I
heard her speak. He spoke English, when he spoke at
all, with a Germanic accent; Spanish the same way.
During the first days of the voyage the only time
anyone saw them at all was at meals, which were
served at a big wooden table bolted to the after-deck
under an awning, or when they went aft to use a toilet
or washbowl. They never said Hello, Good Morning,
or The hell with you. Just pass the beans, or pass the
tortillas. Not even *por favor* or *gracias*. They ate,
patronized the *excusados* and washbowls, disappeared
into their cabin.

Because I was the only other person aboard the
jaula who spoke English, I tried to engage them in
conversation a couple of times. The guy left me cold,
but I felt sorry for the woman. She was such a drab,

dispirited beaten-down thing, obviously afraid of and dominated by her man. I couldn't get any further with her than I could with him. She wasn't having any, at least while he was around, and he was always around. So I gave up. It must have been pretty rough on them, spending all their time in that cramped little hotbox of a cabin while the rest of us were out on deck in the breeze, but it was their choice. Nothing to do about it.

After the sing-fests, which made us thirsty, Magro, Buchisapo and I used to squeeze into my cabin to drink beer. Not because we liked it there but because it was the only thing to do out of consideration for the other passengers. I didn't have enough beer for the whole boatload. As a matter of fact with two cases I could only keep the three of us lubricated for about a week before we ran dry.

There is no beer to be found in obscure little hamlets along the middle reaches of the Amazon, but there's often a store where you can buy demijohns of a ferocious high-test spirit called *cachaça*. It's distilled from sugarcane mixed with old rubber tires, and it tastes like gasoline. In the same store, however, you can frequently buy another drink, *guaraná*, that is probably the best soft drink in the world. Actually it's a kind of low-proof ferment, one or two percent at most, brewed from a native Brazilian berry that grows along the river. It has a refreshing sour-sweet taste, not too much of one or the other, and a slight head that fizzes into life when you uncork the jug, like a good Portuguese *vinho verde*. Both of these drinks, one terrible and strong, the other very good but weak, are cheap, and when mixed together the good taste of one hides the bad taste of the other without diminishing its firepower. Since I still had money I loaded up with enough *cachaça* and *guaraná* to keep not only the trio in good voice for the rest of the trip but the rest of the passenger list tuned up, too. We all got enjoyably varnished on the *guaraná-cachaça* combination every night. All of us, that is, but the oddball couple, who stuck to their hotbox of a cabin while the rest of us were making a cruise out of it.

Then—surprise! One night the wrongo and his woman were there, listening to the evening concert. I can't say they joined our appreciative audience. They sat by themselves, away from the others, and they didn't applaud when the others did. But they were there. On an impulse during a moment when the generator was working and I could see to move around, I filled a couple of glasses with *cachaça-guaraná* and took them over to where they were sitting.

"Have one on the house," I said.

She looked up quickly, looked down again just as quickly, shook her head. No words. *He* said to her, "Take it."

She took the glass obediently. As an afterthought, as if she was remembering words long forgotten, she said, "Thank you." He said nothing at all when he took his glass, nor as much as nodded to show his heartfelt gratitude for the gesture. But he knocked the whole big glass back in about three swallows and had exchanged his empty for her full glass, still untouched, before the generator pooped out and the lights blinked off. I saw that much, and his face briefly afterward in the flare of a match as he lit one of those incense-stick cigarettes. It was the last look I ever had of him. Alive, that is. Dead, he was a lot prettier.

Chapter Nine

Maybe I should have warned him about *cachaça's* high octane content. I don't suppose he'd ever had any experience with it before, or with the smooth deceptiveness of *guaraná* as a mixer. I can't say that my conscience ever bothered me because I didn't explain that I made the mix real strong so it could be taken slow and stretched out, to preclude the need of anybody stumbling around in the dark for refills. With his drink and his woman's, which I hadn't intended for him, he put down in about five minutes the best part of a pint of high-test booze. I didn't see him go to his cabin, which I assume he somehow managed to reach under his own power or with his woman's help before passing out. I did see him leave it feet first some time later. They found him face down on his bunk in the morning, a butcher-knife from the galley sticking out from between his shoulder-blades. His woman sat there looking at the body, as expressionless as ever.

She gave no trouble. "Yes, I killed him," she said, at a kind of semi-formal hearing around the table under the awning on the after-deck where meals were served. The captain presided, Buchisapo took notes, Magro and I were witnesses to the proceedings. Coroner's jury, kind of.

"Why did you kill him?" the captain asked.

"I hated him."

"Was he your husband?"

"Yes, I think so."

"What was his name?"

"He didn't use his right name. I don't know what it was."

"Where did he come from?"

"I don't know."

"Where do you come from?"

"I don't remember."

"What is your name?"

"Mary Smith."

"Are you North American?"

"I think so. I'm not sure."

It was that kind of question-and-answer; pointless. She was passively cooperative. She'd give some kind of an answer to each question, but there was no information in it. Neither one of them had any papers, any money to amount to anything, any ascertainable identity or much in the way of personal possessions. She had murdered the guy because she hated him, and that was the end of it. She didn't give a damn what came next. I mean she *really* didn't give a damn.

The captain was essentially a gentleman. After the pointless hearing, which got nobody anyplace, he said, "I regret it, señora, but I must turn you over to the authorities. I have no choice. However, if you will permit me to confine you to your cabin, I will wait until we reach Santarem before doing so. You will receive better treatment and—accommodation—there than elsewhere. Are you agreeable?"

She shrugged. She still didn't give a damn one way or another.

My cabin, to return now to the padlock, had the
only door on the boat that could be locked from the
outside. I gave the cabin up to the woman, along with
the jug of throat-lubricator mix and what was left of
the groceries. If she wanted any of them, she was
welcome to help herself. Then I persuaded the captain
to let me talk to her in the cabin. I was, after all, her
countryman—probably—and spoke her native language. Maybe I could get something out of her that he
hadn't been able to. I'd like to try, anyway. He said it
was all right, giving me the key I had turned over to
him (neglecting to mention the existence of a second
key in my pants pocket) but warning me not to indulge
in any *tontería* with the process of justice like helping
her sneak ashore when we put in to Obidos to unload
the body for burial. That had to be done quickly,
because of the jungle heat.

"She has my sympathy, as she has yours," he said. "I
regret that I must do what I must do. But I am respon-
sible for what happens aboard my command, and she
does not deny the fact of the murder. I must ask for
your word of honor as a gentleman that you will do
nothing to help her escape justice."

"You have my word of honor," I said, not bothering
to cross my fingers. A confidence man, by definition,
has no honor. He is a cheat, a fake and a thief of other
people's worldly goods. I couldn't give the captain
what I didn't have, but he didn't know that. He thought
I was a gentleman, like himself.

If I'd had any compunction at all about breaking
my word to begin with, I would have lost it after
hearing the woman's story. I got it out of her by get-

ting her drunk. Not as drunk as the wrongo had got before she pushed him off, but drunk enough to talk. It was hot in the little cabin; hot and close and sticky. She was dehydrated and thirsty. She asked me to bring her a pitcher or bottle of water. I said I had something a lot better than river water right there in the cabin, a jug of cool refreshing *guaraná*, and slipped her a good shot of the mix without telling her there was anything in it besides *guaraná*. Two or three of those and she began to come unraveled. She hadn't had anybody to talk to for a long time. After a while, little by little, she let her hair down.

It took quite a while, so I'll condense it. Part of it is guesswork, hers or my own, but logical guesswork. She came from California, where she had been recruited as a missionary by some crackpot religious order that wanted to convert Peru to its own brand of Christianity. The wrongo had stumbled across her at a forlorn little outpost of a missionary school on the high *altiplano* near Lake Titicaca. In the years after World War II a lot of Nazi war criminals got away to South America, where they surfaced later as Austrians, Lichtensteiners, Swiss, Sudeten Czechs, anything Germanic that wasn't German. He was one of them. He claimed to be German-Swiss, although of course he had no papers to prove it. What he wanted was to acquire American citizenship, which he figured he could safely hide behind for the rest of his life. Somehow he heard about a law just passed in the U.S.—this was early in '59—that made it quite easy for the alien spouses of American missionaries stationed abroad to obtain citizenship. He had persuaded the

girl to marry him, but he couldn't persuade her to go
back to the States with him, as she had to do if he was
to get his papers. She had a vocation to bring the
Lord's word to the *altiplano*, and she meant to follow it
come what may. She was a real dedicated Christian,
just as he was a real dedicated son of a bitch.

To force her hand, he had burned the mission one
night. It wasn't much of a building, but it had a schoolroom, a little chapel, living quarters of a kind for the
missionary and, in this case, the missionary's husband.
She had been letting some of her pupils, illiterate
Indian kids, many of them homeless, use the schoolroom as a place to sleep—unofficially. It had no beds
or anything, but it was a lot better dormitory for the
kids than out there on the *altiplano* at twelve or thirteen thousand feet. The kids didn't get out of the
place when it burned. She was convinced, and I agreed
with her conviction, that the wrongo had deliberately
trapped them inside. I never saw a bunch of active
kids that wouldn't boil out of a burning building like
water coming through a sieve unless they were re-
strained from it somehow. He wanted to destroy her in
Peru. He destroyed more than he had figured on. She
escaped the fire, because he saw to that. But everything
that was her life went up in the flames; her papers,
money, personal possessions, accomplishments, hopes,
her reason for being, everything. When she tried to
get the kids out, he prevented her. To keep her from
sacrificing herself uselessly, he said later. He held her
while she listened to the noises that came out of the
schoolroom as the kids burned.

The mission had never been more than grudgingly

tolerated by the Peruvian church and authorities, all strongly Catholic. The fire finished it as it finished her. The wrongo persuaded her that the only way she could escape prison for arson, murder and several other charges was to break and run with him. Stunned, unthinking, numbed by the horror of the tragedy, she had done it. They had got away and out of the country, as I had, by its Amazonian back door.

"I shouldn't have gone with him," she said dully, dopey with the sticky heat of the cabin and the booze I had poured into her. "I should have stayed and faced whatever I had to face. But I couldn't seem to think straight, those first few days. I thought God had punished me for something I had done or failed to do. Then, when I began to think, I knew it was not the Lord's work but the devil's. No merciful God would have permitted those children to burn. The devil himself had burned them."

She was sitting on my bunk, her face shiny with sweat. I was sweating heavily myself, only partly from the heat. Her eyes closed and her head drooped.

I said, "Do you want to sleep now?"

"Not yet." She went on talking with her eyes closed, drowsily. "What he wanted was for me to go back to the States with him. When I realized at last that my husband was the devil on earth, I swore I would never go back until he was dead. I promised him I would see him where he belonged first, burning in the everlasting fires of hell. As he had burned those poor children. To punish me, and because I defied him, he—he—he—"

Her head drooped again. Her body swayed. I didn't

know whether she was going to drop off to sleep, fall off the bed or what. She was almost gone. But she stood up—creaking, as she always moved—to lift her skirt, high above her waist. She wore nothing underneath. On the insides and front of her upper thighs, on her belly, I would judge also within the perimeter of her pubic hair from its patchy moth-eaten look, were burn scars; some old and healed, white-puckered cicatrices, some new, still fresh and sore, still leaking serum. They were just the right size to have been put there by the red-hot coal of a burning cigarette pressed into the flesh.

While I stood there staring, my mouth open, unable to comprehend for a moment the awfulness of what I was looking at, she turned around to let me see her buttocks. He had used a whip on her there; something fine and limber, a thin cane perhaps, that had cut the flesh, scarred it and stung it cruelly. When she had let me see what there was to see, she dropped the skirt and sat down again. Creakily.

After a while I could talk again, although it took a heavy shot of lubricator to moisten my mouth for it first. I said, "You must have been able to escape him somewhere along the way. Even here on the boat, you could have turned to any of us for help. We would have protected you."

"I didn't want to escape him." Her voice was as dull and emotionless as it had been ever since she started talking. "I wanted to kill him before he could escape me. I'll go to hell for him willingly, now." A moment later she added, "Thank you for helping me do it."

"Thank me for—*what*?"

"You made him drunk. He wasn't used to drinking. He didn't realize how strong those drinks were you gave us. You've made me drunk, too, haven't you?"

"It will do you good, help you rest. You ought to try to get some sleep." I was still shaken by her thanks.

I took her back aft to use the *excusado* before locking her in again. She was almost out before I got her into the bottom bunk. I don't think she even heard me when I said I'd be back in a little while.

About that time the *jaula* was putting into Obidos to unload the body and load firewood. It was getting along in the day and the channel was tricky. I figured the captain would be eager to get in and out of port and back on the river again before nightfall trapped him until daylight. To make sure, I checked with him when I gave him back the padlock key, before he went ashore with the body and the cops. (They would have been just as happy if he had kept the murderee as well as the murderess on board as far as Santarem, but recognized his pressing need to unload one if not both in view of the heat.) He said, Yes, he'd be back just as fast as he could get through the *papeleo*. Anybody else who went ashore could count on one free hour. It would take at least that long to get a load of wood aboard. More than one hour was strictly at the passenger's risk. The *jaula* would push off just as soon as he could arrange for it to do so, not one minute later.

An hour was plenty for what I had in mind. I went ashore as soon as we tied up, walked into town, made a few purchases, asked a few questions, went back to the river bank with a package under my arm. The deck-crew was loading fore and aft, carrying big loads of

three-foot billets up the springy gangplanks on their
shoulders. They all wore split-out gunny sacks draped
over their heads and down their backs for padding as
well as for protection against the fire ants, tarantulas,
ticks, centipedes and other wildlife that crawled out of
the wood to feed on them during the fueling operation. Most everyone else aboard had jumped at the
opportunity to go ashore to explore for something
edible. The *práctico* was doing a repair job of some
kind on the forward deck, the engineer was at his
deathbed watch below decks as usual. Buchisapo was
on the river bank checking the wood as it went aboard.
I unlocked the padlock with my private key and went
in, after first arranging the padlock and hasp in a way
to give the impression that the cabin was still locked if
nobody gave it more than a casual glance.

She was sound asleep, sprawled half on her side,
half on her back in what I supposed was the nearest
she could get to a comfortable position. She didn't
wake when I went into the cabin, or even twitch. She
was drugged by fatigue, pain, emotional stress, *cachaça*,
you name it. So drugged in fact that she still didn't
wake when I lifted her skirt and went to work on the
burns with the ointment I had bought in town. Her
breath was bad, her teeth were bad, her skin was bad,
her hair was dirty, her dress was filthy, she stank of
sour body-sweat, she was as skinny as a starved rat. All
in all she was a pretty miserable Christian missionary. I
hoped the wrongo had had time to wake up and feel
the knife going in before he died. I didn't have her
faith in the fires of hell.

When I had finished with the burns, those I could

get at without shaving her pubic hair, and bandaged those that needed bandaging, I woke her. I couldn't turn her over without hurting her enough to wake her anyway, and I wanted to look at her behind. When she had turned over as instructed, I saw there was nothing much to do for it but put on more of the ointment, which I did. Then I took a pair of panties out of the package I had brought.

"Put these on," I said. "And this." I took off the money-belt, which I wore next to my skin, and gave it to her. "Strap it around you under your dress, where it won't be seen."

She still didn't give a damn, one way or another. She put on the panties, wincing a bit, then the belt. But she was curious enough to ask about the belt, "What is it?"

"Travel insurance," I said. "Cinch it up as far as it will go."

She was too thin to fill it, even cinched up to the last hole, but she had woman's hips to hold it up. It wouldn't fall down to lasso her around the ankles.

"Listen to me," I said. "Listen close. If I say something that isn't entirely clear to you, stop me. Otherwise, don't interrupt. In that belt around your middle is a fair chunk of cash; not a fortune, but enough to carry you a good way; mostly dollars, some *soles*, some *cruzeiros*. In this bundle you'll find a dirty pair of pants and a dirty shirt like those the crew wear, with a gunnysack hood like those they pull over their heads to load wood. As they're doing now." We could hear the thumps and bangs of the billets being dumped on deck. "Your own shoes are ratty enough to pass inspection. Also in the bundle you'll find a clean dress, another pair of underpants, a pair of sandals that should fit you more or less, a few other things; cosmetics, a comb, soap, a towel. In about one minute I'm going to take you and the bundle to the *excusado*. Lock yourself in there, change into the pants, the shirt and the gunnysack. I'll allow you the time you need. When things are right I'll knock twice on the door, like this." I rapped on the table, one, two, to fix her attention. I could see she was about to interrupt. "When I do that, you come out, hand me the clothes you have just taken off and go down the gangplank like any other deckhand who has just brought a load of wood aboard. Don't move too fast, no hurry. Keep the gunnysack pulled forward and your face turned left, because the *sobrecargo* will be out there on your right as you come off the plank. He's nothing to worry about, but look away from him."

"No," she said. Still dull, still dopey, but definite.

"No what?"

"I won't do it."

"What won't you do?"

"I won't run from punishment. I have sinned. I must atone for my sin."

"Killing that scum was no sin. You did a public service."

She shook her head. "No."

"You consider yourself a Christian, don't you?"

She thought about it for a moment, then shook her head again.

"No. Not anymore. Christ preached forgiveness. I am an instrument of the Lord's vengeance."

"You could be an instrument of the Lord's mercy as well, now that you've completed the other assignment. There are plenty of illiterate Indian kids that need schooling and mothering right here in Brazil. Why throw yourself away? If you want to atone, atone that way. Don't just quit your job without finishing it."

I worked on her like a fundamentalist preacher thumping the Bible at a revival meeting. It took some doing and more sweat, but I knew I had her when she said, "What's going to happen to you when they find out you've helped me?"

"They won't find out. I'm going to fake your presence aboard ship until the last possible minute, then make it look as if you got away on your own just before we reach Santarem. It will give you a fair head start. After you go down the gangplank, keep moving, no hurry, until you can get under cover without being seen doing it. Change to the new dress and sandals, wrap the cosmetics and things in the towel, ditch your shoes. A mile or so to the other side of town there's a little airport where planes leave now and then for a few other places, all of them on the river. You can't get out of any of them except by boat or plane, so take the first flight—it leaves at noon tomorrow—for Belem. From Belem you can take another plane to someplace where you can go on by train or bus. You'll probably have to give a name to buy plane tickets, but—"

"I want to know—"

"You'll know all you have to know when I've done talking. Stop interrupting and listen. You'll probably have to give a name to get plane tickets. Make it something like Jane Jones, here, but in Belem and after-

wards change it to something Spanish. It might be a
good idea to change the name from time to time as you
move around. While you're here in Obidos don't show
your face any more than you have to. Staying out of
sight until tomorrow and getting out to the airport are
your own problems, but there'll be a ladies' room of
some kind at the airport where you can hide out after
you've bought your ticket. Use the time to clean yourself up. Wash your hair, comb the rats out of it, put on
some lipstick, make yourself look like a human being.
Got it all straight?"

She still wanted to argue about running off and
leaving me, as she thought, holding the bag. It was a
good sign that she had enough spunk left to put up an
argument, but time was running out. I beat her down.
Any time I couldn't con a bunch of simple backwoods
Brazilians I'd turn in my conning suit. I didn't tell her
that, though. Instead, I lied freely about the money,
friends and political clout waiting for me in Santarem
(a town I'd never seen before and would just as lief
never see again). Still talking, I took a quick peek out
the door of the cabin, made sure the coast was clear
and led her back to the portside *excusado* after carefully locking the cabin door behind the stolen horse.

She made it. At least I never heard that she failed to
make it, and if they didn't catch up with her during the
first few days while they still had a chance—working
as they were without a photo, fingerprints, a proper
description or even a phony name to go on after she
stopped taking planes—they never would. She'd need
papers of some kind to get out of the country if she
wanted to get out of the country, but I couldn't help

her there. All I could give her was a sendoff and a running start.

This I accomplished by conning the whole boat for the best part of two days and nights, the time it took us to get to Santarem. Working for me I had the advantage a successful hustler always has over the marks; their confidence in the hustler. Particularly the captain's confidence, which was of prime importance. When he came back from town, still with the key to the padlock in his pocket, I borrowed it so I could look in on the prisoner and see how she was doing. She'd been quiet a long time. Sleeping, I thought, but I wanted to make sure. When I had made sure, I gave him the key back, reporting that she was very tired, emotionally drained, asking to be left alone but O.K. I thought I'd try to get her to eat something a little later on. If it was all right with the captain.

He was preoccupied with working the ship out of the channel into the river before the light faded—night comes down like a quick curtain that close to the equator—and more than willing to leave the prisoner's feeding to me. She ate a bowl of canned soup and some crackers later that evening. By proxy, in a manner of speaking. I reported her dinner to the captain, and that she'd asked for a cup of tea. Tea I had among my supplies, but I had to go to the galley for hot water. Carefully and conspicuously locking the cabin door behind me each time I left it.

We talked for a long time after she'd had her tea, with the door barred from the inside so we wouldn't be interrupted. I suppose my voice was more audible than hers from outside the cabin, and I did most of the talking anyway. We spoke English, of course. When it was dark enough and the generator seemed to have pooped out for the evening, I reported to the captain that I'd just taken her back to the *excusado* before locking her in for the night. I didn't think she'd be needing anything more that night.

When I gave him back the key, he suggested—hesitantly—that maybe I ought to keep it in case she *did* want something during the night.

"No, sir, captain," I said firmly. "Thank you for the gesture, but I wouldn't feel comfortable with it. If anything comes up, I'll ask you for it."

It just goes to show how dumb you can be if you work at it.

He wanted to look in on her himself the next morning. It was a bad moment. I was keeping watch on the door, and I stepped in front of it before he could unlock it. Her plane wasn't due to take off from Obidos for another two hours, and wouldn't get to Belem for at least another couple of hours after that. The *jaula* had no radio communication, of course, but I didn't know how close we might be to some dump of a river port where there might be a telegraph or phone, or even radio. If he went into the cabin prematurely, we were both cooked.

I said earnestly, "Captain, I don't think you should try to talk to her. I've calmed her down, encouraged her, lied to her about her chances of getting off with a short prison term. I know she has no such chance, but I did it to give her peace of mind. You can't lie to her as I have. You are a man of honor. If she asks you questions, you'll have to tell her the truth. Let her have

peace and hope for the few hours left to her. I ask it of
you as a personal favor to me."

He looked at me for a long moment without
speaking. I squeezed every drop of chicanery in my
whole being into the man-to-man look I gave him back.
After a moment he said, "Señor, it is a privilege to
know such a *caballero*," and went away. I went into the
cabin and had a quick jolt of the lubricator to quiet my
jangling nerves.

By one trick or another I kept the hoax going until
the following morning. It came to an end when we had
only hours to go to Santarem.

My plan had been to fix it to look as if she had
jumped ship at our last fueling stop before Santarem.
How she might have managed it was someone else's
job to figure. I meant to help the someone else to a
conclusion by leaving her discarded clothes in the
cabin. It shouldn't be too hard to reason that she had
gone down the gangplank disguised as one of the
wood-loaders. Her escape from the cabin would almost
certainly be blamed to my carelessness, which I would
freely confess. I might pull a couple of weeks in the
bin for that, but a couple of weeks in the bin never
hurt anybody. I could do a couple of weeks standing on
my head.

I had it all figured, as smooth as silk, when I got the
key from the captain for the last time. As usual, I
opened the cabin door just enough to slip through,
and barred it behind me immediately. Also as usual, I
went into my spiel immediately, with, "Good morning,
my, you're looking well this morning, I'm going to
bring you your tea in just a minute—"

That's as far as I got. Turning around from the door-barring, I looked Buchisapo in the eye. Without a word he brushed past me to unbar the door. The captain came in.

Neither of them seemed to want to say anything. The stricken look on their faces made me think of a couple of kids who'd just seen someone murder Santa Claus. I said, as brightly as I could, "Why, she doesn't seem to be here, does she? I wonder what could have happened to her?"

It was no good. They had me with *los pantalones bajados*. The captain, good guy that he was, hadn't been able not to say a private goodbye and apologize again for having to do his duty in turning her over to the cops. He'd entered the cabin while I wasn't watching it, guessed the true situation immediately, planted Buchisapo as a witness when I gave myself away. The possible two-week holiday I had planned to spend standing on my head began to look like something more than a holiday.

Magro and the other passengers lined the *jaula's* rail when the cops took me away wearing that old wrist-jewelry they lend you without charge. Nobody said goodbye, although Magro and Buchisapo did come to see me in jail before the *jaula* went on its way downstream. Buchisapo brought what was left of my stuff from the cabin, Magro his guitar. I thought jail was an odd place for us to have a final songfest, but that wasn't what Magro had in mind. He gave me the guitar as a present.

"It will keep you company," he said, and when I

tried to decline the gift, pushed it at me. "Take it. I will get another."

"I don't know how to play it," I said.

"You will have plenty of time to learn. Take it."

I took it, together with what Buchisapo had brought. Things were a little awkward after that, but they didn't stay long. They had to get back to the *jaula*, which the captain was holding for them. I asked them to thank him for the gesture. Magro and I shook hands, my hand disappearing to the wrist in his great black mitt. We gave each other an *abrazo*, the Latin embrace exchanged between male friends like a handshake. Then I went through the same routine with Buchisapo.

Nothing at all was said about the deception I had brought off or its consequences until just before they left. I should say until just before Buchisapo, who lingered for a moment after Magro, followed him.

"Why did you do it?" he asked. "To satisfy my curiosity and the captain's. Had you known the woman before? Did she mean something to you?"

I had asked myself the first question at intervals since learning that what I had thought would be an easy short-term fall for carelessness could well turn out to be a stiff five years for accessory after the fact. I hadn't been able to arrive at a satisfactory answer for myself, so I couldn't very well supply him with one. Not an honest one, anyway. I gave him a dishonest one that he and the captain would understand.

I said, "The man did me an injustice, years ago. I had planned to kill him myself. When she took my crime upon herself, I had no choice but to help her escape the consequences. It was a matter of honor."

His troubled face cleared immediately.

"Of course," he said. "It is easy to understand as a matter of honor. Thank you."

People will even con themselves, if you give them the right mouthful of words to do it with. The words don't have to mean anything in particular. Just so long as they sound good.

Chapter Ten

I pulled eighteen months. It was a lot more than I had thought I'd be risking when I gave Miserable a hand in escaping from the *jaula*, but then again it wasn't as bad a fall as I'd been afraid of since my foot slipped.

The cause of my drawing such a relatively easy pop was the *jaula's* captain. Talk about Christian forgiveness, turning the other cheek and so forth. He couldn't wait arou.nd for the trial, but he filed a sworn statement with the court that his own failure to take proper precautions for the prisoner's security had been contributing negligence, without which she could not have got away even with my help. In a way it hurt my professional pride. Contributory negligence my eye; he'd been conned, and conned good. But I was grateful for the three-and-a-half year discount. Five years in stir can be less than exciting, from what I've heard.

The eighteen months weren't too bad, all in all. Day for day they were a lot better than a freighter's fire-room, in many ways better than the U.S. Army. You didn't have to salute every time a piece of brass went by, or take daily *scheisse* from a hard top-sergeant. I served my time not in prison but in a prison camp; a work camp. The Brazilian government operated an experimental rubber plantation near Belterra, on the Tapajoz tributary south of Santarem, and the labor was done by convicts because the local river-people, *caboclos*, wouldn't work for what the government wanted to pay them. Us lags they got for free.

The camp was known to its house-guests as O Caldeirão; The Cauldron. The name was appropriate. Almost on the equator, hemmed in all around by rain forest or river, the place was hot, steamy and sticky. It had more than its share of insect life, too, and they weren't all big beautiful butterflies. Bolts, bars, barbed wire and similar restraints on voluntary leave-taking were few. To get away from the camp all you had to overcome were a couple of million square miles of jungle surrounding it on three sides, with the huge river (populated by flesh-eating *piranhas*, among other finny friends) on the fourth. Nobody had been known to get beyond those barriers alive, although some had tried it.

I had not thought of becoming one of the volunteers. Working as we did surrounded by jungle, much of the time slashing away at it with machetes to keep it from overrunning the plantation, we frequently saw anacondas, boa constrictors and other interesting reptiles large enough to swallow a lousy convict like a grape. Also out there were those Indians you've read about; the ones who shrink your head to the size of an orange and mount it over their mantelpieces. A year and a half of my youthful existence weren't important enough for me to gamble it against what might be left over afterward.

Camp discipline, like bolts and bars, was negligible. No time off was allowed for good behavior, only time added on for bad behavior. But it you gave no trouble and did your work without too much goofing off on the job, the guards left you alone. It was always too hot and steamy at O Caldeirão, for guards and prisoners alike, to get charged up over inconsequentialities. As a result, there was little of the constant brawling that goes on in some other prison camps. Arguments now and then, of course; a few fights, occasional stabbings with home-made pig-stickers the men whacked out of bamboo. Two slashes of a machete at a half-inch cane would do it; a diagonal chop to give the cane a point and edge, a horizontal chop to lop off the length you wanted to hide in your shirt. If a guard took one away from you, you made another just as easily, and you could kill a man just by sticking him in the throat.

I saw it happen a couple of times. The proper technique for killing with a pig-sticker, although I never tried it myself, appears to be to go in from the side of the throat rather than directly from the front. That way you cut the arteries and major veins at the same time you get the guy through the windpipe so he can't yell for help before he bleeds to death. It didn't happen as often as you might have expected in a camp as tough as O Caldeirão. The heat and the overwhelming humidity were good peace-keepers. Even when a fight started it was an even bet that it would run out of energy before anybody got hurt enough to count.

Anther thing that helped to keep trouble to a minimum among the lags was their once-a-week marital privileges. Their "wives" were *cabocla* women who came into the camp every Sunday afternoon to do the prisoners' laundry and take care of their other needs

for a few extra *cruzeiros*. Anybody with the money
to pay for the merchandise could buy a weekly wife,
cigarettes, *cachaça*, special food, whatever he wanted
that was available in Belterra. The problem was whom
to trust with your cash to take into Belterra to spend
for you, and how to get up the cash to give him in the
first place.

I asked an old-timer around camp about these
things. He was a *colombiano* in for murder, and he
spoke Spanish. About twenty-five percent of the lags
were Spanish-speakers, so I had no trouble communi-
cating while I was learning jailhouse Portuguese.

He said, "Don't worry about the first part, friend.
We've got a tame guard who does the shopping for us.
He gets a cut but he knows he'll get another kind of
cut if he pulls any *porquerías* with the money. It keeps
him reasonably honest."

I said, "Where and how would I get some money to
give him?"

"Where and how did you get it when you were
Outside?"

I told him. He shook his head. "I wouldn't try that
kind of thing here. Too dangerous."

"I wouldn't try it anywhere I couldn't run faster and
farther than the guy coming after me," I said. "What
else is there to do—gainfully, and without too much
physical effort?"

As it turned out, there were a number of small
money-making industries around camp. Six days a
week we were worked pretty much from sunup to
sundown; chopping at the jungle, planting new trees,
taking out old trees, bringing in the latex in buckets

slung from both ends of a carrying pole, loosening the duff that was allowed to collect around the trees to hold water at their roots (and breed big fat mosquitoes), other chores. They kept us busy enough. But we got a one-hour break in the middle of the day for *o matabicho*, the midday meal—the word means 'bug-killer'—and a lot of the lags used some of this time as well as some of their Sunday time (to the extent it was not taken up by mass, confession, gambling or weekend wives) to make things; baskets, palm-fiber mats, string hammocks, carved and decorated gourds, carved wood, small carpentries, *cabocla* dolls, other handicrafts. Another tame guard took them into Santarem and sold them for a cut.

Other prisoners worked as house-servants for the camp governor and guards; no pay, but many opportunities for negotiable loot from the kitchen and pantry. Others hired themselves out as *maricões*, although homosexuality in the camp was minimal because of the availability of the *caboclas*. Still others had other ways of making money.

There was very little thievery or double-dealing among the crooks in camp. This was true for the same reason the tame guards refrained from *porquerías* with the funds entrusted to them. O Caldeirão offered nowhere to run, no place to hide from justice. If you cheated the man who habitually swung a three-foot machete at your side from day to day, and he found out about it, he just might come after you with a pig-sticker on his own time.

I saw that happen too, once. I think the guy must have crossed up a lot of his pals, because his execution had an air of community effort. Like a quilting bee, or a roof-raising. One minute he was working along with the rest of us, the next his head was bouncing at his feet. It was a real well-honed machete. The body kind of teetered there for a moment, half bent over in the position in which it had been working, jets of blood pumping out of the severed arteries of the neck, before it toppled.

No guard was around to see it when it happened. Four men took the body, still spouting, by its arms and legs and ran it off into the jungle. Another, the man who had done the chopping, followed along carrying the head by an ear. (None of us had any hair to amount to anything. They treated us to the old billiard-ball bob regularly once a week, for hygienic reasons.) Other men began methodically scraping up dirt and duff to hide the blood. Ants or anacondas or some other jungle scavenger would have taken care of the remains in a short time, and that was officially the end of it except for a nose missing at the evening count. Nobody got excited about it. He was written off as another would-be escapee who would never make it.

Unofficially, I made inquiries. Not for the purpose of bringing the miscreants to justice or anything stupid like that, but for my own protection. I figured that if there were rules and regulations in the camp that I didn't know about, I'd better learn them. I asked what the guy had done to lose his head like that. Tactfully, of course.

The lag who had swung the chopper, a chocolate-colored man from Pará who had learned his swing cutting bananas, said, "Why do you want to know?"

I said, "I don't want to make any mistakes by mistake."

"You haven't made any mistake that I've heard about."

"Would you hear about it if I did?"

"Probably."

"Will you tell me about it if you do?"

"No."

"Why not?"

"You're afraid of a *machetaço, verdade*?"

"You're damn right I'm afraid of a *machetaço*."

"Good." He nodded. "Stay that way. You'll be careful not to make mistakes, and we'll have no trouble with you."

He had something there. You never saw such an honest bunch of crooks as we were after the chopping. We hardly even liberated each other's cigarettes except now and then. When I established my own cottage industry, a standing blackjack game, it was strictly on the up and up. All I had working for me was the house percentage, small but useful.

I had to sell Magro's guitar to get the money for cards and to start a bank, but it was no loss. The lag who bought it was a much better player than I could ever hope to be. It was a real pleasure to listen to him. Another pleasure, for me, was the same lag's habit of standing on a short count, twelve or thirteen or fourteen, hoping the dealer would go bust. Sometimes I did, of course, but more often not. On the whole, the inhabitants of O Caldeirão were not good blackjack players. They had hunches, they believed in lucky days and unlucky days, they thought that if you cursed loudly enough and filthily enough at bad cards they would come to heel. Blackjack was a very popular game at O Caldeirão after I had introduced it and explained the rules as it was played in the U.S. Army (although in the U.S. Army I would have had a fat chance of keeping the deal permanently in my own hands). Until I joined the prison population the principal amusements had been a weird kind of poker with a stripped deck, and Sunday afternoon *cabocla* screwing with stripped *caboclas*.

The house limit, which I had to impose both because of the anemia of the bank with which I started and to restrain the doublers and re-doublers of losing bets, was twenty *cruzeiros*. It kept the game toned down so that it remained a game instead of turning into a blood, guts and feathers operation that could have resulted in bruised feelings. Once, only, I had real trouble.

There was a guy in camp, an ugly plug from Santos, another murderer, on whom sweet reasonableness was wasted. He didn't get along with anybody very well, but with me he didn't get along twice as well. He was a lousy loser. A lousy winner, too, as far as that goes, but worse when he was in a bad streak. Three or four bad hands in a row, not uncommon in any game against a bank, would drive him into a black fury. Another on top of the three or four and he'd curse, crumple the cards, accuse me of cheating, raise hell generally. I ran an honest game, as everyone in camp knew, so irresponsible accusations didn't bother me. What did bother me was the way he balled up my cards. Sometimes I could straighten them out well enough to play again, sometimes not. When I couldn't, the deck was ruined and the game closed down until I could get the tame guard to buy me a new deck. Both the interruption and the expenditure cut into profits. But I didn't want any more trouble with him than I wanted with anyone else, so I put up with him, his cursing and his card-crumpling until the afternoon when, after a run of hard luck, he tore his cards in half.

The game stopped of its own accord, in the middle of a deal. The other players sat there looking at me, waiting.

I said, "All right, you ugly mistake of a diseased whore, that does it. You're going to buy me a new deck, and you're out of the game for good. Beat it."

"Do you say so?" He reached inside his shirt and took out a pig-sticker about ten inches long, baring his dirty teeth like a dog. "Say it again. I don't hear so good."

Nobody moved. We were seated, five or six of us, around the crate we used as a card table. It wasn't a very big crate, and I had my back to the wall of the cookhouse. I always sat that way so no one could stand behind me and maybe see the corner of my down card when I lifted it for a peek, enough for a signal to a buddy. The way this one held his pig-sticker, its point was only about a foot from my eyeballs. With my back, as they say, against the wall.

Cut bamboo, mature bamboo, holds a point and an edge like a knife. All this thug had to do was jab and I'd lose an eyeball. If nothing worse came of it. Kicking the crate over was out of the question. He was leaning his weight on it ready to lunge if I took up his

challenge. I had the deck I'd been dealing from in my
left hand. I squeezed the cards until they were well
bowed, then let the spring of the bow shoot them in a
stream at his face. They didn't hit as accurately as I
had hoped but they startled him, put him off balance
long enough for me to scramble out from behind the
crate. After that it was only a question of letting him
chase me with his pig-sticker long enough for me
to find a stick with which to knock the thing out of
his hand.

I beat him up good, with prisoners and guards
looking on. He wasn't difficult to do it to. I was bigger
than he was, and knew more about what I was doing.
Knife-carriers and gun-carriers, by and large, tend to
come apart when deprived of their weapons. They rely
on them so much that their loss is crippling. I marked
this guy up in part as an object lesson, in part because
he'd scared the living hell out of me, in part because I
wanted him to know I'd meant what I'd said about
his buying me a new deck of cards, in part because I
wanted him to be afraid of me instead of my being
afraid of him, in part because I plain didn't like him—
all this *ex post facto*, of course; in afterthought. While
I was doing it I was just doing it.

Equally mechanical were occasional weekend work-
outs I had with one or the other of the *cabocla* women.
I was young, in good health with normal appetites.
They fed us plainly but well; plenty of river fish for
protein, pork or beef now and then, manioc flour and
rice, quantities of fruits like pineapple, mango, chiri-
moya, bananas, melons, oranges, avocados teeming
with vitamins; all the Brazil nuts we wanted to crack

for ourselves, horrible Brazilian coffee as black and bitter as printer's ink with lots of unrefined sugar in it to make it taste worse. We were also allowed to brew our own *chicha*, a fermented drink made—at O Caldeirão; there were other varieties—of pineapple pulp and peelings. It came out of the tub about as strong as beer. By common consent it was saved for Sundays.

I drank my share, and reacted to it as a man does when there are grass-skirted, bare-to-the-waist women who are ready, willing and able. When the itch got too strong, I'd pay a *cabocla* to scratch it. But they were ugly women, squat, dark and dirty, and many of them had skin infections ranging from fungus to yaws, a disease far too similar to syphilis to play around with. Some had other diseases as well. Every time I took a chance I'd swear to myself it would be the last, fiercely scrubbing myself all over with the jungle root-bulb we used for soap. It always was the last time until the itch got too strong again.

Skin infections and venereal disease weren't the only things you had to look out for in our garden spot. So many men had lived, defecated and sometimes died there that the ground was infected; with hookworm, liver flukes, elephantiasis, other worm-borne diseases. After our shoes wore out we worked in *chinelos*, a kind of loose rubber boot-slipper made by wrapping a square of cloth around your foot, fastening it there with a thorn for a pin, then dipping foot, cloth and all, into liquid latex enough times to give it body and sole while you wiggled your foot to keep it loose. *Chinelos* didn't last long, what with the barbs, hooks, spines, thorns and stickers in the muck we worked in and around, but they were easy to make. Their worst drawback was their impermeability. Because they were of rubber and seamless, they didn't breathe. The result was that our feet sweated heavily. Most of the lags would kick off their *chinelos* as soon as they got into camp and go around barefoot for the relief it gave them. The *least* they ever caught were foot fungi that attacked not only their skin but their toenails. A few of us, the smart ones, kept an extra pair of *chinelos*, holed for ventilation, in camp for what might be called leisure wear. A simple, easy precaution, you'd say? Ninety percent of the lags never bothered with it. Too much trouble. Ninety percent of the lags had something wrong with them before they'd been in O Caldeirão for a year. I came out of it, after serving eighteen months to the day, with nothing worse than a normal quota of mosquito bites, tick-bites, chigger-bites, fly-bites, spider-bites, leech-bites and other nibblings.

Also on the credit side, I had nearly a hundred and fifty dollars worth of *cruzeiros* that I had saved from my blackjack winnings. This was very close to the amount that had been in the money-belt strapped around Miserable's skinny waist when she walked off the *jaula*. Looking at it philosophically and from the bright side, my year and a half in camp had repaid me for my unwise investment in her escape. I had also put on about fifteen pounds, after first sweating off almost the same amount. The additional weight was all solid meat, no fat.

In Santarem I took passage on another *jaula* going

downstream. I figured a big seaport like Belem would hold promising opportunities as soon as I'd acquired some decent clothes and grown enough hair to hide the fact that I had just matriculated from college. Arriving in Belem, a pretty city with wide streets and avenues shaded by mango trees, I walked, just for the pleasure of a *passeio* of my own choosing, from the docks to the Praça do República in the center of town; a mile or more.

It was late afternoon, the mangos were ripe, many had fallen to smash on the pavement beneath the trees. Bees buzzed happily around the pulp of the fruit. They left me alone, I left them alone. But while I was walking I heard a rattling sound in the branches over my head and looked up in time to see a big mango coming my way. I caught it, my supper, straight from heaven.

It was a good sign, I thought. At least it showed that my reflexes were still quick. I could probably still shift into getaway gear as quickly as ever, although if I couldn't sell the simple citizenry of Belem a gold brick or two without repercussions I wasn't half the slicker I thought I was. All in all I was feeling quite euphoric that afternoon when I sat down on a shaded bench in the Praça, kicked my *chinelos* off so I could scratch the bites on my feet and ankles with my toenails, and began to eat my mango. Life was worth living, even in Belem's heat and humidity.

A mango is a messy meal to cope with manually. That job is best attempted while you are stark naked in a bathtub, because then if the slippery fruit pops out of your grip, as it most often does, no real harm is done

either to you or it. In whatever circumstances you take
a mango on hand to hand, however, you are going to
get the fruit on your face. It's impossible not to. You
have to burrow into it and gnaw the pulp off the pit.
I was well burrowed in and gnawing when a pair of
attractive female legs passing my bench came to an
abrupt stop, in front of me. Dead, as if their owner had
run into something impassable.

I went on gnawing. The legs, their shoes and the
bottom part of a short white skirt spelled Class loud
and clear. They did not belong within the ken of an
unshaven scabby bum sitting on a park bench eating
a gratis mango. Whatever they stopped for, it wasn't
me. But then a voice I had heard before—although
never with the same timid, uncertain, questioning,
shocked, incredulous, almost frightened, tone to it—
said, whispered rather, "Curly!" and I looked up from
my supper into the startled, unbelieving face of
Nemesis. The Honorable Regina Forbes-Jones.

"Curly!" she said again, in the same choked incredulous whisper. "Curly!"

My first thought, so help me, was of the warrant she
had sworn out for my arrest in France. I guess it's true
that the guilty flee where no man pursueth, or however it goes. Quite spontaneously, without reflection,
myself as startled as she was, I said, "Oh, for God's
sake, Reggie. Halfway across the world for a lousy suit
of clothes? You're crazy!"

"Curly!" she said again; inaudibly this time. I saw
her lips form the word, although no sound came. She
was thinner that I remembered her, and had lost some
of her Mediterranean suntan. Otherwise she looked

the same; as chic and patrician and cool of appearance in tropical white as I was hot, sticky and sloppy.

"Curly!" she said, or tried to say, again. Her eyes had a stunned look, as if she had been hit hard on the head. Then, as I watched, her face crumpled, the eyes filled with tears and she began to bawl. Not noisily, but with a little whimpering sound. She put her hands over her face and made mewing noises behind them like a cat locked in a closet.

I didn't have a handkerchief to offer her, or anything else that would serve except the sleeve of a dirty shirt. Not knowing what to do or what it was all about, but feeling contrite because of what I had apparently said to bring on the storm, I stood up and went over to her. To apologize or something. I'm not quite certain what, except that I had no intention of laying a finger on her. In the first place I was too dirty and sweaty and smelly to touch her, in the second place I remembered the boff on the chin I had got the other time I tried it as well as her promise of what I would get if I ever tried it again, in the third place I just didn't have it in mind in the first place. What happened in Belem's Praça do República and thereafter did so because she made it happen, and if I'm a cad and a rotter for saying it, so be it. The truth is the truth. Not that I didn't cooperate after we were launched.

I said, "Ah, Reggie, look, I didn't mean—" but got no further. The Honorable Regina took her hands from her face. With her eyes tightly but ineffectually closed against the tears that continued to leak from them, she reached blindly to grab me around the neck with both arms like an anaconda immobilizing its

breakfast. Clinging to that anchorage, she plastered
her clean tropical whites against me as if she was trying
to fit her buttons into my buttonholes and began bab-
bling, "Curly Curly Curly I thought you were dead I
thought you were dead!" She didn't even pause for
punctuation. She did take one deep breath before she
hitched another reef in her headlock, then began to
kiss me. Her lips were warm and soft and trembly;
salty with the salt of her tears, sweet with the taste of
the mango on my mouth. It's God's truth, the whole
truth, nothing but the truth, may I buy the Brooklyn
Bridge five times over if it's not. She kissed me so
long and hard and uninterruptedly through the three-
eighths of an inch of stiff beard that it irritated the skin
of her chin and around her lips, so that she had to wear
special makeup for days afterward to hide what looked
like heat rash. Tie that for a greeting from a former
employer who has a warrant out for your arrest.

As might be expected, I was less than prepared for
the reception, but I refrained from fighting her off. A
gentleman's stature as such is not measured by the
length of the stubble on his chin or the sweat-stains on
his only shirt, and no gentleman would twist a lady's
wrists to win release from circumstances like those. To
tell the truth, I hadn't been properly kissed for so long
that I enjoyed the novelty. As long as she wanted to
keep it up, I was willing to hold still even if I got
boffed for it afterward.

When she did let go of my neck at long last, it was
not to boff me but to take hold of my arm and start
tugging me across the *praça*. She had stopped crying,
although the evidence of tears was plain on her face.

So was the mango. Her eyes and nose were red as well as the skin of her face where I had sandpapered her.

"What?" I asked, unable to think of anything more coherent as she continued to haul at my arm.

All she could say, kind of desperately, was, "Come! Oh, please come!"

"Wait for my shoes!" It wasn't exactly what I meant to say, but it was at least understandable. She paid no attention, just kept hauling away at my arm and saying desperately, "Come, oh, please come!" She was still teary, although no longer tearful.

I went where she dragged me. Short of breaking her fingers one by one to get free, there was nothing else I could do. It wasn't far, just across the street from the *praça* to the Hotel Grande.

The Grande was then and may still be for all I know the best hotel in Belem, a big pretentious-looking place. A number of people, mostly tourists from their appearance, sat around sidewalk tables under an awning killing time the way people do at sidewalk tables all over the world; with a drink or a coffee at their elbows, reading a paper, writing postcards to the home-folks, gossiping or just watching the passersby. Whatever they were doing, they lost interest in it when the Honorable Reggie in her chic tailored whites, her lipstick smeared and with second-hand mango on her face, came sniffling across the street from the *praça* dragging by the arm a large, ragged, dirty, barefoot, smelly bum with a prison haircut and a stubble of beard, also with smeared lipstick. We may not have stopped traffic, but we sure focused a lot of stares.

Reggie paid not a bit of attention to the gawpers. Still telling me to come along, still tugging to make sure I did, she dragged me into the hotel lobby, over to the desk to get her key, into an elevator, out of it again several floors higher up and into an old-fashioned but elegant and roomy suite where a couple of clattery window air-conditioners had wrung the humidity out of the air and were keeping it cool and dry. It was a welcome change from O Caldeirão. Even though I still didn't know which way was up.

I found out soon enough. Not to put too fine a point on it, Reggie ravished me. Ruthlessly, repeatedly, unstintingly and without hesitation the minute she got me behind closed doors. I have already admitted that I cooperated willingly in the effort once we got started, but she did take me by surprise. Before I knew what was happening to me, to us that is, it had happened and was on its way to happening again. And again. And again. After eighteen months in dead storage except for a *cabocla* now and then, my fires were banked but ready to blaze forth when fanned. Reggie was a great little fanner. Behind the cool patrician front lurked a whirlwind, a cyclone, a tornado, a hurricane. She didn't even give me time to shave, or bathe, or dab cologne on my earlobes, gestures you'd think a lady of her background and breeding would insist upon. I got around to those things about sixteen hours later, the following morning.

Long before morning came I made a discovery. It was kind of startling. As noted, I was charged up and full of fire after being too long without a genuine woman, and when the wraps came off I didn't pay a hell of a lot of attention to anything but the immediate lusts of the flesh. Reggie didn't really give me a chance even to be considerate about it, or gentle. But after I'd glutted the flesh satisfactorily I had to get up to go into the bathroom, and the evidence of what had taken place was plain; on me, on Reggie when I went back to look at her, in the bed. She had bled a lot. At least it looked like a lot to me, who had never before participated in the defloration of a virgin.

I said, "Reggie, for Christ's sake! I—you—I—you—"

"Do stop gabbling," she said. She was lying on her back with her forearm over her eyes, smiling in a kind of relaxed, secretive way. "What is it you're trying to say?"

"You—I—you—I—"

She moved her forearm to look up at me. I was waving my arms at her, at myself, at the bed. She said indifferently, "Oh, that. I suppose I really should do something about it, shouldn't I? Give me a kiss first and I'll take steps."

I gave her a kiss, still not knowing what in hell to say. The thought that smooth, sleek, sophisticated woman-of-the-world Reggie might be virginal had never—I just hadn't *thought* about it. I hadn't even thought about Reggie for so long that—well, it was all pretty rattling, to have a woman like that drop out of the past like a mango falling from a tree and practically force her virginity on me within ten minutes after our meeting.

She knew I was rattled, too. She took me by both ears to hold me stooped over her in a kissing—and observant—position. She had beautiful breasts; erect, pointed, symmetrical, lily-white in contrast to the still-remaining pigmentation of the rest of her sun-tanned skin.

"Curly, love," she said gently. "I swore I would make it happen like this if I ever found you again, and that if I didn't find you no one would have me. I found you. That's all. Now we'll not talk about it further."

She got out of bed. We did not talk about it further.

But we did talk about a lot of other things before morning came. We also ate from time to time, meals that Lady Forbes-Jones ordered sent up to the room along with several bottles of indifferent but well-chilled Chileno champagne, the best the hotel could offer. I hadn't had anything cold to drink for over a year and a half. Or slept in a bed instead of a string hammock, or felt cool air blow on my skin. With Reggie unbelievingly in my arms, no mosquitoes gnawing at me, and no need to roll out before sun-up, it was all an incredible, impossible pipe-dream, but wonderful as long as it lasted.

She lay with her head on my shoulder, nibbling my ear while she talked to it. Several times I suggested that I would smell better if she would let me up long enough to take a hot bath (another first for me since jumping ship at Callao, the best part of two years earlier). She wouldn't let me go even that long. For a girl who had never had any practice at it, she was damn near as insatiable for me as I was for her. Even the roughness and stiffness of the bristly beard that was sandpapering her face didn't hold her back.

"I've waited too long already," she said, when I

suggested that shaving was in order as well as a bath. "More. More. More."

"Just as a matter of curiosity," I asked, when I had got my mouth back. "How long have you been carrying this torch for me?"

"How long have I been *what*?"

I had to translate. It wasn't an Americanism she knew. She said, "I don't know, actually. I suppose ever since I saw you on the beach at Cannes with that frightful old American harridan you were sleeping with. Otherwise I wouldn't have spoken to you as I did, would I?"

"She wasn't a frightful old harridan. She was nice and kind and generous. And I wasn't sleeping with her, whatever you believe. Ours was a platonic friendship."

"Bloody likely."

"You certainly managed to conceal your true feeling for me."

"I didn't know what my true feeling for you was. I couldn't believe, I refused to believe, that I was hopelessly smitten with a common gigolo, a horrid little spiv, a—a—"

"You needn't continue. I understand."

She nibbled my ear for a while before she said, thoughtfully, "I couldn't. Understand, I mean. For a long time. All I wanted to do was hurt you because somehow you were hurting me. Until the night of the charity ball, remember? When you kissed me?"

"I remember that you kissed me right back with a right hook and promised you'd put me in jail if I ever touched you again. I'm touching you."

"So you are, aren't you? I was upset. That kiss infuriated me. You were so smug and sure of yourself, so—so—confident. As if I were some common little shop-girl you had honored with your company for the evening, and would now take to bed. What was even more humiliating, I—"

She stopped. For a long moment she said nothing. I said nothing. Then, barely whispering, she said, "It was frightful! I *wanted* you to take me to bed. That's when I knew."

The air-conditioners clattered on, sending a breeze of cool dry air to fan the bed. I reached out my free arm for the champagne glasses, gave her hers, picked up my own.

"*A la tienne*," I said. "I'm sorry I made you unhappy. I never meant to."

"*A la tienne*. You're making me happy now. The other doesn't matter. Remember the night on the Grande Corniche?"

"I remember."

"I wanted you that night so dreadfully that I hurt. I had made up my mind to seduce you. In the car, in a ditch, by the side of the road, anywhere. But I just couldn't bring myself to—to—"

She never did get to finish the sentence. She was humbling herself beyond reason. I shut her mouth the best way I knew how and tried to prove to her by good works what she would never allow me to try to put into words, then or later.

Because the Honorable Reggie, however deeply smitten, enamored, infatuated or just plain torch-bearing, was still the Honorable Reggie, nobody's fool.

She knew what I was, what I had been, most probably what I would continue to be in spite of her best efforts; a hustler. Whatever I told her, whatever I promised, whatever I swore to, she wasn't going to believe it. Trying to tell her that I felt about her the way she felt about me was useless. She knew better, and she disliked being gulled, as she put it, about a matter as important to her as our relationship with each other.

"I don't want to hear it, Curly," she said, that first afternoon when we became lovers with all the love on her side. "Lie to me about other things, if you must, but not that. You don't have to lie about it. It's enough for me that you're alive and in my arms. Promise me just one thing, only one, truthfully, and I'll forgive you a thousand lies. Please."

"I promise. What is it I promise?"

"Wherever you go, whatever you do, whatever trouble you get into, please let me know that you're still alive. You don't have to tell me where you are, or whom you are with, or what you are doing or have done; just that you are alive. Don't just disappear. I couldn't stand it again, thinking you were dead, that I'd never see you again. I-I-I can't tell you—"

She choked up. I said, "I promise, I promise, I promise, I promise. Please stop it."

All in all, it was a hell of a situation; to be in bed with a lovely woman who loved me enough to bare her soul as well as her body for me but refused to listen to anything I had to offer in return. All my talents as a bunco artist weren't enough to sell her the simplest little bunco in the world. It made me feel downright inferior. Just as the doggedness of purpose with which she had set out to find me when I left France made me grateful she hadn't been coming after me with a gun.

She had tracked me easily enough to Tangier. The *juge* in Marseilles had issued a warrant and put her on to Interpol when she had asked for his help, although he himself wasn't particularly interested in pulling me in, and warned her that the warrant was no good outside France. She didn't care. The Milquetoast who came after me in Tangier was an Interpol clerk she had bribed to try to con me during his summer holiday. She knew nothing about him, and nothing at all about Boda. It had been a good bit more difficult for her to track me back to the States, but she'd managed it about the time I shipped out for South America. More than a year went by after that before she picked up my trail again in Lima, where my passport had surfaced.

I said, "Wait a minute. All this must have cost you a potful of money."

"Of course it did, silly. A bloody fortune."

"All for me?"

"All for you. I had to hire detectives to discover where you were, where you were supposed to be. After the fiasco in Tangier I never let them go any further than that, but followed them to look for you myself. In Lima the police had lost interest in you, but regained interest when I offered a large enough reward. They finally traced you to Iquitos, and I went there. I learned that a man answering your description had bought passage to Belem on a riverboat, almost two years ago—"

"It's only a few weeks over eighteen months, but go on."

"I flew here, it's been about a month now, but there was no trace of you, no indication that you had ever arrived. And I heard horrible things about the Amazon jungle, about men who had disappeared in it, been lost, captured by Indians, other things. I began having nightmares, horrible dreams in which I could see you, things happening to you, being done to you—"

I shut her up again. Her voice had gone thin and she was talking too fast. Holding her tightly, I could feel her heart banging in her ribcage behind the beautiful breasts. When it had quieted down a bit, I let her talk again.

"So then I saw you sitting in the park, eating a mango and scratching yourself with your toes," she went on. "For a moment I thought it was another dream. But then I knew you were real, alive, that I had found you at last, and I did what I had been promising myself for two and a half years I would do right away, without hesitation, if I ever got you back. So here we are. Where have you been? Where did you disappear? After Iquitos, I mean."

I'd been waiting for the question, mulling over various answers to it while she talked. One of them was the truth. But getting myself into O Caldeirão the way I had was such a dumbheaded thing to do that I was ashamed to confess it, and besides she would have read romantic overtones into my gesture toward poor bedraggled Miserable. Since she knew the police had been after me in Lima anyway, I told her that the Brazilian fuzz had put me away as a favor to their Peruvian buddies.

She listened without comment until I finished

talking. When I said, "That's all. I've been out long enough to grow the beard I've been scratching your face with; four days. I've got no papers, no money to amount to anything, no shoes since you lost mine for me, no other clothes but the ones you stripped off me in your unseemly haste, and no immediate prospects. However, within the next few days I'll con one of the local suckers out of his life savings and be back in business. Will you marry me?"

"Bloody likely. Bloody likely story, too. It rings just enough of the truth to sound plausible. Except for the picture of you performing honest labor for a year and a half, even under compulsion."

"If you'll kindly take a look at the calluses on my hands—"

"I don't have to look at the calluses on your hands. They're imprinted all over me. You probably got them dealing dishonest *vingt-et-un* to your fellow prisoners."

It was odd how close she could come to the truth without hitting it bang on. For lack of a better retort, I said, "They don't call it that here. It's *vinte-e-um*."

It sounded kind of lame even to me. Somehow I had a feeling that the Honorable Regina Forbes-Jones was back in the pitcher's box again, and I was catching for her.

Chapter Eleven

Whatever doubts I may have had about it vanished in the morning. I was soaking in a hot tub, examining my bug-bites and enjoying the caress of real soap, when she got on the horn and began wreaking her will on the hotel desk.

The Honorable Reggie wouldn't have been too bad at the bunco game herself. After ordering practically everything there was in the kitchen sent up for our breakfast, she said, "Lord Forbes-Jones has just returned from a trip into the bush. His kit has been misplaced. Please have a hairdresser and someone to do his nails here exactly one hour after breakfast has been served. Also the best available tailor—a *British* tailor, if possible—and a cobbler to take his foot measurements. His Lordship will also wish to order shirts, hose, underwear and the other things. Please attend to it. Exactly one hour after breakfast has been served, mind."

From the luxury of the tub I yelled, "And a doctor! His Lordship has tick heads."

"You've *what*?" her phony Ladyship called back.

"Tick heads. They ought to come out, if I'm going to look pretty for you."

"What in heaven's name are tick heads?"

"The heads of ticks. Just say you want a doctor, doll. The intimate details aren't necessary."

She passed on the order, but she was still curious. I

had to show her. Ticks are inescapable in the Amazonian bush. They aren't very big when they grab on to
you, but they get to be as fat as plums after they've
drunk enough of your blood. This they do by sinking
their heads into your flesh, very often going for the
groin and what they refuse to recognize as the private
parts. If you're careless about pulling them off, or
scratch them loose by accident in your sleep, the head
remains under your skin and festers.

I had half a dozen of them in me that the doctor had
to go after with a scalpel. Then I was shaved, sham-
pooed, cologned, massaged, pedicured—no fooling; I
felt like a pet poodle—measured, fitted, clothed, shod
and turned out looking exactly like a freshly sprung
convict made up as a British lord.

Trying to fit into the part, I picked up the phone to
order something, I forget what it was. I said, "Lord
Forbes-Jones heah," to the operator in my best imitation of Reggie's accent and delivery. She jumped up.

"A peer doesn't identify himself as such in conversation," she said critically. "You're simply Forbes-Jones.
And do please refrain from affecting that atrocious
accent. It's grotesque. If you want anything, I'll order
it for you."

"Yes, ma'am," I said. "May I use my own judgment
about wiping my nose, or are you going to do that for
me, too?"

"I only meant to say—"

"I'm saying now. You listen. I'm not on probation to
you anymore, Reggie, and I'm not going to be your
stooge. I appreciate your feeling for me, and what
you've done, and why you're doing it. I'm grateful to

you. But I'm going to pay you back for all this lettuce and mayonnaise you've hung on me, and until I do I'm still my own man."

"Curly, I only want—"

"I know what you want. I'm trying to tell you that I'm not it and I won't be it. Get it through your obstinate head. If you want me, stop shoving. Otherwise you're going to shove me right out of bed."

Her face went white and stiff as she listened to me. I suppose it was the only time in her life she had held still for a slap in the mouth like that. But she took it, and it was she who said "I'm sorry" first. I apologized in my own turn. The subject was dropped, for the time being.

She asked me, in a nice way, if I would please go back to France with her. Before the slap in the mouth she'd have told me we were going back to France. We discussed the pros and cons. I brought up several objections, which she knocked down. The warrant had been withdrawn, my minor connection with the de Lille swindle had apparently not come to light—at least she hadn't heard of it, as she would have if it had been known—and no charges were outstanding against me. When I said I had no passport, she said I did, too. The old one she had pinched in France. She'd carried it everywhere she went since getting it back from Mr. Uh Uh. It had expired but was renewable.

While I was getting it renewed at the consulate, she got us plane tickets for Paris, after first making sure I knew she was doing it and approved of her schedule. I had no real objection to France as long as I wasn't going to be flung back into the *violon* as soon as I got

there, but somehow I had a feeling that the Honorable
Regina was being entirely too sweet and obliging and
dutiful to His Lordship's wishes since His Lordship
had pinned her ears back. I can't say I had any solid
grounds for complaint in any direction, though. Anything I wanted from her or of her was mine without
hesitation. We had a tacit understanding that a day
of reckoning would come, but it was never again
discussed after our *tête à tête*.

There are various ways to get to Paris from Belem
by air. I don't know that she picked the route that went
by way of Cayenne, in French Guiana, deliberately. I
suspect that she did, for the moral effect it would have
on me when the plane came in low over Devil's Island
for its landing and I could look down on the sorry sons
of bitches doomed to die there. Not every *transporté*
sent to l'Île du Diable during the years it functioned as
a penal colony was a lifer. But a lot of them were, and
escape from it was just about as tough as escape from
O Caldeirão. Sitting there in the plane—first class,
no less—in my snappy British tailoring, with a good-
looking heiress who loved me at my side, cute dolls
running up and down the aisle to gratify my every
whim whenever I raised a languid hand and Devil's
Island as an object lesson to remind me of the wages of
sin, I'd have been a thorough horse's ass to contemplate returning to a life of crime, wouldn't I?

I was a horse's ass. I had figured out a new con, with
Reggie's help, before we reached Paris.

She didn't know she was helping me, but the come-
on was a fake identity as a British peer, the getaway
gimmick a disappearance of the British peer into the

identity of an American G.I. (She had brought my army papers with her, too.) I set myself to studying her accent and diction from then on to be able to bring off the imitation convincingly. I could speak good French, pretty good Spanish, Occupation Army German, jailhouse Portuguese and gutter Arabic as well as American. I didn't think it would be too hard for me to learn to speak English as well.

In France we set up housekeeping in a pleasant little villa Reggie rented in the hills back of Mougins, a few kilometers from the Mediterranean shore. A lot of flowers are grown in that area for the perfume factories in Grasse—carnations, roses, tuberoses, jasmine, others—and we were right across a back road from the flower fields. When they had freshly blossomed and were ready for gathering, early in the morning, they were pretty heady. The villa was rather too close for my comfort to the Cap d'Antibes, where the Marquis and Marquise de Lille du Rocher had *their* villa, until I learned that the horselaughs engendered by the trial had driven them from the Côte. Bernard and his pals had been put away for a solid rap, so no trouble would be coming from that direction. All in all it seemed that I had found *le filon*, as the French say of someone who has stumbled onto a good thing.

There was one fly in the otherwise enjoyable ointment. That was Reggie's obduracy. She had stopped pushing her muscle at me since I cut her down for it in Belem, but her views and attitudes hadn't changed a bit. She was still determined to make something out of me I wasn't and didn't want to be; a silk purse, you might say. Fighting her on those—or any—grounds was like fighting a feather mattress. She took all my best shots, absorbed them, smothered them and was unaffected by them. No matter how much I screamed, howled and protested that I wanted to live my own life, make my own mistakes, win my own prizes and pay my own penalties, she was bound and determined to set my feet in the path of righteousness. Not religious righteousness, nothing like that. She was irreligious as I was. Legal righteousness. Economic righteousness. Moral righteousness. The old nine-to-five straight and narrow.

She didn't care a groat, as she put it, what the neighbors thought about our living together without any pretense of being married. As a matter of fact our neighbors, being French, wouldn't have cared a groat themselves, if they'd thought about us at all. But Reggie didn't want anybody to get the idea she was keeping me as a house pet. She *was* keeping me, of course, in a way; she paid all the bills and gave me spending money. But everything was noted in an account book she kept of my indebtedness to her, and our agreement still stood. She would get her money back in time.

I planned to raise the *grisbi* with the British Peer swindle I had figured out, as soon as I was ready for it. My Lord Haw Haw delivery was getting better every day, although I never let her catch me practicing it.

She had different ideas, naturally.

"I'm going to lend you five thousand pounds," she said. "It's not a gift, mind, and you'll have to pay me some kind of interest on it when you're able to. We'll talk about that later. You can put it into anything you like, just so long as it's honest."

"How about a baccarat game?" I asked. "That's reasonably honest."

"Don't be flippant. You have a good mind, Curly love. Please use it intelligently for both of us."

"Uh huh," I said. "Yes, ma'am. I'll invest in a shoe store. I always wanted to sell shoes. Look up the girls' legs and all. Boy!"

"You're not old enough to be a dirty old man. You're a dirty young man."

What I bought was Riviera real estate. There wasn't even much of a gamble in it. All the French capital that was then being repatriated from Indochina, Algiers, Morocco, Tunisia and other former overseas colonies was looking for a new place in the sun to settle down. A lot of it found its way to the Côte d'Azur. Property values, which had been depressed by France's troubles abroad, doubled, doubled again, doubled again after that and still rose. A lot of landholders took their profits too soon, then kicked themselves as more profits accumulated for the buyers. I took profits as fast as they could be realized, but I didn't kick myself for it afterward. By turning them over quickly without ever taking title I made Reggie's five thousand pounds do the work of fifty thousand. Sometimes I'd buy, sell and re-buy an option on the same piece of property two or three times, ride it up a way each time, sell off, get onto something else and maybe go back to look at the first piece again after a while. If it sounds screwy, so is the in-and-out trading by which smart operators make killings in a steadily rising stock market. I made a killing. Not an enormous one, but a nice pile of *braise* that kept right on snowballing.

Reggie was still paying the bills and jotting the amounts down in her little account book, so I didn't have to take anything out of the pot to live on. Life was so smooth and the living so easy at the Villa Parfumée that it was dull. I had everything anybody could ask for, just for the asking; a loving woman, a comfortable home, a Mercedes-Benz to drive, money, plenty of food and booze, all the entertainments I could use— my God, it was as bad as driving a bus. Sometimes I got so damned bored with it I thought of signing my investments over to Reggie and shipping out again. Not as a fireman this time, that would be no improvement, but on deck. Reggie would miss me, probably, but I'd come back in time. Probably. Or maybe not. We didn't have any contract of cohabitation, express or implied. I had suggested that we get married, three or four times by then, because I thought she expected it of me. The answer was always a firm Nyet.

"No, love," she would say, always giving me a nice kiss and a pat to take the sting out of it. "When I marry it will be for love. Not to an unscrupulous fortune-hunter."

"Goddamn it, Reggie," I said, the last time she gave me that same brush. "I'm not after your goddamn money! I don't want your goddamn money! I've got money of my own. You say you love me, but when I try to tell you I—"

"Don't try. And please don't swear at me."

"I'll swear all the bloody hell I like whenever I goddamn well feel like it, at you or anyone else! And if I goddamn well want to say I goddamn well lo—"

She shut my mouth the way I had shut hers when I

was depriving her of her virginity in a hotel room in Belem. It was a real sweet loving lovely kiss.

"I do love you, Curly," she said afterward. "I'll always love you, whatever you do. I just don't want you to lie to me about important things."

"*Goddamn it all to hell and back!*" I yelled. "*I'm going to ship out! The hell with you!*" and went somewhere else. I really *was* going to ship out, on the first available ship. I didn't give a good goddamn where it went. I'd even sign on as a fireman, by God, if I had to. I couldn't take the Honorable mulehead Regina for another ten minutes.

Somewhere about this time I ran into Jean-Pierre, my old *pote* and jail-mate. He had put on a good bit of lard since I saw him last, and was doing business behind the *zinc* of a bar-and-grill in Golfe Juan, where I had gone to look at a piece of property. Watering the scotch as usual, I assumed. But after we had greeted each other and bought each other a drink, one of the waiters working the tables in the place called him '*patron*' while bringing him the money to settle an *addition*.

I said, "Nobody in his right mind would let you handle the cash if you *weren't* the patron, so I guess you have to own the joint. Whom did you rob?"

He grinned, shaking his head. A couple of extra chins he had grown wobbled when he did it.

"Got lucky at the casino one night," he said. "And drunk. Too drunk to quit while I was ahead, so I got further ahead. I put it into this place quick before I could lose it back. Got a real good buy. The *mec* who had it before me died, and his widow wanted to unload."

"I'll bet she unloaded more than she'd counted on."

"Not a bit. I gave her a fair deal. I'm legitimate now, Curly. Those bullets the Spanish bastards shot at us that night with The Boar—remember?—scared the piss out of me. I didn't like the *violon* too well, either."

"How legitimate is legitimate?"

"Oh, I push a little contraband booze, a few cigarettes, change a few black-market dollars, maybe pass a word to the right people now and then when I hear a pigeon flying around loose. It's good for business. But that's all."

"No H? For The Boar, maybe?"

He gave me a sharp look. "Not on your life. The *flics* beat you up for that first and lock you up for it afterwards. I told you, I'm legitimate. Even if I wasn't, I wouldn't have any more to do with those stinking Corsican bastards than I have to. Let me tell you about Corsicans, Curly. Of all the low-down rotten dirty cutthroat scum in the world—"

He shut up as if he'd been shot. He wasn't looking at me, but over my shoulder at someone who had just come into the bar. His face had the same kind of sick look on it as the face of the warehouse checker in Tangier when The Boar gave him the hard eye. I turned around to have a look for myself and stared straight into those same chill Corsican goat-turds that had curdled the checker's blood.

He recognized me immediately, for all the months that had passed and the expensive British threads that clothed me. He looked pretty prosperous himself, as befitted the heroin king of the Marseille waterfront. His suit was a bit on the *gangstaire* side, flashy, but the big diamond he wore on his pinky looked like the real article. He came up to the *zinc* and ordered a Pernod.

Jean-Pierre's hands were shaking as he put out the bottle, the glass and a carafe of water. Whatever he had been about to tell me further about the Corsicans, he had almost told it at the wrong moment.

"You?" The Boar said to me in his expressionless, scar-tissued voice, holding up the bottle.

"I'm drinking whiskey," I said. "Nothing but the best for me, nowadays. Thanks, anyway."

"Give him another whiskey." The Boar said it without bothering to look at Jean-Pierre. "You're doing all right, eh?"

"I'm doing all right."

"That your Mercedes outside?"

"I drive it."

"What's your *truc*?"

"No *truc*. I'm legitimate. Like Jean-Pierre here."

"Who's keeping you?"

I didn't bang him for several reasons. One of the best was that anyone who banged on The Boar was going to get himself killed. It was enough to make the other reasons unimportant. Besides, he hadn't meant the crack as an insult. In his vocabulary it was actually a kind of compliment. It implied that I was smart enough to arrange for somebody else's money to support me; in his dung-drop eyes, a commendable accomplishment.

I said, "Oh, I flit around. Flower to flower."

"Ever flit as far as Marseille?"

"Not lately. Not since the *violon*."

"I've got business going in Marseille. I could use an

American with a front like yours to carry merchandise aboard American ships."

Jean-Pierre slid the whiskey in front of me, sloshing part of it on the bar. He was still shaky.

I took the time to finish my old drink and start on the new one while I thought of the right thing to say. It wasn't going to be a wisecrack, and it wasn't going to reflect my honest opinion of people who deal in heroin. He had no more sense of humor than a rattlesnake, but his Corsican code of honor, if you call it that, demanded at least one cut throat in answer to a slight. Jean-Pierre mopped at the bar; seeing no evil, hearing no evil, speaking not at all. He would have been happy to go into the kitchen and hide under a stove.

I said, "Well, thanks. Maybe some day. Right now I've got a *poulet* who doesn't give me much time off."

"There's money in it for you."

"I've got all the money I can use. Thanks anyway."

"Nobody ever has all the money he can use. Any time you want to work for me again, this one knows how to get in touch with me." 'This one' was Jean-Pierre, to whom he bent a finger telling him he was now being called upon to speak. "Anything new?"

"No, sir. Nothing."

"Make a call once a week anyway. I don't like to come by here for nothing."

"Yes, sir. I tried to call a couple of days ago, but—"

"*Merde.* Someone is always at the number I gave you. Next time, get through."

"Yes, sir."

The Boar left us. He hadn't said hello, he didn't say

goodbye, he didn't pay for the drinks he had ordered, mine or his own. He put his glass down and walked out. Nobody said him Nay.

I said to Jean-Pierre, who still looked sick, "You were telling me about Corsicans?"

He finished what he had to say about Corsicans in six words, of which the least virulent was *con*. In French this is by no means the equivalent of 'con' as in swindle, or *con* as in *chile con carne*. After that he shut up like a clam.

About a week after that Reggie's father died. Suddenly and unexpectedly. She had to go back to England for the funeral and to do something about the estate of which she was either sole heir or principal heir. She wouldn't know which it was until the will was read, but she stood to come into a bigger potful than she already had. I put her on the plane at Nice airport.

We didn't have much to say to each other while we waited for her flight-call. I was thinking that the gap between us was going to be wider now that she was stinking rich instead of merely rich. She may have been thinking along the same lines. After a silence between us that lasted a good ten or fifteen minutes, she said abruptly, "Don't forget your promise."

"What promise?"

"The one you made in Belem."

"I'm sorry. I just don't remember what it was. Give me a hint."

"Wherever you go, whatever you do, wherever you are, whatever you have done—"

"I'm not going anywhere, Reggie. You're going. To England. Remember?" I took her by the arms to make her look at me, which she seemed disinclined to do. "I'll come with you, if you want. We don't have to live together. I'll be just another guy you met over here, passing through."

"No. I don't want that. I wouldn't want to see you if I couldn't love you." She was still reluctant to look at me, for some reason. "Promise that you won't forget your promise."

"I promise, I promise, I promise, I promise, I promise, I promise. What's this all about, anyway? I'll be right here waiting when you get back. All you have to do is let me know—".

Her flight-call came booming out of the box before the conversation could go any further. I took her as far as I could go, the check-in gate, and kissed her goodbye. She hung on to me for a moment as if she were a barnacle hanging to a rock.

"I'll love you until I die, Curly," she said into my ear. I think she was crying, although she turned away from me so fast I didn't get to see her face. "Whatever happens. Goodbye."

With that, she was gone. She didn't look back. I thought, Now I wonder what that was all about, she's only going to be gone a month or two or three, she plays it like "Kathleen Mavourneen."

It didn't bother me long. The warm, welcome wave of relief from restraint that came over me when I had waved her plane off from the observation deck and watched it fade safely into the distance was wonderful. I felt as if I'd just come out of O Caldeirão again. Reggie was a doll, but a demanding doll. Sweet, loving, attentive, attractive, at once a lady and a good lay but

as inexorable as a glacier in having her way. Marriage
to her would be a fate worse than death, no question
about it. At least in a *de facto* arrangement such as
ours I could walk out whenever I wanted to. I would,
too. Some day. In the meantime, I was free, free, free,
free of her for at least a month, maybe two or three
months. To do whatever I wanted.

I'd gotten a better idea than the Lord Haw Haw
bunco. François André wasn't the type to be taken in
by that, and François André was the fattest pigeon in
the south of France with the possible exception of
Onassis, Niarchos and a couple of maharajahs. He may
have been even fatter than they were. Just the thought
of plucking his feathers brought my theretofore languid
pulse-rate up. I didn't know just how I was going to do
it, but he was well worth a flim-flam tailored to fit him.

André is dead now. He led a long, full and satisfying
life turning himself from a penniless barrel-maker's
boy into a multi-multi-multi-millionaire. He was something of a con man himself. He used to boast that he
got his start by betting that he could roll a barrel in a
straight line although the other guy couldn't. Suckers
who saw how easy it looked when he did it—it *is* easy,
if you've been doing it since you were six—financed
his initial venture into professional gambling during
the years when games like roulette were illegal in
France, therefore unregulated and untaxed. Young
François, who was big for a Frenchman, long-legged
and fast on his feet, ran a crossroads roulette game in a
suitcase. Some said that his habit in later years of
always carrying an umbrella outdoors, rain or shine,
stemmed from the days when the umbrella opened up

into a roulette layout with two or three extra zeros on it to sweeten the house percentage. He could set up for business in two minutes, fold up and run from the *flics* in thirty seconds.

From the crossroads game he went on to start a bootleg casino on the outskirts of Paris, from there onward and upward until he owned and/or operated casinos in Cannes, Juan-les-Pins, Aix-les-Bains, La Baule, Deauville and several other places. He also owned hotels, nightclubs, sports grounds and other ancillary properties in these popular resorts, and banked two highly profitable *circles privés*, private gambling clubs, in Paris, where casino gambling is still outlawed. He was literally so wealthy he didn't know what his wealth amounted to.

"How can I possibly say?" he told me when I asked the question. "It changes from moment to moment. Since we have been talking I may have won or lost a milliard of francs."

A *milliard* is what we could call a billion, and a billion francs in those days was worth something in the neighborhood of a quarter of a million dollars. It was nice to know the old boy had that kind of money to spare without hurting. A *milliard* or two would satisfy my ambitions nicely.

I said, "But day by day you are of course richer rather than poorer. Is that a fair statement?"

"Of course. I will give you without charge the one infallible system for consistently winning at roulette, young man. Operate the wheel."

I got to ask him personal questions like these by producing credentials to show I was a freelance writer on assignment from a well-known American magazine to do a biographical piece about him. The credentials took a bit of forgery, but they looked good when I finished them. I hired a photographer and went through channels until I got to the office André was then occupying, a plain little barely furnished cubbyhole up under the eaves of the winter casino in Cannes. His only watchdog there was a little old moth-eaten secretary, male, in a smaller ante-cubbyhole who somehow gave the impression that he wrote letters with a quill pen. I thought it strange that a man who was such an obvious target for crooks like me should be so easily accessible, but later found out he wasn't as easy as I had thought. André was a wily old boy, past eighty when I knew him but shrewd and sharp as a tack with a mind as quick as a rat-trap. He still had his own hair, teeth, hearing and eyesight, all without artificial aid.

"So, young man," he said, when I first presented myself and my phony credentials. He called all males *jeunes hommes*, all females *jeunes filles*, regardless of their age. "You want to interview me. Of what possible interest could I be to your readers?"

"A man who has come as far as you have from such an unpromising start in life as yours, sir, is the epitome of the American idea of success. We are great admirers of success."

"How do you know of my beginnings, and how far I have come?"

"The basics of your career are a matter of public knowledge, sir, as you must be aware. My readers would like to know more of the details."

"You will let me see what you write before it is published?"

"Of course. I will also want photographs, but I have a man to take those. Any time at your convenience."

"Very well. Where shall we begin?"

"To answer that, sir, I'd need to know how much of your time I may have."

"As much as you like." He waved a hand indifferently. "I have little else to do with it. Few activities but the accumulation of more money than I can possibly use are still left open to me."

I must say I liked the old boy's attitude about money, although the truth is I didn't get even one lousy milliard of it. I didn't even come close. But the stimulation and satisfaction of a good swindle are as much in the preliminaries to the grab as in the grab itself; in some ways, more so. Setting up the store, telling the tale, sinking the gaff, teasing the mark down to the finishing wire, all these things call for the exercise of artistry, adaptability, sound judgment, ingenuity, applied psychology, steady nerves, showmanship, gall, further talents. While the operation is going on you're like a gambler in a game where the stakes are high enough to make you sweat. Win or lose, one thing you don't get is bored. I'm not now talking about tired old cut-and-dried cons like the Spanish Prisoner bunco, the Wire House, the Envelope Switch, the Money-Making Machine, hocuses that always follow the same pattern. They still work and will continue to work because Barnum underestimated the boob birthrate by about ninety percent. A *good* con is one you build to order around a mark who isn't a natural-born sucker but a shrewd, successful, hard-headed wise old fox like François André, and while I didn't get his money I got a hell of a lot of enjoyment out of figuring ways and means to take it away from him. Since my plans never got off the ground, or even shaped themselves fully in my mind before I had to give them up, there's nothing more to be said about what they might have been.

However, as a start I had to know a whole lot about him that I didn't know; his strengths, weaknesses, idiosyncrasies, vanities, traits of character, the other things. I got him started talking about himself easily enough, but he began as far back as he could remember, when he was rolling barrels higher than himself. To cover the next seventy-five years even sketchily would have taken seventy-five years. I asked him please to stick to the dramatic highlights of his career.

He said, "Well, once I bluffed four kings in a poker game. Is that a dramatic highlight?"

"Yes, sir," I said. "It certainly is. But I wouldn't call four kings exactly a bluffing hand."

"No, no. Four real kings, all at one of my tables. Belgium, Portugal, Denmark and Sweden." He laughed at the memory. "I had a small pair, as I remember. At least two of Their Highnesses had better hands. But they couldn't believe that a poor barrel-maker's boy would have the temerity, the brass, to challenge them without an adequacy to challenge with, and I took their money by throwing in an enormous bet any one of them could have had with a call. *Lèse majesté*, they would have said if I had let them know the truth. Of course I never did."

"You sound like a fine poker-player, sir."

"Experienced, you could say. I will give you another gambling secret that may be of value to you, young man. It is: *L'audace, l'audace, et toujours l'audace*. If you do not have the courage to risk whatever must be risked to win the stakes of the game, then you are best off out of it. Because a bolder player, which is to say a better player, will beat you every time if you play against him long enough."

"It sounds like good advice from an expert, sir."

"Thank you." He smiled at me in a gentle, friendly way. "But let us return to the subject of bluffing, which holds a strong fascination for me. What are you going to say when I tell you that I know your credentials are false and you are in no way what you have represented yourself to be? Eh?"

Chapter Twelve

This small bombshell fell in my lap after I had been interviewing him steadily for three days, several hours each day, and my photographer had taken up several further hours of his time with picture-snapping. André had at all times been gracious, cooperative and charming. He was *still* gracious, cooperative and charming, by God. At least if he felt otherwise inside he didn't show it. He was quite a man, the old barrel-maker's boy, as well as one hell of a poker player.

I sat facing him across his desk, my notebook spread open in front of me, a pencil in my hand for note-taking. I closed the book, stuck it in my pocket, put the pencil away and stood up.

"I would say that my chances of convincing you that you are wrong are poor," I said. "I'll not waste any more of your time. Thank you for what you have given me, and good afternoon."

"Sit down," he said amiably. "You aren't wasting my time. Or your own. What did you have in mind in mounting this masquerade?"

"I should think that would be obvious, sir. Your money."

"That *is* obvious. By what means did you hope to take it from me?"

He was so pleasant, so frankly interested in what I'd been working up to, that I told him what there was to tell. Namely, not much, except that he'd looked like a good mark for a score if I could work out the right pitch. There wasn't anything he could do with the confession that he couldn't do without it. If he wanted to do anything.

He said, "Young man, there is a basic error in your psychology. To swindle anybody, it is necessary that you present him with a temptation. Your fish must have greed in his soul for the lure that will bring him into your trap. Is it not so?"

"If you mean to suggest that you can't cheat an honest man—"

"I don't. Honest men are cheated every day. My games are honest, and I have been cheated many times. My roulette wheels and card tables represent my greed for the money of the people who choose to play at them. They make me cheatable. They are the tangible evidence of my greed—as it once existed." He was still gently amiable, still smiling, but somehow he managed to look sad. "I have no children. My wife is well provided for if I should die before she does. I am in good health and good appetite for a man of my age. I have more money than I can possibly count. With such great wealth, so few desires left to gratify, what can I possibly want that I do not possess? What can you tempt me with that you are able to give me, or even pretend to be able to give me?"

"Not a thing," I said. "I see your point. I could never get your money today. I might have, years ago."

He nodded. "Possibly. But it would have been difficult. I am always cautious. And never trusting."

It had been mere mechanical routine for his protective force to begin running a check on me as soon as the old boy got word that I wanted to meet him. He had known that I and my credentials were phonies within twenty-four hours after I first entered his office. But he had been bored and curious at first, later hopeful of being able to use me in a scheme of his own if I lived up to his expectations. All the time I'd been getting into *his* character, he'd been getting into mine. Now he made his own pitch.

He said, "While I no longer have greed in my soul, I do have a peasant's stubborn determination to cling to what is my own. That is bred in my bones. I would like to enlist your help in a venture for which a certain deviousness I detect in your character will be useful. You will be well rewarded, and I believe you may enjoy the occupation I have in mind for you. Will you cooperate with me, young man?"

I said, "Sir, I believe I am your pigeon. Before I commit myself, however, tell me the tale."

What I really said was, *"Glissez-moi l'appât."* (He spoke no English to amount to anything.) It means, Slip me the come-on, more or less, and is best said out of the side of the mouth without moving the lips. He smiled and told me the tale.

He had built the popular summer resort of La Baule, in Brittany, out of a fishing village, a sand dune and a fine empty beach. It had cost him a potful, but he gained large income-tax advantages from investing his profits in such projects, and of course they returned even larger profits to him in time. From his viewpoint, which I could easily understand, the project had been worthwhile for the enjoyment of doing it. It gave him an interest, and activity, other than watching the

money roll in. It was a pleasure to him to roll the money
out and see the town, his town, grow with his planting;
its sproutings of casino, hotels, *boîtes*, golf course,
tennis courts, parks, pretty villas, all the incidentals.
He wanted to do the same kind of thing on an even
bigger scale with the Costa Smeralda, on the northeast
coast of Sardinia; the so-called Emerald Coast. (He
didn't live long enough, but the project was ultimately
carried out by the Aga Khan, young Karim.)

To do it as he wanted to do it, he had to buy the
whole until-then undeveloped coast outright, and he
knew damn good and well what would happen to prices
if word got about that François André's millions were
bidding for the land. He was willing to pay a fair price,
even a generous price, but not a sky-high stick-up.
What he wanted me to do, since I was already in the
land-buying business, was front for him while ostensibly fronting for an American syndicate with plenty of
dollars to put into land speculation but no firm ideas
what or where the speculation should be.

I couldn't grab it fast enough. It was a con without
any of the risks or drawbacks of a con. Even Reggie
couldn't disapprove if I brought it off. I didn't even
care what kind of a score I made out of it for myself, it
was that attractive. Sure, it would lack some of the
spice of a real swindle, but on the other hand it had
interesting fringe benefits. I sat down to write Reggie
that I had a new and interesting land deal coming up,
that I missed her, that I was well, that I hoped she
was well and that our *bonne à tout faire* at the Villa
Parfumée had had a toothache but was no longer
complaining about it.

I couldn't think of anything else to report. How the hell people manage to fill up four pages of stationery, letter after letter after letter, beats me. I wrote about twice a week, and all I had to say could have been put on the back of the stamp. Reggie wrote every day, acres of driddle about death duties and chancery courts and probate courts and entail and solicitors and her family estate down in dear old Kent and what people I'd never heard of were doing. Cecil and Bunny and Tony and Roger and Lord Poopsy and Lady Bickerstaff, Christ knows who or what else. She never repeated herself, either, except in her regular sign-off: I love you Curly. Once, only, I wrote back, I love you, too, Reggie. Her reply covered six pages instead of the usual four. The two extra ones crisped me like so much fried bacon for having the temerity to lie to her in writing. It was even worse, she said, than lying to her orally.

I didn't tell her about the fringe benefits of André's job because they would have been too hard to explain. His people had already done all the necessary spade work for me, working very quietly. The biggest and most important piece of the property he wanted for his project was owned by a wealthy Italian industrialist named Petruzzi. It had been in his family for generations without exploitation. He and his signora spent a lot of time on the Côte d'Azur, much of it in André's gambling rooms and other playground areas. Petruzzi was the kind of industrialist who let other people be industrious for him, although I don't mean to imply he was any worse than the rest of us capitalists. Actually he was a nice guy, good company when I got to know him.

I did that easily enough at the baccarat tables. He was a nut for baccarat. *Tout va*, the big no-limit game.

His signora, Stefana, was also attractive in a kind of full-blown, spaghetti-fed way. She called me Cici, pronounced chee-chee, short for *cicisbeo*. The word is often used in Italy as roughly equivalent to gigolo, although strictly speaking a *cicisbeo* is a married woman's public escort who may or may not be her lover in private as well. Because Stefi was easily bored by the gambling that had her husband hooked, she got her kicks out of pretending we were having a heavy affair behind his back. I would take her to some *boîte* to dance—at Petruzzi's request; he wanted to play baccarat, she wanted to play something else—where she would cling fast and wiggle her crotch against me on the dance floor, croon Neapolitan *spumoni* in my ear and whisper, "Ah, Cici, *amore*, do you burn so with passion for me, then?" Glued to me the way she stayed glued when we danced, she knew damn good and well I was burning with something for somebody. It couldn't very well be concealed from her. She was only teasing, it never went any further than that, but I could neither brush her off nor try to follow through. Staying on the right side of Petruzzi was too important. But Stefi had me charged up for action the way they charge a stallion on a horse-breeding farm with a brood-mare in heat to get him snorting for the lady who is going to get the real workout. When Odile came along—but events first, alibis afterward.

To assist me with Petruzzi, André gave me one of his personal cards. On it he wrote, in a beautiful clear flowing hand you would never think to associate with a barrel-maker's boy, *Le porteur est notre invité.* That's all, but my God, what a passport it was. I couldn't pay a check or a bill or buy a drink or a meal or anything else anywhere within the old man's empire. Every casino has one or more spotters always watching the people who come in to play, on the lookout for sharpies and troublemakers but with an eye open as well for the big wheels. In France these housemen are called *physiognomistes*, and they never forget a face or its connotations. The first time I flashed André's card at one of his pleasure domes—it was the same winter casino in Cannes where he had his birdnest office up under the eaves—the receptionist's eyes widened slightly before she bowed and said, "*Bienvenu, m'sieur.*" I don't know what went on after that, but before I left the gambling rooms a couple of hours later everybody in the joint from the *caissier* to the *chasseurs* who empty the ashtrays knew I was with it, for it and of it. I couldn't even tip the hatcheck girl, or the doorman who called me a cab. When you can't do *that* on the Côte d'Azur, you are really riding a reserved seat on the gravy train.

There were even fringe benefits to the fringe benefits. I had to move slowly and cautiously with the Petruzzis—slowly with him, cautiously with her—because I could not show interest in his property, or even indicate that I knew it existed. He knew that I was interested in buying land, and had the money behind me for large-scale dealing. It was as far as I could go on openers. The next play had to come from his side of the table.

Evening after evening I waited for it in one casino

or another while he bucked the *tout va* bank, the cynosure of all eyes. I mean I was the cynosure of all eyes, not Petruzzi. I wore the faultlessly tailored evening clothes that had set Reggie back at least a hundred quid, and always had a generous pocketful of hundred-thousand *jetons* (André's, naturally) to toss negligently into a game whenever I felt like it. Always I got more than my share of bowing and scraping from the minions. Inevitably I caught the eyes of other people like myself, crooks and swindlers, every one, eager to take me into camp and pluck my gorgeous feathers.

Many of the hustlers were female. One in particular was markedly so. Her name, let's say the name she used with me, was Odile Lumaye. Madame Odile Lumaye. Husband, dead; a war casualty. Age, indefinite, but several years more than my own, probably in the early thirties. Height, about five-four or five-five, along in there. Weight, perfect, and well balanced. Color of hair, a kind a light pink, very attractive. Color of eyes, greenish. Color of lipstick, approximately the same as her hair, and tasty. Perfume, Ma Griffe, I think, although I'm not an expert. Sex, oh, yes, indeed.

In my whole life I never knew a woman who radiated sex as Odile did. Not even Boda. Boda's sex was simple, uncomplicated, a natural aura surrounding her. Odile's sex was polarized, or maybe laserized; focused, concentrated and projected in a beam that could burn the suspender buttons off a man's pants if she chose to turn it that way. When she smiled her thanks at a waiter or *chasseur* for bringing her something, he would bump into tables going back to wherever it was he came from. She made men, including me, dizzy with her impact. She was as crooked as a bolt of lightning, but with four times the voltage.

She picked me up at a baccarat table. I don't even remember exactly how it was done. That's how dizzying she was. I do remember that before I looked up from the play to fall drowning into the big green eyes, the Greek who was dealing for the Greek syndicate fumbled a card in taking it out of the shoe. Any time a dealer for the Greek syndicate fumbles a card you can bet he's just had a coronary occlusion or worse. This one had been hit by Odile's lightning. As I was immediately thereafter. My next conscious recollection is of buying her a drink at the bar. After that we were in bed in her hotel.

I don't remember any prolonged intervals between steps A, B and C, but intervals must have existed. Shortly after stage C, I got a wire reading: ARE YOU ALL RIGHT. WHY DON'T YOU ANSWER MY LETTERS. HAVE TRIED VAINLY SEVERAL TIMES TO REACH YOU BY PHONE. PLEASE CALL WRITE WIRE ANYTHING EVERYTHING. TERRIBLY WORRIED. LOVE YOU ALWAYS. REGGIE.

By then I was back in my own bed with plenty of time for sending wires, writing letters and the other things you do in bed, like convalescing. I cabled that I had been involved in a land deal, out of town for a while, now back, in good shape (ow!), letter follows.

Have you ever slept with a bolt of lightning? Sweet Odile knew tricks of her trade I'd never heard of, or even imagined. Where Boda had been as simple and

unaffected and joyously wholehearted as a bunny rabbit
about screwing for the sake of screwing, and Reggie
was a lusty lady in love, Odile made a technique of it. It
was part of her planning, I believe, so to drain a man's
vitality in bed that he would have no resistance to her
in other departments, and could only cooperate as she
wanted him to. She was much like The Boar in this
respect, an extortionist, except she used sex where he
used brutality. I had about fifteen hundred dollars
worth of André's *jetons* in my clothes when we launched
our first orgy, and if she'd been working a badger game
I wouldn't even have been sorrowful about losing them
when the outraged husband broke in on us with a gun.
Provided he didn't break in too soon, of course. That's
how good she was. I mean bad.

She was after more than a lousy fifteen hundred.
When she had reduced me to will-less pulp, she went
into her pitch. We were still in bed. The only way I
could have got out of it was by falling out.

"*Mon coeur*," she said. She had a pleasantly husky
voice like a tiger's purr. It went with the green cat's-
eyes. "Listen to me. Would you like to make a lot of
braise? A great quantity of *braise*?"

"No," I said. "I'd like to sleep. Good night."

"Do not sleep yet. There is a fortune within our
grasp, if you will but take it."

"I haven't the strength left to grasp five francs.
Good night."

"If you do not listen to me, *mon ange*," she purred.
"I shall do to you thus-and-so-and-thus-and-so and
thus-and-so—"

I listened. She was perfectly capable of doing thus-

and-so to me for the rest of the night, and it would have killed me stone cold dead.

She wanted me to help her swindle André. She had in mind a gimmick that had been successfully worked years before in Monte Carlo. She knew I was André's fair-haired lad from observing the treatment I got from his hired help, although not why. She sensed, knew instinctively with that it-takes-one-to-know-one instinct, that I was a hustler like herself. She was also without doubt that she could buy me with her body and tricks. I listened to her pitch because I was too debilitated not to, also from professional curiosity.

Her gimmick was to counterfeit André's *jetons*. The big ones, nothing less than a hundred thousand francs. At the time, a hundred thousand francs were worth between two hundred and two hundred and fifty dollars, and the *jetons* were as good as cash in whatever casino had its name on them, either for play or for redemption at the *caissier's* window. A couple of hundred of the fakes, as Odile pointed out unnecessarily in her wicked purr, would make a nice score for us to split between us. We didn't have to stop at a couple hundred, either. With my *entrée* and my favored position with André—

"*Eh alors*, what is it with you and the old goat, *mon chou*? What do you have on him, that he gives you the keys to his kingdom? If he likes pretty boys, you are no *tournedos*. Of that I have reason to be certain. Tell me the truth."

A *tournedos* is a cut of filet mignon. But the word is also obscure argot for a male homosexual, passive posture, although not known in this usage to polite

society, or even semi-polite society. Scrumptious sexy
Odile had to have been around, to have learned about
things like *tournedos*. Furthermore, a doll like that on
the crook wouldn't be allowed to freelance even if she
wanted to. She was too valuable a property. She would
have hard-case pals lurking somewhere in the wood-
work, ready to pop out and take over when the time
came for us to split the grab. I had a strong feeling that
I was being set up for a fall, somehow.

I said, "*Mon âme*, André and I are good friends, no
more. We used to roll barrels together. I know nothing
about counterfeiting except that the penalties for it are
rough. Get yourself another boy. Again, good night."

"*Mon amour*, wake up or else. All you have to do
is help me pass the fakes. I will attend to everything
else. Besides, it is not counterfeiting, only copying.
Counterfeiting is the making of false money. André's
jetons are not money."

"*Ma petite brioche*, is this all your idea, or have you
been coached? You seem well informed."

"*Mes yeux*, it is my idea. I have given it thought and
study. Now listen to me further."

Somebody had sure given it thought and study. The
matrices for shaping the fakes were to be made by
using genuine *jetons* as molds. Plastic of the same
color and texture as the originals would then be
poured into the matrices, and plaques of the size and
shape of the originals would be obtained when the
plastic had hardened. These would be carefully checked
for dimension with a micrometer, since an experienced *caissier*, blindfolded, can run his fingertips up
and down a stack of chips once and pick out phonies if

they vary from the norm by as much as a couple of thousandths of an inch. (The picture of luscious Odile sweating over a hot plastic crucible, then checking the results with a micrometer, was fascinating in its incredibility.) The plaques would then be finished off for denomination and identity by hand. It was not intended that they be good enough for play on a table watched by three or four sharp-eyed *croupiers*. But if size, shape and texture were right, a busy *caissier* could be expected to accept a stack of them topped by one or two genuine *jetons*, count it visually and pay off without taking the stack apart before putting it in his rack.

"Until the fakes end up in a *croupier's* box and are immediately discovered to be fakes," I said. "Then what? The *caissier* will check every *jeton* from then on. And how many people cash in ten million franc stacks of *jetons* without being remembered?"

"We will not cash ten million franc stacks, *mon soleil*," Odile purred. "We will cash half-million franc stacks. Pah, it is a nothing to a *caissier*, half a million. Then, when he does begin to check the *jetons*, we move to another casino until he is no longer alert, and return to do it again. Who will suspect a good friend and favorite of the court of François André of such an activity?"

"François André," I said. "Like a shot." To stay with the swing of the conversation, I added, "*Ma violette*."

"Pah, *mon coquelicot*. You are a sheep. I thought you would be a lion."

"Let me have a few hours rest and I will roar again, *ma pivoine*."

"You will reflect on it, *mon astre*? If you do not

promise I shall do to you thus-and-so-and-thus-and-
so—"

"I promise. For God's sake, let me get some sleep."

"Good night, *lumière de ma vie*. Sleep well."

I reflected on it just long enough to decide that
the best way to handle Odile was to peach on her to
André. I didn't want to get her into any more trouble
than was necessary, but the only way I could see to
keep her from stepping into trouble up to her lovely
lo-lo's was to prevent her from taking the step. Her
scheme had gaping flaws in it. She and her patsy,
whomever she found to help her with the passing,
were almost certain to be spotted sooner or later if
they kept it up long enough to make the deal worth the
effort. André had not operated his empire for the best
part of half a century without knowing the ways of
crooks, and what to do about them.

So I was surprised when, having heard me out in
silence on the subject of Odile, he asked me what I
thought should be done about her.

"I thought you would decide that, sir," I said.

"I am capable of making the decision, young man,"
he said dryly. "First I should like to hear your sugges-
tions for handling the lady."

"Well, she's committed no crime against you, so far.
Wouldn't it be enough just to bar her from your gambling rooms? She can't very well operate if she can't
get in."

"It would be something of a deterrent, yes." He was
sitting at his desk, I was standing in front of it. He
looked up at me from his shaggy white old man's eyebrows. "Having her jailed would be more effective."

"On what charge?"

"Charges can be arranged."

"I'd rather we didn't do it that way, sir."

"Why?"

"Well, I—it's—the thing is—I just wouldn't feel *right* about it—if you see what I mean."

He nodded again, gravely. "I see what you mean."

If he did, he saw more clearly than I did. I guess I just didn't like the idea of putting Odile in jail for something she hadn't yet done. Maybe it was because I had slept with her. I don't know. But André agreed to let me take care of her in my own way, and if he thought I was being unwisely quixotic or downright stupid, he didn't say so.

My way was to wear her on my arm that night to three different casinos. Normally I stuck pretty close to Petruzzi at whatever casino he chose to play, waiting for the run of bad luck that would net him for me. That night I told Odile I wanted to check the different *caissiers*, observe how their procedures varied. The real reason was to give the *physiognomistes* at all three places a good hinge at my lady-friend. The word had gone out from André's office that M. Curly's companion of the evening was to be regarded as *de trop* from then on, and once you are declared *de trop* at one gambling parlor in that part of the world, you are dead at all of them. This kind of news gets around fast. You can't just walk into a French gambling casino as you can into a casino in Las Vegas, for example. You have to identify yourself, prove you're over twenty-one and get a *carte d'admission*. The receptionist, who is also a *physiognomiste*, keeps a record of your membership, to call it that, in his file, although if you are a regular he doesn't have to look you up but bows and greets you, by name if you are somebody of importance, as you pass into the games-rooms. I was of course a regular in all of André's places. So was Odile, probably— until the second evening we went casino-crawling together.

This time I took her to still another casino for the *physiognomistes* to look at. It wasn't necessary. She was already blackballed all the way from Aix-en-Provence to Menton and points north. That's how fast an organization like André's can work when it wants to.

The receptionist bowed, smiled and said, "Good evening, m'sieur et dame," but made no move to pass us on in. "Madame's name?" he asked me politely.

I said, "Lumaye."

"Lemay?"

"Madame Odile Lumaye." I spelled it out for him.

He said, "Thank you, m'sieur. Excuse me one moment," and went to look it up.

Odile's perfect brow was faintly troubled by a frown. She was by no means used to having the personnel of a gambling casino forget her. The receptionist came back too quickly to have looked up anything but his sleeve.

"I regret it, m'sieur, but madame's name is not in our files."

"You are completely mad," Odile snarled at him in her tiger's voice. "I have been here many times, idiot."

The receptionist ignored her, politely. Before Odile could bite him I said, "It doesn't matter. We'll get you another card," and reached for my pocket.

"I regret it, m'sieur," the receptionist said, still polite. "It will first be necessary to talk with the management."

That did it. He hadn't once addressed Odile directly, or even looked at her. The management gag meant that she had just been thrown out of the place on her luscious behind. Figuratively speaking, of course, but effectively. She snarled something at the receptionist that no lady has any right ever to call a gentleman without knowing a whole lot more about the peculiarities of his sex life than she could have known if he was what she said he was, and we left.

She began to get the message at the next place, understood it fully when the same thing happened a third time. I was in the middle of a suggestion that we run down to Monte Carlo and try there when she spat in my face and called me the same thing she had called the receptionist.

"You did this to me, you piece of filth!" She sounded more like a cobra than a tiger now, or maybe a green mamba. "But I will make you pay!"

She left me wiping her venom from my face.

You may say I was a pretty clumsy bunco artist not to be able to keep my face from being spat in. I was, but with reason. You've got to love your work in the hocus business trade. You've got to be with and for a con to bring it off properly. You can't go at it half-heartedly or you'll flop as badly as any other salesman who knows in his heart that his product is a turkey. Although I'd done Odile a favor in keeping her out of jail, my heart wasn't in the way I had done it. I felt guilty about it. As I had never felt guilty for the small-town banker who had wanted to bribe his way into a

phony franchise, or the Daddies and Mommies in
Marrakech, or the marks Smitty and I had circularized
with the Spanish Prisoner letter in Lima. So I bobbled
it, and got spat on.

I also got banged on by some of Odile's hard-case
friends. It happened two nights after the spitting.

They got me in Nice, where Petruzzi had gone to
tackle the Greeks at the Palais Méditerranée. His luck
was running discouragingly well, and I didn't feel like
putting up with Stefi's horseplay on the dance floor.
She had seen me squiring Odile around and was in a
mood to give me a hard time. I went for a stroll up the
Promenade des Anglais to get a breath of fresh sea air
while I thought about Reggie's letter of the day.

She had written her usual four pages of news. She
thought she might be able to come home in about
another month or so. Lady Bickerstaff had gout, Tony
had asked her to marry him, Simon had asked her to
marry him the week before, somebody else the week
before that. Every cheap grifter in London including a
couple with titles had either asked her to marry him or
was standing in line waiting his turn. Who the hell did
those guys think they were, mousing around with my
girl? She said she'd only marry for love and she loved
me, although she wouldn't marry me. That left it tied
up nothing to nothing, but I didn't need outside help
to break the tie, by God.

My thoughts along these lines were terminated by a
casse-tête or something equally hard that took me in
the back of the head and put me away. For this I had
reason to be grateful rather than otherwise. I didn't

feel what they were doing to me while they were doing it, only afterward.

They didn't try to kill or cripple me, just worked me over good. With their feet, probably. They cracked three ribs and my left cheekbone, loosened several teeth, broke one off. Nothing serious, and no damage either internally or to the family jewels. But when I woke up my face was so swollen I could see out of only one eye, not very well with that one. There wasn't much to look at in the room where I was but a big bunch of beautiful pink roses.

When a nurse came in to do what nurses do to patients, I gestured toward the roses. I didn't want to use my mouth unnecessarily. They'd torn my lip, too. She brought over a plain white card that had come with the bouquet. I pried my good eye open enough to read what was on the card.

It said, *Pour me rappeler, mon coeur.* To remember me, my heart. No signature, just the imprint of a kiss in pink lipstick.

Chapter Thirteen

Petruzzi's luck held while I was healing enough to get out of bed and creak around. If it had changed while I was still laid up I could have missed getting the gaff into him. But it didn't, and I did.

I'd sent word to the *bonne* at the Villa Parfumée that I'd been called away on business, then rented a room in Cannes near the office of the dentist who was going to rearrange my teeth. Driving back and forth to Mougins with three cracked ribs would have been no pleasure. Besides, if I had let the *bonne* see my face as it looked for a couple of weeks she'd have told Reggie I'd been brawling in her absence and got me a chewing out.

I let Stefi see my face at its worst, while it still looked like a stuffed ripe eggplant. It served her right. If it hadn't been for her—but I'd only be conning myself to blame her for the beating. I'd asked for it when I stepped between Odile and the jail André wanted to send her to. I told Stefi and anyone else who asked that I'd fallen off a roulette wheel. If they didn't believe me, it was their privilege.

Tout va is one of the roughest games in the world, as well as one of the simplest. It's nothing more than baccarat with a bank that stays in one man's hands instead of moving around the table as in *chemin de fer*, with no limit on the amount you can bet against it.

French law, for reasons of its own probably having to do with the no-limit rule, says that no casino operator can bank a *tout va* game. He can have a *tout va* on the premises, as he usually does, but the players do not bet against house money. In southern France most *tout va* games are banked by the so-called Greek Syndicate, which is not to be confused with the Syndicate that runs the numbers racket in the U.S.A. Nobody has ever charged the Greek Syndicate with dishonesty or double-dealing or tough stuff, anything like that. They're strictly legitimate. They have a small percentage going for them with the bank, a whole lot of money behind them. You want to bet a hundred thousand dollars at a Syndicate dealer on two cards and an optional one-card draw? Go right ahead, pal, you're faded. And the next time. And the next time. And the next. Paid off then and there if you win, too, with no expression on the banker's face even when he's just finished laying out half a million dollars of his own and his partner's money. As long as you keep bringing it back to play again, friend, you're welcome.

Petruzzi's streak had lasted most of the month before it fell apart, as I had been waiting for it to do. He was a moderately high roller; not up there with Jack Warner, Darryl Zanuck, Farouk, the Argentine millionaires, and La Môme Moineau, people who couldn't enjoy the game unless they won or lost a fortune, but heavy enough. He must have been into the Syndicate for the equivalent of around a hundred thousand dollars when the percentages caught up with him.

I was there when it happened. Not playing, just watching the game. Stefi was ignoring me, thank God, in favor of another Cici she had picked up to tease on the dance floor. Petruzzi lost four consecutive bets of two hundred thousand francs each when the dealer turned eight, seven, eight, nine. He doubled his bets, lost twice more, won once, lost twice again. I never saw a bank with such a run. The dealer was beating both sides of the table three times out of five, losing to both sides only about once out of five.

Most of the other players, recognizing the developing run, reduced their bets to ride it out. Not Petruzzi. He kept doubling up. In *tout va*, if you've got inexhaustible funds and nerves of vanadium steel, you can ride out any run of bad luck until it turns for you. There's no ceiling on the amount you can bet except the one you set for yourself or your cash reserve sets for you. In Petruzzi's case, he ran out of money before he ran out of nerve.

I could see what might be going to happen when it started happening. Stefi and her Cici came by the baccarat table, but I herded them both into the bar for a champagne cocktail before Stefi could see what was happening and try to get her husband to stop play. I needn't have worried. Only one thing in the whole wide world could have got him away from that table. As it did in about thirty minutes.

He came into the bar looking white, shaken and as clean as an empty piggy bank.

"Have a drink," I said hospitably. "What'll it be?"

The way he looked, he might have ordered hemlock. He said, "Scotch. Double. Straight," and threw down the drink in a gulp.

"How did it go, *amore*?" said Stefi.

"Not well."

He fiddled with his empty glass for a while, then said he had to go to the *vater*, meaning water-closet. He gave me the look that says, Come along, *amico*. We excused ourselves and went to the *vater*.

He was blunt and to the point.

"I need money," he said. "How well do you know François André?"

"He'll cash a check for a reasonable amount for a steady customer. You don't need any help from me for that."

"I don't want to cash a check. I want to borrow."

I didn't crowd him to find out what had happened to his finances besides a bad streak of luck at cards. It didn't matter. He was coming up to the gaff nicely.

I said, "I can let you have four or five thousand."

He made a quick gesture of dismissal. "Thanks, but I need at least ten million, fast. That game is just about to turn around and run the other way. I've got to get back in."

"André doesn't lend money to bet against his money. No gambler does. You know that."

"It's not his money I'm betting against, *pazzo*! It's the Syndicate's money. For God's sake, you've got to help me! I'm desperate!"

"Gee, that's right. It *is* the Syndicate's money, isn't it? I'd forgotten that. Well, I'll speak to André, but I don't know. Ten million is a lot. I'll try, though."

I went away looking dubious and thoughtful.

If Petruzzi hadn't already used the *pissoir* while we talked, he'd have wet his pants for sure waiting for me to come back. I stalled around for half an hour or so to let him sweat, then came back to find him hanging over the *tout va* table like a man nailed to a cross. The luck was running the other way now, against the bank. Every time a player took a *coup* Petruzzi would flinch as if he'd been hit with a whip. When I came up beside him he whispered hoarsely, "Did you get it? Did you get it?" almost without taking his eyes from the game that was killing him.

"No," I said, feeling sorry for the poor bastard. Gambling can be worse than dope or even love, when you're badly hooked. "But I can get it for you. Part of it, anyway."

I had him. Gaffed and hanging on the wire. He'd have sold me his wife, his mother, his children, his balls, anything in the world to get back into that game with a fair stake. The tale I told was that André wasn't lending because he was superstitious about such things. He would cash my check for five million, which I would myself lend Petruzzi out of friendship and fellow feeling. However, since the money was not mine but funds of the land-buying syndicate of which I was the front-man, I would of course have to have some kind of solid security for my principals. It would have to be real estate, naturally, since that was all I had authority to deal in, but if he had anything to put up, a piece of speculative land maybe—?

He didn't even haggle about valuation, he was burning so with eagerness to clobber the Greeks. André had told me how high he was prepared to go for the land, a fair price that Petruzzi settled on like a shot. André's lawyers had typed up, on plain stationery with a few artful erasures, non-invalidating mistakes

and typeovers, an air-tight agreement which made me
the option holder for my "principal or principals";
during such and such a period, with such and such
terms of payment if the option was exercised after
examination of the property, a recovery clause if the
property or its title was not in every way as represented (more window dressing since everything had
been carefully checked out), the other things. It was
quite clearly an option to purchase, not just a pledge
of collateral he could redeem if he chose, but he raised
no fuss about that. A lousy piece of Sardinian coastline
that had been kicking around in his family for generations, what was that compared to a quick pocketful of
cash when he needed cash in a hurry? He signed the
agreement without hesitation in front of two barmen
as witnesses, and I brought him five million francs
worth of *jetons* from the *caisse* simply by signing a
receipt. I could have easily have got him the ten million he wanted, or fifty million, or a hundred million. I
just didn't want him to lose more than another five
million on top of what he'd already lost.

He made a comeback. Not a big one as far as I know,
and certainly not to the point where he was into the
Greeks as big as before, but a pretty fair recovery. I
watched him pile a few more millions on top of the
working capital I had got for him, then left the *tout va*
table feeling that I had done my daily good deed.

André was pleased with the news when I reported
it. I had been avoiding him since the pounding I had
taken from Odile's friends, not wanting to confess that
if I had sabotaged her his way instead of my own it
wouldn't have happened to me. My face looked a lot

better, my teeth had been repaired, I could see out of both eyes. Some of the discoloration still remained. When I had finished reporting he said, "You did well. What happened to your face?"

"I fell off a roulette wheel."

He looked at me sharply from under his shaggy eyebrows, but only said, "They do spin a bit rapidly at times. Tell me, young man. You have done me two favors, I suspect at some cost to yourself. What do you think your reward should be? Within the limits of my purse, you understand."

He'd promised me a reward, and I knew that whatever it cost short of the contents of the French National Treasury he could afford it. What I hadn't expected was to be asked to name it myself. I thought fast and hard.

"Would this piece of property you have acquired include a small island or two, sir?"

"I believe so. Even one or two fairly large islands, I am told. I have not seen the land myself, only photographs of it."

"A small island would do me nicely."

He gave another sharp look from under the eyebrows. "You may have your choice of the availabilities. Will you tell me *why* you want an island?"

"Well, sir, it seems like a good investment if you are going to develop the coast off which the island lies. Aside from that, I've always wanted an island of my own. Like Onassis."

"A yacht to go with it, perhaps? A tame opera singer? A fortune to spend?"

"No, sir. I'll take care of the small incidentals myself. Just the island."

"Very well. You shall have it. Go select the one you want and let me know."

That night I wrote Reggie a longer letter than usual. Nearly a whole page. I told her I had a surprise for her which I would give her when she came back to the Villa Parfumée, that I had had some dental work done, that the *bonne* was fine, I was fine, I missed her, best regards.

The surprise was to be the island. There isn't a hell of a lot you can give an heiress as rich as the Honorable Regina. (I added a postscript to the letter: Are you still an Honorable, or did your father's death change your status? Are you an earl or female equivalent thereof?) But I was pretty sure she didn't own any islands, and the value of the one she would get from me would more than repay what I owed her little black account book. Furthermore, it was honestly come by—more or less—and the fruit of my own efforts rather than her capital. I felt real good about it when I flew over to Olbia, hired a launch and went island-cruising.

Six days later I'd made my choice. It had about twenty-five acres of land with a nice little land-locked bay, several good small beaches, a couple of good springs, a hill and a fine growth of the wonderful fragrant *maquis* that grows on Corsica and Sardinia, redolent of sage, thyme, arbutus, fennel, rosemary, heather and other aromatics. No buildings, no people, rabbits so tame they sat up on the hill and watched me without alarm, many birds including quail calling in the *maquis*, shellfish in the sea, signs of *sangliers* in the withered bushes they had ripped up with their tusks to get at the edible roots. The *sangliers* would have to go, they were too dangerous for Reggie on a small island, but the rest of the livestock contributed to the wild charm of the place. I planted a sign-post on the beach that said, ISOLA REGINA, the hell with any name it had had before that, then went back to France feeling like—like—I don't know what I felt like. But I felt *good*. Better than I had ever felt in my whole life. Briefly.

After the dental work was finished I had gone back to the Villa Parfumée, given the *bonne* a plausible story to account for my still-battered face and read the mail that had accumulated for me. All from Reggie, four pages a day and I love you at the end. Now there was another week's accumulation. I sorted the letters into order by their mailing dates and read through the usual driddle until I got to the last letter.

It was almost as short as my longest one to her. It read:

Dear Curly—

You sound in good spirits and health. I am happy for you. I'm sure I'll be surprised and pleased by your surprise for me.

I have a surprise of my own for you. I have decided to marry. Legal and other pressing reasons have caused me to modify the strong views I have long held on this subject, as you know. I have given it a great deal of thought and am not to be dissuaded. Even if you truly wished to dissuade me.

*I expect to return to France in about three weeks
to say goodbye to a way of life which, in its fashion,
has been one of the most rewarding I have ever
known.*

I'll love you always.

Reggie

*P.S. No, I am no longer an Honorable, as you put it,
or anything other than plain Miss Forbes-Jones. It
is one of the reasons I have come to the decision you
now know.*

It was like getting slugged with the *casse-tête* all over
again. I was really stunned. How do you figure a doll
like that, telling you in one breath she's going to marry
some prick called Simon or Eustace or Percy, in the
next that she'll love you forever? I'll bet I read that
letter forty times, trying to make some kind of sense
out of it, but all it said was just what it said. She would
love me always, and she was going to marry a jerk who
had stabbed me in the back when I wasn't looking.

The next three weeks are kind of hazy in my memory.
The highlights I do remember aren't among my most
treasured recollections. I spent a lot of time in the
casinos going from bar to baccarat game and back.
I lost more money than I could afford, had to sell a
couple of my good options before they were ripe, got
involved in several brawls. Not at the baccarat table or
because of the options but with guys whose girls I took
or tried to take away from them. I was still being hustled by every high-class *poule* working the Riviera, but
I didn't want any popsy who could be had for the
taking. I wanted somebody who was hanging on some

other guy's arm, as my girl was hanging on some other guy's arm. More often than not the arms would start swinging, I'd swing back, and yo-heave-ho. If it started out in one of André's places the other guy would go out on his can. Anyplace else, we'd both go out on our cans and finish the brawl in the gutter. Sometimes I'd lick the other guy, sometimes he'd lick me, but I never won anything in any real sense. Even when I took the doll home with me to the Villa Parfumée for fun and games. In Reggie's bed, as a matter of principle.

I didn't try to hide anything from the *bonne*, Rose. She was stiff with disapproval and spoke to me only when there was no possible way to avoid it. I'm pretty sure she would have quit except that she wanted to be around when Reggie got home so she could tell on me. The hell with you, I thought. Go ahead and blab all you want. The hell with Reggie, too. The hell with everything. She'd love me always, and she was going to marry some shit named Tony or Roger or Reginald or Cuthbert. Probably some kind of puky peer.

That's what it was, by God. It came to me in a flash. She didn't want to be just plain Miss Forbes-Jones, she wanted to be a Lady. She was always pretending to be a Lady, now she had a chance to grab off the real thing. I hoped she got stuck with somebody named Lord Athol. It would serve her right. Lady Athol, hah. The hell with them both. I hope they ended up knee-deep in little Athols.

During those three weeks she wrote only occasionally, maybe half a dozen times in all. No more four-page letters, either. Half a page or a page at most. She said she was terribly busy trying to get "things" in order. There was a lot to do before she could get married. She sure seemed to be hot to get hitched to that Athol character. I pictured him with buckteeth, no chin and dishwater-colored hair parted in the middle. How anybody of Reggie's taste, discrimination and sensitivity could fall for a slob like that—but she *couldn't* have fallen for him, damn it. She loved *me*. She said so regularly in every letter, however sketchy it was otherwise. The hell with her and her love.

I didn't write her at all. Screw writing. Screw Reggie. Screw everybody. Screw everything.

Then, about a week before she was due—she still hadn't given me a definite date—I cracked up the Mercedes-Benz. No overwhelming damage, either to the car or to me, but a ruined fender, a bashed-in headlight, chromium ripped loose, bumper twisted, things like that. It was raining and I'd had too much to drink at Jean-Pierre's bar, where I'd gone to vent my indignation at the lousy world. Jean-Pierre had no choice but to listen to me cry into my drinks, as long as I paid for the drinks. I paid for too many, that's all.

The nearest place where I could get a proper repair job was Marseille. I drove there and ran into a police roadblock that had the whole port cordoned off, as far as I could make out. The cops were stopping only cars coming from the city, but they were checking those out carefully. They weren't answering any questions I heard asked, just going about their business. I asked no questions myself. Screw the cops, too. The hell with everything. I would have felt terrible even without the constant hangover that rode with me those days.

There were more cops in the city, police cars dash-

ing about giving those hee-haw noises they emit in
Europe in place of sirens, uproar everywhere. I took
the car to the shop where it was to be fixed and turned
it over to a mechanic.

He said he thought I could have it by the next afternoon, if the repair parts were in the stockroom. He
couldn't say without checking. About the *bagarre* in
the streets, he knew no more than I did.

"The *flics*, they are always boiling up a shit-storm
over something," he said, indifferently. "Me, I ask no
questions and keep my nose clean. *On se défend.*"

One defends oneself. With the implication attached.
Screw everybody else. It was a philosophy that closely
fitted with my own.

I went to a lousy hotel, had a lousy dinner with a
lousy bottle of wine, read a couple of lousy newspapers
before going to sleep in a lousy bed with rocks in the
mattress. According to the papers, the *bagarre* had
been a well-planned, widespread strike by the police
against Marseille's heroin traffic. Several hundred
kilograms of the finished product had been taken, a
whole lot more of the unprocessed morphine base,
much processing equipment, more than two hundred
and fifty people jailed. Among them was noticeably
not a Corsican criminal known to police and the
milieu as Le Sanglier, uncrowned heroin king of the
Marseille waterfront. (No 'allegeds,' 'reputeds,' or
'rumoreds' for the French press. They call a crook a
crook.) The king's reign had ended with the seizure of
a large stock of the drug in a warehouse where he had
been accumulating it for overseas shipment. His own

arrest was predicted within a matter of hours. He had shot two policemen, killing one, in making an escape from the warehouse. One of his own mob had been killed by the police when Le Sanglier used him as a shield in his getaway.

I would have been such a pretty carrier pigeon for you, Le Sanglier, I thought. Me and my American front. Screw you, too. I went to bed and slept miserably.

They hadn't caught up with him by the time the morning papers came out, but it was nothing to me. I had troubles of my own. The parts the mechanic needed to put the Mercedes-Benz back in shape weren't in his stockroom. They had to be ordered. Might take a week before the car was ready, the mechanic said.

Reggie was due back in a week or less, although I still didn't know the date. I phoned the Villa Parfumée. Rose's voice was as icily disapproving as ever when she said that no word had come from her mistress. I explained that I was tied up in Marseille, gave her the number of the hotel where I was staying and told her to call me as soon as she heard anything. Over a hundred miles of telephone wire, without saying a word about it, she managed to convey her conviction that I was calling from a cheap waterfront whorehouse.

Screw you, too, I thought, hanging up. A cheap waterfront whorehouse was just about right for my mood, but somehow I couldn't bring myself to it. I was too depressed and miserable and crestfallen, I guess you might say. Reggie had hit me where it hurt, in my masculine pride. I was good enough for an earl's daughter to love, she couldn't help loving me because you can't do anything about love. I just wasn't good enough for her to marry. So goodbye, Curly love, I'll adore you forever but that's all of it. It would have been different if I'd given her the brush, of course. I'd walked out on plenty of girls before her, and if they'd wept in their pillows about it afterwards, *tant pis*. A girl here, a girl there, who cares? Reggie was no different from the others. But for *her* to leave *me*, and for a silly slob like that Athol prick—

Misery, misery. Groan, groan. Grinding of teeth. Gloom.

The job on the Mercedes-Benz took four days. I called the villa every morning to learn if she had sent word of her return. I didn't trust Rose to call me as I had told her to. For three mornings, nothing. On the fourth day, a cable had arrived from London.

It was in French, the easiest way to get a telegram delivered in France without garbling. Rose could read it to me. Translated, it said: ARRIVE NICE FRIDAY BEA FLIGHT 078 ETA 1410 PLEASE MEET PLANE SURPRISE SURPRISE SURPRISE LOVE YOU ALWAYS REGGIE.

Holy Mother of God, I thought. She's bringing the slob *with* her!

That did it, once and for all. If she thought for a minute I was going to chauffeur her and that chinless bucktoothed dishwater-colored son of a bitch around the way I'd chauffeured her around when she had me on a leash, she could think again. Let Athol worry about Lady Athol-to-be. Or was she already Lady Athol? Jesus, I could just picture the three of us at the airport: "Lord Athol, may I present the man I love? Curly, this is my husband, Lord Athol. Charmed I'm sure. Up yours, too." The woman was crazy, that's all. She had to be crazy. She *deserved* someone like Athol.

Friday, her arrival date, was the day after I got the message in Marseille and the day after the repairs to the car were finished. I could easily have made it to the airport in plenty of time to meet BEA 078 in the afternoon. Instead, I called Rose the night before from a bar where a jukebox blared background music, let her think I was drunk and told her I was too busy to meet the plane. I'd probably be home in a day or two, maybe three, I said, and hung up. If she wanted to report to Reggie that I was carousing in a Marseille whorehouse, it was all right with me. Then I tried to get drunk but only managed to get sodden.

I slept late the next day, most of the morning, and took my time about driving back to Mougins in the afternoon. I wanted to be sure Reggie and the slob were there when I nonchalantly walked in after a night of debauchery. I hadn't shaved or bathed, my eyes were bloodshot, my shirt was dirty, anybody could see I'd been having a whole lot of fun. I even took along a bottle of cognac so I could belt a couple at the last minute and breathe booze-fumes on them. With care and forethought I planned how I would walk in, say an indifferent "Hi" to her, sneer at her choice of a husband and walk out of her life forever. Screw everybody, everything and all combinations of both.

It was raining, not heavily but steadily, when I reached the villa. Even in the drizzle I could smell the fragrance of the blooming flower fields. For some reason, it was terribly depressing. A car I didn't know, a Peugeot, was parked in the graveled turn-around in front of the house. Rose's bike, which she pedaled into the village most mornings to do her marketing and kept stabled in a shed near her kitchen entrance the rest of the time, lay in the middle of the path that went around to the back of the house. It looked as if she had started to go into town, changed her mind and gone back into the house. But it was totally unlike her to leave the bike like that, even if it hadn't been getting rained on.

To postpone the moment when I would have to face Reggie and the slob long enough for my two belts of Dutch courage to take effect, I picked up the bike, wheeled it around to its shed, stabled it and banged through the kitchen door good and loud to step a few preliminary rounds with Rose before moving on to the main bout.

Rose was beyond tattling on me. She lay on the floor of her kitchen in a lake of bright blood that stained most of the linoleum she had always kept clean and well-waxed. She was on her back, her mouth open in a frozen scream. Her throat had been slit. Not slashed across, but pierced in the way you pierce a man's throat with a pig-sticker to slice the main blood vessels and cut his windpipe so he can't yell for help before he bleeds to death. A steak knife, one of the villa's own, lay in the blood near her outstretched hand. She had got it out before she died, but it had done her no good.

Jean-Pierre was there, too. He hadn't been able to get his steak knife out. It stood hilt-deep from his back, thrust upward and inward under the left shoulder blade to split his heart. I could see enough of his face, cheek down on the linoleum, to identify him. He had bled less than Rose, although enough.

A photograph of the kitchen and bodies, in black and white, later appeared under the headlines on the front page of *Nice-Matin* for Saturday, February 14, 1959. I'll always remember the date, for various reasons including the fact that it was Valentine's Day as well as for the events narrated here. Just as I'll always remember the scene in the kitchen as it photographed itself on my eyeballs in vivid Technicolor an instant before a familiar inflectionless voice from somewhere not within the scope of my vision said, "*Vas-y*. Straight ahead, through the door."

He never joked, he never made threats, he just gutted people when they crossed him. The wild boar with the razor-sharp tusks. I walked straight ahead as instructed, even though by a circumvention I could have avoided stepping in the stickiness of the blood on the floor. I was scared absolutely silly, both for myself and for what I might find on the other side of the door when I went through it.

Chapter Fourteen

Reggie was there. Unmurdered. Tied to a chair with what looked like several of my neckties, gagged with another. The gag was a tight one, stretching her lips at the corners, and her eyes were full of pain. Not fear. Nevah feeyah, as she might have said if she'd been able to say anything. The stiff British upper lip is a wonderful thing when you've got it. My own upper lip was fluttering in the breeze like a loose windowblind.

There was no sign of the Athol character about, dead or alive, or baggage that could have been his. Hers, which I recognized except for a purse that had been emptied and tossed aside and one of those pencil-thin rolled British umbrellas, was dumped in a corner of the room as if it had been thrown there without much care for the arrangement. I still hadn't been invited to turn around, or told to do anything else but march through the door. I marched, conscious of the stickiness of my shoe soles as well as the cause of it until I stood in front of Reggie's chair.

The room we were in we called the sunroom because it got a lot of sun in the morning when there was sun to be had. Two walls were of glass, overlooking the villa's garden and the road that went down to the village, up over the hills to Grasse. The place had originally been a conservatory. We used it as a breakfast room, after having venetian blinds installed to cut down some of the glare and give us privacy. With the blinds drawn, as they were when I came into the room from that awful slaughterhouse of a kitchen with a gun pointed at my kidneys—I didn't have to see it, I could sense it with the antennae of the hairs standing stiff on the back of my neck—you could see out without being seen. The sunroom with its tiled floors impervious to blood, sweat, tears and prayer was an even better place to slit a brace of throats than the kitchen.

"Untie the gag," the inflectionless voice said behind me. "No tricks."

I untied the gag, having some trouble with my fingers. They fluttered like my upper lip. Reggie worked her mouth to ease the discomfort of her lips, then tried to smile. It wasn't a success.

"Hello, love," she said. "You look dreadful. Been out on the tiles?"

"Speak French," The Boar said. "You talk." This was to Reggie. "You listen," was for me, although how we were supposed to know which order was which I can't say. But we knew.

Reggie said, "We communicate better in English."

"French," The Boar said. "Keep it short."

"Very well. He wants a hundred thousand pounds to let me go. That's over a milliard of francs. I haven't got that much money, either in francs or in pounds. I can raise it through my bankers in London by liquidating securities, but they won't act on an oral authorization. They won't release that much cash without a proper receipt, either. I've already discussed it with them by telephone. You'll have to go to London and get the money for me."

I gave her an incredulous stare.

"It has to be done, love. We're in no position to bargain. I'm into my fifth month, and it's not a good time to be bashed about. Or even tied to a chair for too long."

"You're in your fifth month of what?"

She really did smile, this time. It was wan, but it was real.

"Surprise, surprise," she said. "Haven't you noticed?"

"Haven't I noticed—?"

"That's all," The Boar said. "Put back the gag."

Reggie said nothing. She wouldn't stoop to plead with a pig like him. But her eyes pleaded, with me. I stood there, a pillar of salt, taking it all in with my mouth open; the soft new fullness of her throat, the new swell of the beautiful breasts, the boastful beginning bulge of the belly that had always been trim and flat. I got it in about a second and a half. Another second and a half after that I had counted back five months and put the finger on the contemptible bastard who had knocked up the Honorable Regina Forbes-Jones higher than the Tour Eiffel. Me! She was carrying *my* child! And with my child in her—

"Put back the gag," The Boar said again.

I heard him, but the command didn't register. My head was still going round in cartwheels. *My child!* But then what—why—who—where—how the hell— that Athol character…?

"Put back the gag," The Boar said again.

That time, I caught it.

I caught something else, too. He had told me three times to do something I hadn't done, and I was still alive. Your mind can shift gears awfully fast at a time like that. I suppose maybe the responsibilities of incipient parenthood had something to do with it. I turned around to face him and said, or tried to say, "No." A lion defying death to protect the mother of his young.

The trouble was, I didn't have enough lion in me to get it out. But I did face him, and made no move to obey his order.

Behind me Reggie sucked in her breath. He had a gun all right. Held at just the right height to give me an extra navel if he twitched his finger, and at the right distance to discourage any foolhardy ideas I might have about trying to get it from him before he could use it. But the villa wasn't so isolated that a gunshot might not attract the attention of the neighbors, as he would have figured when he did Rose and Jean-Pierre in the way he had, and he needed me; for a while at least. One hundred thousand pounds worth. Until I got that for him and unless I did something directly to endanger him, he just couldn't afford to shoot me. Any more than he could afford to shoot Reggie.

I can't say I was as confident of my reasoning as it sounds in the writing. I defy anybody to be confident while standing bellybutton to bellybutton with a gun in the fist of a killer who has just cut the throats of two people. But the fact of their deaths and my survival when he could have got me quickly and quietly with a stab under the short ribs as I stormed into the kitchen spoke for itself. I had a while to live yet. If I didn't challenge his security, and did nothing stupid.

"Be reasonable," I said, having sold myself the bill of goods. "She isn't going to ask for a bang in the mouth and the gag put back by screaming. I'll get the money for you as long as nothing happens to her or the baby she's carrying. If anything does happen, all bets are off."

No response. But he didn't tell me again to put back the gag.

"I'll help you get out of the country afterward, too," I said. "You'll need all the help you can get for that. You're a cop-killer now. You know what that means."

He knew. D.O.A., when the *flics* caught up with him. French cops feel about cop-killers the way other cops feel about cop-killers.

Still no reaction, for all of half a minute. His pocked face showed nothing of what he was thinking, just fatigue and strain. Then he said abruptly, "For a time. But no talking, and no tricks."

"I must say something," Reggie spoke up. "I have to use the toilet."

She must have been really desperate to say it like that. But as fastidious as she always was about such things, she was above all a realist. She went on talking about it while she had a chance to talk.

"I have to use it at least as often as every two hours, sometimes more often. It's because I'm pregnant. If you'd lock me in the bathroom instead of tying me up like a—"

"No," The Boar said. "You stay there."

"But I've just told you—"

"Untie her," The Boar said. "Take her to the *pissoir*. Leave the door open. No talking, no tricks. Bring her back."

I did what I could to give her an illusion of privacy, standing with my back turned in the open doorway while she did what she had to do. Then I tied her to the chair again, as directed. The Boar tested the knots afterward to make sure I hadn't fudged them. I hadn't. I wanted her immobilized and out of the way while I thought further about guns and things. I was still scared, but not scared silly. There's a difference.

The Boar's flashy clothes weren't so flashy anymore. They were stained with what looked like paint, engine oil and something else. Blood, undoubtedly. He wore a clean shirt I recognized as my own, and one of my neckties. Some time that day he had shaved and laid a thick layer of pancake makeup over his pig's face to diminish the conspicuousness of the pockmarks. My raincoat, enough too long for him to hide the disreputable appearance of his clothes, with a beret I carried in one of the coat pockets, had been tossed on a chair. His shoes were muddy and, like mine, tracked blood on the tile of the sunroom whenever he went to the window to peer cautiously up and down the road, as he did every few minutes. He smoked constantly, lighting one Gauloise from the butt of another before tossing the butt on the tiles to step on it. The butt tended to cling to his shoe sole until it disintegrated.

His diamond pinkie ring was gone; the price, possibly, of escape from Marseille. He'd have to buy his way out of France now. It would cost a lot of money; the money I had to live long enough to get for him. After that, no reason at all for me to survive. Or Reggie. Or her baby—*my child!* (It flashed in my brain like a neon sign every time I thought it.) Poor Reggie, who had to pee for two every two hours on the hour or oftener, tied to a chair in the power of a monster,

trying to smile to show that the old British upper lip
was still stiff, there'll always be an England, chin up,
old boy, good show—it was pointless even to consider
the possibility that he might let us survive our immediate usefulness to him. When the usefulness would
end in Reggie's case was something I didn't want to
think about. But I dared not leave her without protection, even a protection as inadequate as mine was in
the circumstances. Come what may, somehow, some
way, I had to con that cutthroat Corsican son of a
bitch out of control of the situation in which we were
trapped.

The Boar said, "Pick up the phone. Call the airport
at Nice. Ask for information."

I picked up the extension phone we kept by the
breakfast table, called the airport and asked for information. Information about what, the other end of the
line wanted to know? I passed it along.

"Put the phone on the table," The Boar said. "Move
back against the wall."

When I had done that he took the phone to ask his
own questions; never taking his eyes from me, never
permitting the pistol to waver from its unblinking
stare at the part of me a bullet would hurt most. I listened to his end of the conversation, learned what I
could from it, and tried to figure a gaff to hook him
with. It was no good. My mind wouldn't track. I just
couldn't seem to think my way around, over, under or
behind that damn alert gun.

I like to believe that it was solely my concern for
Reggie and what she carried inside her that made me
decide to go for broke. Other reasons could logically

have influenced me, although I don't remember whether they occurred to me then or later. My chances of walking into a London bank, handing over a note and walking out again unmolested with the cash equivalent of more than a quarter of a million dollars were non-existent. The bobbies would have the arm on me faster than you can say Old Bailey, shake me down, bust me open and put the whole story on the wire to the Sûreté Nationale within an hour. Even a hog's mentality like The Boar's should have been able to see that. Of course, he was desperate, and knew he was going to die the moment the law caught up with him unless he got out of France first. His death would be fine by me. But I didn't want him to die in a hail of bullets poured into the Villa Parfumée while Reggie sat there helplessly gestating our joint effort, most probably being used as a shield by the son of a bitch. So you might say that even if this reasoning did help me decide, it was still my feeling for her and her baby—*our child!*—that made me decide to try for the gun.

Having bravely made up my mind to it, I got the shakes all over again when The Boar made a reservation in my name for the first available plane to London. The time-clock had begun to tick.

"BEA has a flight at seventeen-thirty hours," he said, hanging up the phone. "Check-in is from an hour to half an hour before the flight. It will take you half an hour to get there. Toss me your watch."

I tossed him the watch, first checking the time. Twelve minutes to four. One hour and forty-two minutes to takeoff. Less a minimum half-hour wait after check-in and a minimum half-hour to get there. Forty-two minutes left at the outside to put together the most important con of my life. Her life. Our lives.

The watch had an expandable band, no clasp or fastener. Getting it on his own wrist didn't cause the pistol barrel to waver perceptibly. If he'd had a watch of his own at one time, it must have gone the way of the pinkie-ring. Engraved on the back of the one he now wore were the words: *To Curly from Reggie. I'll love you always*, and the date of my last birthday. I mean my *latest* birthday. It didn't help the shakes at all to think about last birthdays. Forty-two minutes. Nearer forty-one now. Still no new thoughts. Tick, tick, tick, tick, tick, tick. I couldn't hear my watch running, but I could feel it.

"Get moving," The Boar said. "Your ticket is at the BEA window."

"There's plenty of time," I said. "Let me take her to the *pissoir* once more first."

"She doesn't have to go. Move. *Vite!*"

"Just to make her more comfortable."

I've said before that he never made threats. Like his piggish namesake, he acted where a dog might have growled a threat or a rattlesnake buzzed a warning. When I still argued after his second order he took a single quick step toward Reggie and slapped her so hard in the face with his free hand that he almost knocked her to the floor, chair and all. The pistol remained unwaveringly pointed at me.

"Move," he said. "*Vite!*"

The cracking blow had spun Reggie's head away from me, so that for a moment I couldn't see her face.

I was just as glad. My own would have looked sick. I knew what was going to follow, what had to follow.

Still without moving, I said, "The—"

He hit her again, backhand this time, just as hard as before but with knuckles on it. Her head snapped around. Her mouth had been knocked open and lopsided by the force of the blow, but she never let out a whimper. I may have. I don't remember. Her lip began to leak blood while I watched, and her eyes made me cringe. They were full of fear as well as pain now. I'm certain it was not so much fear for herself as fear of what might happen to her baby if she were bashed about, as she had said it. But the eyes held no recrimination, no reproach for what I was submitting her to. *I'll love you always, Curly.*

"—receipt," I said, trying to keep it steady, hoping the single word would stop him. "Her signature. I can't do anything without it."

He heard it, he got it, but his hand was already lifted to smack her again. He smacked her again, as hard as before, before backing off. It would have been out of character for him to waste a blow already started.

The need for a receipt had slipped his mind. It was a good sign. He was under too much strain for his pig's brain to function at its best. Maybe something else important would slip his mind in the next forty minutes, if I had as much as forty minutes left. How long could I stall him without subjecting Reggie to more punishment than she could take? Twenty minutes, maybe? Ten? Five? Two? God, give me a gaff of some kind to sucker him with. I just haven't got the nerve to jump the gun cold without a gaff. Please. While there's still time.

Following instructions, I brought a sheet of Reggie's monogrammed notepaper, a pen and a small table, then untied one hand so she could write. Then I gagged her again, also as instructed, after first wiping the blood from her chin and mouth. Blood still leaked from her split lip. My face was only inches from hers, flushed bright red now from the force of the slaps, when I knotted the gag at the back of her head. It wasn't the time to say what I wanted to say aloud, but I shaped the words with my lips. She couldn't chew me out for it with a gag in her mouth.

She gave no indication that she read me. Her eyes were dim, dazed, frightened. I think for the first time she had begun to realize the kind of animal that had her in his cage, and how dismal her chances were of escaping it alive.

I held the paper unmoving on the table for her while she wrote. The Boar stood by the venetian blinds where he could watch the road as he told her what to write. Outside, the drizzle continued steadily.

While I still stood between him and Reggie's chair I said, "If I'm to get the money without trouble I have to shave and change my clothes. Slapping her won't change that. Receipt or no receipt, no British banker is going to hand over a hundred thousand pounds to a *clochard* with a dirty shirt and a two-day beard."

"Tie her again," he said. The receipt was finished. "Leave the paper where it is. Step back."

I thought he was going to hit her again, but all he wanted was to make sure the receipt was right. He knew enough English to spell it out as she had written it from his French dictation. It contained no trickery, simply acknowledged receipt from Barclay's Bank, Ltd., King St., Covent Garden, London, of one hundred thousand pounds sterling in cash, chargeable to her account, to be paid to the bearer of the receipt without question, and was signed with Reggie's normal signature. A little shakier than usual, understandably. How many minutes did I have left? The gaff, God, the gaff. Send it to me. I can't think.

"*D'accord*," The Boar said, folding the receipt before looking at my watch. "Shave and change your clothes. *Vite!*"

I shaved—my razor was still dirty with his hog bristles—and changed with as little *vitesse* as I could arrange under his watchful goat-turd eyes. The message came down from heaven, exactly as the mango had come down that day in Belem, when a lace snapped while I was putting on a pair of shoes unsoiled by mud or blood. Of such small things are fateful decisions made. I made mine while I fitted a new lace.

When I had finished dressing, The Boar tossed the receipt on the floor where I could pick it up without coming too close to him.

"On your way," he said. "No more *blague*. Move."

I moved, ahead of him and the pistol back to the sunless sunroom. *L'audace, l'audace, et toujours l'audace*, the old barrel-maker's boy had said, that day in his office. If you don't have the guts to play for the stakes of the game, then you don't belong in it. Something like that. It would make a lovely epitaph.

He said, "Not that way," behind me, but I kept on

going until it was obvious that I was going on through the sunroom into the kitchen. At that point, he said, "Stop."

I stopped.

"The front door," he said. "The other way."

"I'm going to get her a glass of water before I go."

"No."

I turned around.

Reggie's head had fallen forward so that her chin rested on her chest. Enough of the gag remained visible to show how the blood from her lip had stained it. Her whole body slumped with defeat. I couldn't tell if she was conscious or unconscious, but I hoped she could hear me.

"Look at her," I said. "I'm going to bring her a glass of water and wash her mouth. Nothing you can do will stop me except a bullet, and that will finish your chances for escape. I won't miss the plane. I told you I'd cooperate to get you the money as long as nothing happened to her or her baby. Those slaps are the last mistreatment she is going to take from you. Because if I come back to find that you haven't fed her or given her water or taken her to the *pissoir* when she has to go, or have harmed her again in any way, you don't get a centime. Don't think I'm going to walk in here carrying it in a satchel for you to grab. We make an exchange; the money for the woman. In good shape. *Assure-toi.*"

On that bold exit line I bravely turned my cringing back on him and went into the kitchen, letting the swinging door swing shut behind me. I knew it wouldn't stay shut for more than a second or so, but that was all right, too. I wanted him to see that I was doing exactly what I had said I was going to do.

I had to pick my way carefully around the edge of things and over things to keep from getting blood on my clean shoes. One of the things I had to step over was Rose, her mouth still open in her last vain effort to scream with the knife in her gullet. She lay by the stove, which offered me a handhold as I stretched across her body without stepping on it. I got a glass from a kitchen cabinet, rinsed it at the sink, filled it, wiped its outside with a clean dishtowel, moistened half the dishtowel in warm water to serve as a washcloth, picked my way carefully back as I had come carrying glass and towel in one hand so the other would be free to accept the stove's support again. The Boar watched me from the doorway, tracking me with the pistol as a compass-needle tracks north.

He had to back away, into the blood again, to keep his distance while I went through the swinging door ahead of him. I heard it swish shut behind us, open again, swish shut again, then the snap, snap of his blood-tacky shoe soles on the tiles behind me. Always at a cautious distance a bullet would cover faster than I could.

Reggie was as before, her head still slumped on her chest, her eyes closed. After I got the gag loose I had to hold her chin up with my free hand to clean it and her mouth. The bleeding had stopped, but her lips were bruised, swollen and dry. She drank greedily when I put the glass to her mouth. Her eyes remained closed. She was conscious but withdrawn, I think, down inside herself to where the baby was, there to crouch over it protectively against the awful things that were happening outside.

I gagged her again, quickly. She could have used more than a single glass of water, but I had already spent more time than I liked with my back toward the kitchen door and The Boar. The moment of truth was almost upon us. When it came I had to be ready, willing and able to move fast; quick, or dead.

What I had done in the kitchen was set a time bomb. Even in death Rose had served her mistress faithfully. Her body, lying as it did by the stove in front of which she had died, had provided me with the camouflage I needed to open the gas-jet of the oven. She had herself twice done this, inadvertently and unknowingly, by catching her apron pocket on the oven gas-valve and pulling it open while working at the stove. The oven had taken an unknown interval to fill with enough gas to leak as far as the pilot light on the top of the stove. The resulting explosion had weakened the hinges of the oven door the first time, blown it across the kitchen the second time, scared the hell out of everyone in the house both times. Rose most of all, of course. She hadn't suffered injury in either blast, but she had been so shaken that Reggie had had to give her a couple of days off. After the second explosion I had tightened the screw that held the valve in its seat until it couldn't be opened by accident. The next time Rose hooked it, it snapped her apron string just as Kismet had snapped my shoestring as a reminder. Of such small things are fateful decisions made.

What I didn't know was how long it would take to happen. I had to stall until it did. But The Boar knew

as well as I did that my bold words about brutality to
Reggie were meaningless, and if he began banging her
around again to force me to leave for the airport I
would have to stand there and let her take it. I had less
doubt about her ability to absorb punishment than
about my own lesser ability to watch it happen. When
you have just discovered, surprisingly, that you are
hopelessly hooked, gaffed and grabbed by the woman
who is carrying your child, you become damn sensitive
to pain. Her pain, which can hurt you a lot worse than
your own.

"Move," The Boar said from where he stood sentry
duty by the venetian blinds. He had run out of cigarettes and was more wound up than ever. A nerve had
begun to jerk in his left eyelid. "*Vas-y*. The sooner you
get back with the *grisbi*, the sooner your woman gets
out of the chair."

Nerves had begun to jerk all over me. My heart was
going thud, thud, thud in my chest, my mouth was dry,
my palms were wet, my knees were shaky, I'd never
felt so scared, unheroic and short of *audace* in my life.
A con man isn't built for direct action in the face of
a gun. It's against his principles. And I had only
moments to go, seconds perhaps, God only knew, I
surely didn't, before I would have to act, instanta-
neously and irretrievably. Quick, or dead. It was too
much, I couldn't take it. I was going to give myself
away by wetting my pants.

The fear of it, the imminence of the disclosure, was
so real that I sidled over to the chair where the raincoat had been thrown. It put me no farther from him
than I had been before, and the coat would hide what

was about to happen to betray me if the big boom didn't come fast. Thud, thud, thud, said my craven heart as I reached for the coat.

"Leave it," The Boar said tensely. He was watching me like a hawk. I mean a pig. He knew, sensed, that something was cooking. He didn't know what it was, but he was ready for it.

"It's raining," I said, foolishly.

"Leave the coat," he said. "Take the umbrella. Get out of here. Now."

He took the three steps that were between him and Reggie's chair and began slapping her again. Methodically, back and forth, forehand and backhand, looking at her only once to get the range, his little goat-turd eyes as steady on me afterward as the pistol muzzle was on my belly, smack-smack, smack-smack, smack-smack, her head rolling loosely back and forth with the blows. Her eyes were closed, no sound came from her. She had to be unconscious after the first few smacks, he hit her so hard, but I wasn't. I couldn't take it. I knew he was going to keep it up until I left the house.

Someone with more guts than Chickenshit Curly might have jumped him then and there, taken a chance, risked a bullet to stop it. I wasn't the man. The oven wasn't going to cooperate, the pilot light had gone out, something else had gone wrong, I was licked. He beat me by beating Reggie, as he knew he could. I said something, I don't remember what it was, something to indicate capitulation, I hate to think I said, "Please!" to the dirty son of a bitch although I probably did, begging him to stop as I turned away to pick up the umbrella. The oven let go just as I got the umbrella handle in my hand.

If I did say "Please!" to The Boar, as I suspect I did, it was the last word he ever heard. He may not even have heard that one, the explosion followed so fast. An enormous thundering *BLAM* of sound and fury shook the house, set the kitchen door swinging with a gust of hot air, slammed something heavy against the wall between kitchen and sunroom (the oven door again, as it turned out), shattered glass. The Boar was fast and alert. He had spun around to face the kitchen door, his gun leveled at it, ready to take on whatever was coming at him, before the boom of the blast died. I got him hard across the wrist with the steel ferrule of the umbrella, knocking the pistol from his hand. He saw me coming out of the corner of his eye and tried to swing the gun back to bear on me, but the extra reach provided by the umbrella was all I needed. Whether or not I broke his wrist was something I never bothered to find out. He tried to scoop up the gun from the tiles with his other hand, but I had the umbrella ferrule jammed into him by then, forcing him back until I could get the pistol myself. If the ferrule had had a sharp point I'd have killed him like that, as a *sanglier* is killed for sport, with a lance in his pig's guts. As it was, I shot him four times at a range of one umbrella length.

The cops would have given him more if the pleasure had been theirs, as I would have given him more except that the gun held only four loads. They were enough. It was a medium-caliber pistol, heavy enough to knock his body back against the kitchen door before it collapsed. It jammed the door open; half of him in the kitchen with Rose and Jean-Pierre, half remaining in the sunroom. I went to Reggie, found I still held the gun and umbrella when I started to untie her, threw them away, got the ties and the bloodstained gag off her and began rubbing her wrists. I couldn't think of anything else to do except to babble at her, pleading with her to wake up. "Reggie! Reggie! It's all over, everything is all right, hear me, honey, read me, the son of a bitch is dead, Reggie, please come out of it, you're all right, I love you honest and true, honest, cross my heart I do, I'll never leave you, I'll never run away, please wake up, Reggie doll, it's all over, there's nothing to worry about, you're safe, I'm safe, the baby is safe, all God's chillun are safe," I don't know what the hell more of the same kind of gabble until her head lifted at last, her eyes opened and slowly, painfully from the bruised and swollen lips she spoke the words of love I was longing to hear: "I have to go to the toilet."

I helped her into the bathroom, went to the kitchen to turn off the oven—it didn't bother me one little bit to step on The Boar's body—recovered my watch and phoned for the cops. I didn't have to go to the toilet. I'd wet my pants, as predicted. *L'audace, l'audace, et toujours l'audace.*

Chapter Fifteen

A tired device over-used by writers of whodunits is a scene at the end of the yarn in which the bad guy, who has somehow got the drop on the good guy with a gun or otherwise gained a temporary advantage, considerately explains to him—and the reader—all the twists, turns and convolutions of the plot theretofore unexplained. Gloating, so to speak, over his own cleverness before he knocks the good guy off and makes his getaway, triumphant. He never accomplishes this, of course. The good guy always manages to take him after the explanations are done with. Sometimes it's the good guy himself who sums up for the bad guy, but the bad guy never seems to be able to turn the tables on the good guy afterwards. In either case, one or the other of them buttons all the loose ends of the plot up prettily before the final fadeout, and no questions remain unanswered.

In Reggie's case and mine, the bad guy died before he could talk, others who might have known some of the ramifications were either dead or kept their traps shut for other reasons, the good guy—all right, all right, say what you like, compared to The Boar I am a model citizen—has already reported what he knows of the goings-on. Neither Reggie nor anyone else was able to explain how it was that The Boar and Jean-Pierre met her at the airport when I failed to do so, although my own loose talk to Jean-Pierre while I was

in my cups, together with The Boar's desperate need
for getaway money superimposed on Jean-Pierre's
terror of him, could have been it. I never told Reggie
this, and never will.

"I just don't know, love," she told me after things
had settled down to near normal. The rain was over,
the clouds gone, the sun brightly shining, the lark on
the wing, the snail on the thorn, my love in my arms
and I in my bed again. Not the same bed I had occupied with Reggie and a sequence of too many tarts
at the Villa Parfumée. Neither of us ever went back
there again once we got out of it. It was a good bouncy
bed at the Negresco in Nice, a hotel that held no
unpleasant memories for either of us. "They must
have got it out of poor Rose, somehow. It makes me ill
to think—"

"Don't. Thinking about her does no good. Didn't it
occur to you that something funny was going on when
they showed up and I didn't?"

"Not a bit. Oh, I was disappointed that you hadn't
come to meet me, of course. When I came off the
airfield I had my stomach stuck out as far as I could
so you'd notice right away, but I supposed you'd
somehow failed to get my wire. Then they said you
had a bad cold and had asked them to come for me in
your place. I knew that Jean-Pierre was a friend of
yours, and the other one, the—the—" she shuddered,
unable to put a name on him, "—was wearing your
waterproof and beret. It wasn't until—"

"Wait a minute. How did you know Jean-Pierre was
a friend of mine?"

"Why, he was a bartender at the Martinez when you

were living there with that revolting old American harridan. I used to see you talking together often."

"You've seen me talking to a lot of bartenders. They weren't necessarily friends. Come clean, doll."

"I haven't the faintest idea what you mean."

"You know damn well what I mean. You say you knew Jean-Pierre and I were friends. We weren't, only acquaintances and for a time business partners, then fellow jailbirds. What made you so sure we were something more?"

"I think I'm going to have an attack of the vapors." She put her hand to her forehead in the hammiest gesture of ladylike debility you ever saw. "Let me go so I can lie on my back."

"You're going to have an attack of me if you don't come clean, on your back or otherwise. Stop stalling."

"The doctor says that during the fifth month—"

"Stop stalling. Tell me."

She sighed, looked down at her stomach, took my hand to put it on the bulge and said, "Don't forget what's in there, lad. Mine is a delicate condition. I'm not to be shouted at or knocked about, remember? I have a small confession to make."

"I'm waiting."

She hesitated for another moment, her hand on top of mine, before she said, "I paid Jean-Pierre a respectable sum of lolly to make himself your friend."

"Why, in God's name?"

"Because I wanted him to entice you into the cigarette-smuggling operation with him. So you would be arrested and go to jail."

"So I would be arrested and go to jail."

Repeating it, I sounded stupid even to myself. I'd heard it but I couldn't read it. The message failed to percolate. So I would be arrested and go to gibberish.

She patted my hand where it rested on the coming generation.

"Curly, love, I love you. I loved you then. I'll love you forever. I saw the way you were going, with your looks, your charm, your good mind turned to bad ends, your—your—I couldn't let it happen. I wanted to save you. For myself, actually, although I suppose I didn't realize it at the time. Jean-Pierre was another spiv. I knew this from Cedric. I paid him, Jean-Pierre I mean, to entice you into the smuggling operation, then betray it to the police. So you would go to jail. So I could have you paroled to me. So I could try to make the man out of you I wanted you to be. Do you understand now?"

I understood enough of it to say, "My God, didn't you realize the risk you ran, crossing people like The Boar and The Plank? If they'd known they'd have cut you to pieces with a dull knife."

"I didn't know who else would be involved, and I didn't care. Besides, they could only have learned about it from Jean-Pierre. He couldn't have given me away without giving himself away, and I knew that would never happen."

She talked about it as calmly as if she were discussing tea at the Mayfair. I said, "Maybe it *did* happen. Maybe that's why The Boar came after you, to slice you up after he'd squeezed the money out of you. Jesus Holy Christ, you make my blood run cold just talking about it. Of all the goddamn, hare-brained, feather-headed, nitwit—"

"That's no way to talk to the woman you're going to marry, love."

"Who said I was going to marry you?"

"I did. I do. You are going to marry me and give our son a name."

"It's not going to be a son. It will be a girl who looks like her mama but has a lot more sense than to do the dumb things her mama does that her papa has to get her out of at the risk of life and limb."

"It will be a boy, with lovely curls like his father. I'm going to call him Curlilocks."

"If we ever do have a son, he'll be called Curlilocks over my dead body. I'd just as soon name him Athol. Which reminds me. Whatever happened to him?"

"Whatever happened to whom?"

"Athol."

"Who in the world is Athol?" she said, looking bewildered. She pronounced the name a good bit differently than I had done.

I had to explain how Athol had come into being in my mind as a tag for the weak-chinned, buck-toothed, dishwater-colored slob she was going to marry, or had said she was going to marry when she wrote me about it. She shook her head wonderingly.

"Curly, love, you're daft. Who could I possibly ever think of marrying but you?"

"But you said—you kept turning me down—then you wrote me that letter—what the hell, you never said you were giving me the nod, just that you had changed your mind about marriage."

"I sent you a letter saying I had changed my mind about marrying *you*. I had to change my mind, in the circumstances. I wouldn't mind too much flaunting an illegitimate child in the face of London society, but he wouldn't inherit. One has to be practical about such things, doesn't one?"

"Don't say 'he' like that. You are going to whelp me a daughter."

"A son."

"A daughter."

"A son."

"I will bet you five hundred thousand million dollars that our child will be a girl. Statistics are on my side. Besides, it's common knowledge that great lovers produce girls."

"How much is that in pounds?"

"Make it five hundred thousand million pounds."

"Done!"

We shook hands on it. Somehow in bed like that, the handshake turned into an embrace, the embrace to spontaneous disregard for what the doctor had told her about the fifth month, whatever it might have been. As Reggie said, It was loverly to be home.

Later, while we were still in bed, too lazy and content to get up, she asked, "What's your surprise for me, love? You've unveiled nothing new so far."

"Well, it's kind of like Mohammed and the mountain. I can't bring it to you. I'll have to take you to it to show it to you."

"You can tell me about it, can't you?"

"No, ma'am. It remains a surprise until you see it for yourself."

"When?"

"In a couple of days, if you're up to a bit of—*Jesus!*"

I jumped a foot, straight up, from a supine takeoff. Almost as startled as I was, she said, anxiously, "What is it? What is it? What happened?"

"The little bastard kicked me!"

"Oh." She smiled and relaxed. "He does that, now and then. He's anxious to be born."

"She."

"He."

"She."

"He."

And so on.

I got the plane tickets for Olbia that afternoon. The routing went by way of Milan, where we had to lie over for a night and a morning before making the connection. She'd never been to Milan before. I took her to look at the wedding-cake cathedral and *The Last Supper*, in the evening to hear a performance of *Madame Butterfly* at La Scala in which the soprano sang the part of Cio Cio San in German, Lieutenant Pinkerton his part in Italian, his pal the other American, what's his name, in French. It was a pleasant little outing, all in all. Each time I showed her something new she would say, "Is this the surprise?" I'd say, "No, not yet, this is nothing, just an hors d'oeuvre to the *pièce de résistance*."

We were in Olbia the following midday, that same afternoon in a motor launch puttering through the blue, blue water of the Tyrrhenian Sea. By then she was curious enough to be biting her nails, except that a properly brought up British girl doesn't bite her nails. She kept begging me to tell her where we were going,

please, please, please. I told her she'd see when we got
there. It was a beautiful day to spring it on her; warm,
sunny and clear, with a sea breeze that brought the
heady fragrance of the sun-warmed *maquis* across the
water to us while we were still half a mile from the
island. The Villa Parfumée was a bad memory that
would fade like a dying flower scent before the wild
aroma of that strong growth.

When I beached the launch at last in the little cove
where I had set up the sign, the sign had fallen down. I
set it up again, whanging it firmly into the sand with a
rock.

"There," I said. "Welcome to your new home. I'd
carry you across the threshold except that the threshold
hasn't been built. I haven't had time to get around to
it yet."

She looked at me, she looked at the sign that read
ISOLA REGINA, she looked at me again, she looked
back at the sign, she looked around; at the blue, sun-
bright sea across which we had come, the beach, the
maquis full of bees hurrying about gathering honey,
the trees where birds sang, the hill where rabbits
lived and quail called, the rocks under which lobsters
crawled, oysters fattened, fish lurked waiting for the
hook. She said not a word, just took it all in, looking
stunned. Finally she looked back at me again. Still
stunned.

I said, "I was going to give it to you in payment of
the five thousand pounds. With interest. It's worth
more than that now, and will be worth a lot more later.
I've changed my mind since finding out I'm going to
become the head of the family. You'll get your loan

back in cash, although you'll have to wait awhile yet because I've got other things to do with my cash at the moment. The island is a wedding present from me to you, or will be after I've built a house, put in a garden, a few beehives and an acre or two of wine-grapes and bought the boat we're going to have. You may call it Curlilocks if you like. The boat, I mean."

She still didn't say anything. Her mouth was open just enough to make her look stupid, quite an accomplishment for Reggie.

I said, "I came by it honestly, or anyway semi-honestly. The title is mine; free, clear and legal. I've made good money in my real estate dealings, with the start you gave me. I stand to go on making it for a while. When the gravy runs out there, I know plenty of other ways to bring it in. I may not be able to support you in the style to which you have been accustomed, but I'll have a damned good stab at it one way or another. For God's sake, *say* something, will you? Don't just stand there with your mouth open."

She looked at me for another moment; still with the stunned look, still with her mouth open. Then, without a word, she turned her back and walked away down the beach. Leaving me with the lines of that silly verse running through my head:

> *She didn't ask the reason why,*
> *She didn't stop to say goodbye,*
> *She walked right in*
> *And she turned around*
> *And she walked right out again.*

Well, women. What the hell. They're incalculable. I think it must have something to do with their body chemistry. Particularly when they're pregnant or otherwise running out of phase. I didn't know what to do, so I did nothing except sit on a rock to smoke a cigarette and wait. She was still walking down the beach; not hurrying, not running away or anything like that, just walking, stopping now and then to examine something, a shell or a stone or a bit of driftwood, that caught her eye.

I smoked and waited. The sea-breeze blew, the sun shone, the *maquis* radiated its heady perfume, birds sang, bees buzzed, rabbits rabbited, quail quailed, lobsters crawled, oysters fattened, fish lurked, I waited. Two cigarettes worth of wait, which means at least an hour even when I'm nervous because I don't know what the hell is happening or about to happen.

She came back; barefoot, carrying her shoes and stockings. No comment. She sat down on the rock beside me and wiggled her toes to get the sand out from between them. No comment. Sun, breeze, *maquis*, birds, bees, rabbits, quail and the other island livestock went about their business as before. No comment.

She sighed. Not too happily, I thought.

"Curly, love," she said. "I am no longer accustomed to the style of living to which I have been accustomed. It's about time you knew the truth, I think. In case you want to change your plans."

No comment.

"Do you know the meaning of the word 'entail'?"

"I am not entirely illiterate."

"Don't be stiff and proud with me, love. I'm trying to explain something extremely important to both of us. I meant the special meaning of entail under British law. My father's estate was in entail to his male heirs. I was his only child. The property passed, under the entail, to his brother, my uncle, along with my father's title. I inherited his personal possessions and his debts."

"Your uncle—"

"My uncle is a good man. Don't misunderstand his position. The title means little to him, and the estate is a burden more than anything else. Nobody in England today has the money to maintain huge seigniorial halls and their grounds, much less occupy them. Or pay the taxes on them. Even when the entail can be broken, as is sometimes possible by legal action, nobody will buy such a white elephant. You can only get rid of it by giving it to the government trust or some private foundation. If they will accept it. If they won't, and you live long enough before death takes the burden off your back to put it on the back of the next heir in line, it can ruin you."

"It ruined your father?"

She nodded, looking off across the sun-bright blue sea.

"I like to believe it was the estate. Something not his fault, something beyond him. I always believed he was a wealthy man. We always lived well, rather conspicuously well. When I was born he settled a trust on me, adding to it over the years until it was enough to keep me—in the style to which I've been accustomed, as you put it—for as long as I lived."

"That's nice," I said. "You can buy yourself fresh diamonds or a new Mercedes-Benz when you need one. I may not be up to managing those things for a while."

Still looking at the sea, she smiled. A somber smile.

"No more will I," she said. "Ever again. The money is finished. Every shilling except the five thousand pounds I lent you. I gave my father a creditable funeral, paid off those debts I could manage—he was horribly in arrears, poor dear—salvaged what I wanted of his books and pictures, things like that, and came away. Back to you. Because I love you. Not because I'm carrying your child. I don't care a groat about its legitimacy, I'd rather have it as a bastard than feel you married me because of it. You are free to marry me or not, as you choose, and forever after hold your peace in either event. I will not have you telling my children that their mother diddled or tried to diddle their father into marrying her by pretending to be a wealthy heiress when she is not."

We looked at each other for a while, sitting on a rock in the sun on an island in the blue Tyrrhenian sea. Sun, breeze, *maquis*, birds, bees, quail, rabbits, etc., etc., etc., as before. Situation delicate, no humor in it, chips down, serious values only, proper choice of words necessary. She was as solemn as all hell about everything she had said, right down to the finish wire. If it turned out to be the finish wire.

I said, "What about the note, the receipt, I was to take to London to exchange for a hundred thousand pounds?"

"There were no hundred thousand pounds. There

weren't ten pounds left. But I knew I could never make him believe it, and the promise of it was what I had to bargain with to keep from being knocked about. I didn't believe you would leave me alone with him, whatever else happened."

"What makes you believe I might want to leave you now?"

"What I believe doesn't count. It's what you believe. I want to hear what it is, now that you know."

I said, "I believe I'm going to look up that horrid old American harridan I used to lay back in Cannes and start all over again where we were before you led me astray from the paths of spivvery. That's what I believe."

"Bloody likely," Reggie said, sliding off the rock to pull me down to the warm sand with her to demonstrate how bloody likely it was. "Not after I've had my way with you, my lad. Nevah feeyah."

Birds, bees, rabbits, quail, lobsters, oysters, the fish and us. You could set it to music.

We were wed at the *mairie* in Nice a few days later, as soon as we could get the *paperasse* out of the way. *Paperasse*, red tape, is so burdensome and so unnecessarily complicated in France, mainly to keep a large corps of government *fonctionnaires* in jobs they would otherwise not have, that the saying is: Anything illegal is far easier to accomplish than anything legal, because if it's crooked you fill out fewer forms. But our marriage was just as legal as I could make it, *paperasse* and all. There weren't going to be any little bastards in *my* family, by God.

Reggie beat me for five hundred thousand million pounds on the first baby, again for another half-million million on the second. Two boys in a row. We put the whole million million on the third get, double or nothing, and I won. She wanted a girl as much as I did by then, but she took the other side of the bet to be sporting and give me a chance to break even. When number four came along in the course of human events, we didn't bet. We both wanted another girl to balance the family budget (we both won, that time) and neither one of us wanted to jinx the odds on what we meant to be our final *coup*. Four, we had decided, was the house limit.

"I think four will be nice," she said, while she was gestating number three. "Actually I'd like dozens, swarming like bunnies all over the place, but we have to think about the population explosion, proper schools, things like that, don't we? You don't think four are too many, love? I mean, all I do is produce them. You have to get up the lolly for all of us."

I said, "Don't worry about me getting up the lolly as long as you don't drop another boy the next time out. A debt of two million million and five thousand pounds hanging over my head just might discourage me."

"Oh," she said generously. "I'll let you work it back."

I worked. Brother, how I worked; not only in the way she had in mind but at earning a living, getting a home built on Isola Regina and a small farm started on the best land, digging out the springs to feed a reservoir for piped water and a few bass I stocked, seeding lobster spawn to fill the demands of the luxury resorts already sprouting on the Sardinian coast across the channel, finding the boat we had to have at a price I could afford, all the other things. Nine to five? I kept going fourteen or fifteen hours a day, seven days a week, and thrived on it. Once a week, if nothing special came up to change the program, I'd go back to the Côte d'Azur to look into land options, which were still paying off. I'd worked out a schedule by which I would get up early, putt-putt over to Olbia, grab an early plane to Rome, make a fast connection and be in Nice by midday. It gave me all the rest of the day and most of the following day to do business before going back the way I'd come, usually pulling into the island landing-cove before midnight. If I got involved with business and had to stay over, we had a radio transceiver on the island that hooked into the Italian phone system by way of Olbia, so that Reggie and I could always keep in touch.

I tried not to get held over. After the house was built I had four good Sardinians on the island and three *ragazze* in the house: a girl to take care of the kids, a cook-housekeeper and a maid. Reggie was never alone or unprotected or out of touch. Still, the island was my kingdom, and when I wasn't there to reign over it I felt as if I had abdicated. It's funny how a family and a home and property of your own can grab you by the short hairs like that. During my Nice trips and business dealings I met easy marks on the average of once a trip; suckers I could have trimmed as easily as plucking a ripe peach. They made my fingers itch just to see the eager innocence with which they held out money for somebody to take it from them. But when you're on the con you have to be always ready to

blow along fast ahead of trouble, and Isola Regina had
me trapped. No complaints, you understand. It's the
way I wanted it, every bit of it, every minute of it,
everything about it. I wouldn't have exchanged what
I'd got for myself, including the fourteen or fifteen
hour working day, seven days a week, for anything else
in the world. Until I discovered the serpent that was
slithering around my island Eden. It kind of put a
different color on things.

To discover that the woman you are married to,
the mother of your children, is an unregenerate, bare-
faced, shameless liar can be something of a shock.
I couldn't believe it, at first. But the evidence was
overwhelming, beyond refutation. How it came about,
I was returning from one of my business trips to
France, as usual late at night; tired, in need of a bath
and a drink but feeling good. I'd made a respectable
score on a deal, money I needed to put in my vine-
yard and make a few other improvements I had in
mind, also to pay for Reggie's third *accouchement*.
Anyway, the launch wasn't waiting for me in Olbia
harbor as it should have been when I got there. The
Sardinians knew my schedule, and that one or the
other of them was to bring the boat to pick me up
unless he was told otherwise by the *patrona*. I phoned
the island right away to find out what was up. Worried,
naturally.

Reggie's warm placid voice on the transceiver said,
"It's nothing serious, love. Pietro was out planting lobster pots and a wave tossed the boat on a rock. There's
a bit of a hole in it, but he says he'll have it repaired by
morning. Why don't you stay the night there, have a

good rest and come over tomorrow? I'll tell Pietro to be there early."

"I think maybe I'll do that. I'm kind of tired. Everything all right? How are the kids?"

"Everything is fine with everybody. Your daughter is going to be a rugby player. She's kicking me like mad."

"I'll be there to let her kick me in the morning. Anything else? Anything you want me to bring?"

"Just yourself, love."

"O.K. Can I say it?"

"If it's true. No lies, mind."

Can you imagine, this from a woman whose very existence was a living lie, as I had not yet learned but was about to learn? Innocent, credulous, trusting fool that I was, I said the words she had inveigled out of me. She said, "I love you too, Curly. Good night."

I spent the night in Olbia, slept later than was usual for me—on the island I got up with the birds, there was always so much to do—had a good breakfast and went by the post office to pick up the mail. Ordinarily this was done by the Sardinians who drove the launch, since I was always in too much of a hurry to catch the plane for Rome going in one direction, too late to find the *ufficio postale* open when coming from the other. So it was mere chance that it was I rather than my double-dealing wife who first saw the long official-looking envelope addressed to Miss Regina Forbes-Jones by somebody in Her Britannic Majesty's Inland Revenue Service, forwarded from the Villa Parfumée. I know damn well I'd never have seen it otherwise. Because in it was the revelation of Reggie's perfidy; irrefutable, undeniable, unbelievable. Almost unbelievable, anyway.

If anyone chooses to ask why I took it upon myself to open my wife's personal mail without her permission, the answer is, I wanted to protect her. I wasn't going to let her see the letter at all if it contained what I thought it contained. England's Inland Revenue Service is the equivalent of the U.S. Internal Revenue Service, and when you receive official letters from either authority their content is always the same; taxes and trouble. Reggie's father had died broke and in debt, she was broke except for the five thousand quid I still owed her. Inland Revenue Service certainly wasn't writing to say Happy Birthday. The letter looked, smelled and felt like an assessment for death duties on an estate from which she hadn't benefited, and I was damn well going to take care of it in my own way without letting it upset her or my rugby-playing daughter-to-be. Inland Revenue could stay the hell inland where it belonged. I was my own majesty on Isola Regina. I opened the letter.

I can't quote it verbatim. I only read it about a dozen times before I re-sealed it with care so I could give it to that fraud Reggie when I got home. I do remember a figure of something more than twenty-eight hundred pounds, because the pound was then worth $2.80 and twenty-eight times twenty-eight is a multiplication you can approximate in your head without too much trouble. Put the decimal where it belongs and you've got a product of nearly eight thousand. Dollars, that is. Not an assessment but a rebate. Of death duties overpaid on the estate of Lord Forbes-Jones. In accordance with Miss Forbes-Jones' instructions the money had been deposited to her credit with Barclay's Bank, Ltd., King St., Covent Garden, London, W.C. 2. The rebate represented final settlement of the estate's tax liability, Inland Revenue begged to remain Miss Forbes-Jones' obedient servant or some such formal mildew, and I was a bigger, fatter and easier pigeon than any sucker I had ever buncoed in my whole professional career.

As already mentioned, I read the letter about a dozen times. It took me that long to interpret its significance. When you get a refund of something like eight thousand dollars in overpaid death duties, it means that a greater amount of death duties, most probably a hell of a lot greater amount of death duties, was originally paid by the estate of the deceased; in this case, Reggie's daddy. This in turn means that the duties were imposed on a large and valuable estate with enough liquid assets in it to pay Her Britannic Majesty's tax bill in cash, since taxing authorities do not accept baled hay in place of legal tender and entailed real estate is neither taxable to the estate of a life tenant nor subject to lien for the debts of the life tenant's estate. It followed that a goodly portion of said liquid assets had still to remain with the heir or heirs of Lord Forbes-Jones, deceased, since death duties, however high, never absorb one hundred percent of the estate on which they are imposed. Reggie's story about the entail may or may not have been true as far as it went, but she had lied flatly about everything else. My wife, already rolling in the stuff when I married her, was a goddamn heiress with more money than she knew what to do with beyond shoveling it into Barclay's Bank, Ltd., King St., Covent Garden, London, W.C. 2,

where it was undoubtedly regularly invested for her in
gilt-edged securities to make her even richer day after
day after day unto the last syllable of recorded time.
While I, credulous chump that I was, worked my fingers to the elbows fourteen and fifteen hours a day,
Sundays and holidays not excepted, to make both ends
meet for her, myself, two and seven-ninths kids and
another still to come. I had been diddled, conned, flim-
flammed, hocused, swindled, hustled, hornswoggled,
gaffed, gimmicked and played upon like a marimba to
make me marry her and bend my proud neck to the
domestic yoke.

This horrid realization came to me fifteen years
ago, give or take an offspring or two. Reggie and I have
the quota we set for ourselves; two boys, two girls, all
good kids sound of wind and limb, not too hard to look
at and with signs of dawning intelligence. The boys are
in prep school in England, and I must say that when
they come home for holidays, vacations and long
weekends their manners are a lot better than mine
were when I was in their age bracket. They call me
"Sir," believe it or not. The prep school requires it of
them, not I, but for a man who never made it higher
than pfc. in the U.S. Army, "Sir" from the yard-birds
falls sweetly on the ear.

The girls, who spend five days a week in a boarding
school in Rome, are less respectful to their old man.
They call me Ricci, short for *ricciuto*, meaning "curly"
in Italian. All in all, you could say I've got it made. A
good family, a good home, a good life, still a lot to be
done with Isola Regina but a good future with it and
for it, everything good. Except for the festering secret

locked away in my bosom that my wife, the mother of my children, the woman I love in spite of all and am stuck with for better, for worse, for richer, for poorer, in sickness as in health, all the rest of the marital manacle, is a living lie, a bunco-steerer in sheep's clothing. A female Elmer, in short.

Of course, I can't let her get away with it forever, although in fifteen years I have so far been unable to figure out a gaff to hook her with. If I can work a good clean artistic con maybe I'll give Daddy's fortune back to her afterward, just for the *beau geste*. God knows she's never had any need for it nor, as far as the evidence goes, spent a penny of it. Even the five thousand quid I paid her lies untouched in a bank account I opened in her name. When I ask her, as I do from time to time when I'm not too busy with other domestic problems, why she doesn't spend some of it on herself, she smiles with the lazy contentment of a female spider digesting its mate and says, "Curly, love, what could I possibly want that you haven't given me?"

It always makes me think, in a discouraged way, of old François André's comment: If a mark isn't greedy for something he hasn't got, it's impossible to sucker him. But I'll get her yet; some day, somehow. Meanwhile, would any of you ladies or gentlemen like to draw the first match?

Afterword

My father wrote *The Last Match* over thirty years ago in San Miguel de Allende, Mexico, where I now live. He was no longer up to traveling—he died here in 1974—and had always taken seriously the standard advice to authors that they write about what they know, and so he wrote *The Last Match* out of his head, skimming through the memories of a lifetime, combining fact and fiction, real-life personalities and invented characters, landscapes and lovers and life-styles to his heart's content.

A lot of it I remember myself. We played the match game together, he and my mother and I, when I was eight years old and we went down the Amazon on a wood-burning steamer called the *Morey.* It was just like the one in *The Last Match,* and the purser's name was Buchisapo too.

I know that because I read it in a book. When he wasn't writing mysteries my father was putting together travel books, a whole series of autobiographical accounts of the trips we took when I was a little girl. I have such a well-documented childhood that at times I'm not sure whether a thing really happened or it's just something I read in a book, but I know Buchisapo was real because I have a photograph of us together on the *Morey.*

My father wrote about what he knew right from the start. In the late 30s he was working as a CPA in San Francisco and my mother was an editor at Macmillan. She bet him five bucks that he couldn't write a decent mystery, so he wrote a novel about a San Francisco CPA named Whit Whitney who gets involved in a murder. It was called *Death and Taxes,* not surprisingly, and Macmillan, also not surprisingly, published it in 1941.

After three more Whit Whitney books—he was writing at night and holding down a Navy desk job in San Francisco during the war—he decided to leave the Navy and see the world. Our first trip got us as far as Guatemala, and because we were green and inexperienced travelers that book was called *How Green Was My Father.* A few countries and a few books later came *20,000 Leagues Behind the 8 Ball,* in which we went down the Amazon.

We started that trip in Arequipa, Peru, where we lived for a couple of years and where he wrote *Plunder of the Sun* (reprinted last year by the estimable folks at Hard Case Crime, as a matter of fact), a Peruvian thriller about buried Inca gold. Hollywood turned it into a Mexican thriller about Aztec gold, starring Glenn Ford and Patricia Medina (whom my father referred to as the Latin Alan Ladd because she had only two expressions). After decades in oblivion, it's being re-released on DVD this year. I may even take a look at it myself.

The Last Match's Peruvian escapades also gave my father a chance to revisit his late teens, which he spent in the merchant marine on a ship sailing back and forth to Chile. He started out as an oiler, he told me, and patiently explained the difference between an oiler and a wiper and a fireman. He had a blurry blue propeller on his left arm, a lifelong souvenir of the night he and his drunken buddies decided to tattoo themselves with knitting needles and wound up in jail in Antofogasta. My mother hated that tattoo, but he was proud of it and refused to get rid of it.

By 1950 we were in the south of France, where we settled just as a cat burglar started sneaking over rooftops into the bedrooms of the rich and famous and making off with their jewels. When the burglar knocked off the villa next to ours my father figured there had to be a novel in it somewhere and wrote *To Catch a Thief,* which went on to greater glory as a Hitchcock film starring Grace Kelly and Cary Grant.

Most of the stories he tells in the Côte d'Azur section of *The Last Match* are true, sort of. He really did interview François André, the barrel-maker's son who wound up owning most of the casinos in France, although their conversation probably didn't go quite as it does in the book. And the story about the gullible French aristocrat who is persuaded to pony up a fortune to help his government defend itself against the Red Menace is entirely true, although my father changed the poor guy's name, probably to protect him from further ridicule.

The North African sections are pretty accurate too, bolstered by the year my parents spent in Casablanca in the early 60s. The American and

Foreign Bank of Tangier was notorious, and there really was money to be made smuggling cigarettes across the Mediterranean.

As for the fictional characters? They're based on earlier fictional characters, by and large. Reggie is little more than a recycled Francie Stevens—Grace Kelly's unforgettable ice queen from *To Catch a Thief*—with a British accent. Le Sanglier appears as Le Borgne in *To Catch a Thief*, both of them based on a real-life Corsican cigarette smuggler called The Plank. And the nameless hero? The crook who tells the story? Oh, he's just David Dodge, I think, dreaming of long cons. My father—the most scrupulously honest man I've ever known—loved the whole world of con men and bunco rackets and professional card sharks, and worked them into his books over and over again.

There's one aspect of *The Last Match,* though, that troubles me. At this distance, three decades later, it's appallingly sexist. What can one say about our hero's relationship with Boda the sex symbol—or for that matter with leading lady Reggie and her entirely implausible virginity? All the hero's relationships with women—including that dismal battered wife he rescues from the Nazi on the Amazon—strike me as profoundly bogus. How could my father—a liberal to his bones who encouraged me to strike out in any direction I wanted, and so attached to my mother that he died ten months after she did—come up with these broads? Even thirty years ago I think I would have been offended. Now all I can say is: Hey, Papa, we've come a long way, baby.

The decades of our lives, his and mine, blur together. He wrote *The Last Match* in the early 70s, ostensibly about fictional events in the 50s and 60s, but in fact reaching all the way back to his early years in the 20s and 30s, long before I was born. And now here I am in San Miguel—the same age as he was when he died here, come to think of it—reliving our adventures. And still playing the match game.

Kendal Dodge Butler
San Miguel de Allende

Learn more about David Dodge at
www.david-dodge.com